# Murder at the Carnival

*Miss Hayward and the Detective series*

## By Helen Goltz

Atlas Productions

**Murder at the Carnival**
First published in 2021
Copyright © Helen Goltz 2021

Atlas Productions
Greenslopes QLD 4102
Web: www.atlasproductions.com.au
This book is a work of fiction. Names, characters, places and incidents are either the product of the author's imagination or are used fictitiously. Any resemblance to actual persons, living or dead, or to actual events or locales is entirely coincidental. Any medical experiments or results cited in this novel have been fictionalised and any slight of specific people, experiments, research or organisations is unintentional.

Edited by: Sally Odgers.
Cover images by: Shutterstock; Radosław Cieśla and Jazella, Pixabay.
Cover design by: Wassamahmedd and Atlas Productions.

A catalogue record for this book is available from the National Library of Australia

NATIONAL
LIBRARY
OF AUSTRALIA

Dedicated to the early trailblazers – the women of words:

Ada Cambridge (1844 –1926)

Louisa Lawson (1848-1920)

**PLEASE NOTE:** This book is written in British - Australian English.

*Chapter 1*

*"Now on exhibition for a few days only, the strange, the wonderful, sights you have never beheld before – Burnham's Carnival. Including Mrs Anna Tufton, the Giantess. Town Hall Reserve. Admission - 6d. Open from 10.30 a.m. to 11 p.m."*

*—Brisbane Courier, 18 April 1888.*

Matilda Hayward stood well back from the crowds gathered at the entrance to the large tent, her eyes searching faces for that of her brother, Daniel. Beside her, her eldest brother, Amos, shuffled and glanced at his timepiece for the second time in brief succession.

'He's officially late and yet he insisted on coming.' Matilda sighed.

'Daniel is always late; he was born late and has never quite caught up,' Amos said.

Matilda smiled, never taking her eyes from the moving crowd.

'No, it's true,' Amos continued. 'Once when I was complaining about his lateness, Father explained I was on time, so too were the twins – Elijah considerate and punctual as usual and Gideon fashionably on time just after Elijah; you were early, which was no surprise, and Daniel arrived several days later in his own good time. Nothing has changed.'

Matilda laughed. 'Lucky he is loveable,' she said, and Amos made a scoffing sound. 'But you are right, Amos. I know it must be a burden at times being the eldest and having to be the most responsible.'

'That's what Minnie says,' he said, referring to his wife of six months. 'She worries that the family's activities might bring me in to disrepute if not checked.'

Matilda's eyes widened with surprise, and before she could voice her opinion that Amos's new bride was a little harsh, Amos continued.

'Which reminds me, I don't like you doing this story or being here.' He turned his attention from his time piece to Matilda.

'I know.'

'I wish you'd give up that writing job, it is…' he glanced around, searching not for the right word, but for the most diplomatic and not the words his wife had offered.

'Unbecoming?' Matilda suggested.

Amos nodded. 'I blame Father.'

'Of course you do,' she said and rolled her eyes. 'Poor, darling Pa. How frightfully awful of him to raise an independent, thinking daughter, and treat her as an equal to his four sons. Unthinkable!'

Amos sighed. 'I'm not saying you are not an equal, Lord knows you're brighter than Daniel, Gideon, and on a good day, Elijah, but a few lessons in playing the role of a lady and wife—'

'Really, Amos!' Matilda cut him off. 'I may not be keen to rush to the altar, but if you find any of my habits particularly unladylike – like writing for the *Women's Journal* – then don't let me keep you. I'm perfectly capable of waiting alone.' She turned to glare at him. 'You were never this preoccupied with my place in society before meeting Minnie. Sometimes, I wonder where the Amos that was once so affable has gone.'

Amos had the good grace to look as if he regretted his outburst. He bowed slightly. 'I apologise.'

'You are forgiven; after all, you are my favourite first-born brother.'

He allowed himself a small smile.

A handsome man rushed up to the pair, running a hand through his dark hair and straightening his waistcoat.

'Sorry, I'm late,' he panted. 'I have no excuse; I somehow seem to be good at being late.' He grinned.

'That you are,' Matilda said and kissed her brother on the cheek. 'It doesn't matter, here you are.'

'Daniel,' Amos said coolly.

'Amos,' Daniel imitated him, which made Matilda laugh. She looped her arm through Daniel's.

'Are you sure you won't come with us, Amos?' she asked.

'Absolutely not,' he said looking with disdain at the tent and the signage across the top reading, *Mr Alfred E. Burnham's Carnival.*

'I'm sure Minnie will want to know all about it,' Daniel offered, teasing his brother. 'I'm surprised she didn't beg to come with you and wander through the exhibitions.'

'Unlikely,' Amos snapped.

'Thank you for the ride and for waiting with me, it is appreciated,' Matilda said, softening towards him after her outburst.

He nodded and bent to kiss her cheek. They were physically similar – fair of face and hair, with light blue eyes, like their mother. That is where their similarities ended. Matilda was similar in nature to Daniel who resembled his father and two brothers, Elijah and Gideon – tall, dark-haired with brown eyes. One would not pick the remaining Hayward men for relatives of Matilda or Amos.

'Sunday then,' Amos said. It was a ritual to have lunch after mass at the family home. With that, he was off, and Matilda turned to Daniel.

'Shall we?'

'Yes! Thanks for inviting me, and for the work.' He fished his notebook and a pencil from his pocket, prepared to illustrate as requested by Matilda, and with the two entry tickets retrieved from her purse, they queued at the tent's entrance.

'No, thank you for supporting me, for being here for this most odd experience,' she said and waved her arm around at the environment in which they found themselves. The carnival's tent took over a significant piece of the boggy and well-trodden vacant inner-city land that backed onto the mangroves and river. To the side and a little distance from this main tent were several rows of caravans and smaller tents, with a background of a large copse of trees. Nearby, a drinking tent held prime position for patrons to watch the coming and goings.

Matilda returned her attention to Daniel. 'Amos wants me to give up my writing.'

'Of course he does. Amos has become such a stick in the mud. It's a shame he married a society girl and not a show girl,' Daniel joked.

Matilda laughed. 'That was never going to happen. And don't you get thoughts that way. You and Thomas visit far too many of *those* places as it is.' She referred to Thomas Ashdown – Daniel's lifelong best friend, now Detective Ashdown with the Queensland Police Force.

'We were just making sure Elijah and Gideon got home safely,' he said, stretching the truth. 'And anyway, how would you know?' Daniel raised an eyebrow in her direction, as they shuffled forward in the queue.

'I've seen the rouge on both of your collars and on some occasions, the smell of drink from the pair of you would knock a publican over!' Matilda said and then she smiled. 'I'm just envious.'

'Of me being with Thomas? I'm sure it would please him to know you feel that way,' Daniel teased her again – an art of which he had perfected over many years.

'No! Of you going out wherever you so choose,' Matilda said. She waited for a beat before asking, 'Why would Thomas care what I thought of him?'

'Why indeed?' Daniel said. 'He's fancied you since the day he first met you, even if you did cry when he beat you at our foot race.'

'I did no such thing. He tripped me.'

The showman interrupted their exchange and exclaimed loudly on seeing their specially-stamped tickets, 'Ah, from the *Women's Journal*, I see!'

Matilda bristled; any hope of going in anonymously was dashed.

'I'm the hired illustrator,' Daniel corrected the man in case there was some confusion that he worked for the *Women's Journal*.

'Let the newspaper folks through,' he continued. 'Important work to do, and an interview today as well, I believe?' he asked, knowing full well that had been arranged with Mrs Tufton, the giantess.

Matilda nodded. As they entered the tent and stepped into a quieter area, the doorman stopped them before they moved on to the exhibitions.

'Alfred E. Burnham at your service,' he introduced himself with a small bow.

'Mr Burnham, thank you for allowing us to cover your visit to our city. As you know, I am Matilda Hayward from the *Women's Journal*, and this is my illustrator and brother, Mr Daniel Hayward.'

'A pleasure, madam,' he said to Matilda. The gentlemen shook hands.

'I'm sure you would like a few quotes from me, as the owner of this successful theatre of entertainment?'

Matilda smiled; she knew from growing up in a household of males that flattery went a long way to getting her way and means.

'Of course I would.' She accepted his invitation to move a little farther into a quieter welcoming area where a single row of chairs was positioned, most likely for guests willing to pay for a private audience. Matilda sat and readied her notepad and pencil.

'Now madam, what can I tell you?' He didn't wait for Matilda's response. 'Our show has travelled the world and been wildly successful, largely because of our range of artistes.'

Matilda's eyes widened at the term.

'Do tell us about some of your artists and how you have come to work together,' she said.

'Right. Let me start by saying that everyone here is willingly here, and we're one large family.' Mr Burnham put on what Matilda would best describe as a sincere face. She did her best not to look at Daniel whose poker face left a great deal to be desired.

Mr Burnham continued. 'The artists came to me or accepted my offer to tour for different reasons. They might want to earn a respectable income and enjoy their independence; they might enjoy the art of entertaining and the spectacle they provide; and sadly, for some, it is survival if their families abandoned or sold them. Here they have found security and safety with us.'

'I see,' Matilda said. 'And you pay an income?'

'We have a model that includes profits, and of course we provide our artists with accommodation, meals, travel, and that which can't be valued – support and friendship.'

Matilda nodded. 'Of course.' She subtly nudged Daniel's foot as he chuckled. He disguised it as a cough.

Mr Burnham continued, 'Plus, our artists can create opportunities for themselves that allow them to save for their future security. Some of them have trading cards for sale or allow for exclusive visits and appearances at the right fee.'

'And how many *artists* do you have in your exhibition?' Daniel asked, keen to put an end to the interview and see the "artists" for himself.

'We have eight exhibiting artists on this tour, and it is not just a tour for the curious. There are medical marvels and magnificent feats to be seen. Our giantess can pick up two fully grown men at the same time!' Mr Burnham exclaimed in his showman's voice.

'Amazing,' Daniel agreed.

'Thank you, Mr Burnham, that has been most insightful,' Matilda said. 'Daniel and I shall wander through to find Mrs Tufton and let you return to your duties. It appears you have a good crowd outside and are much in demand.'

'Yes, it is so, and we allow only twenty guests through at any one time for comfort. But some guests need encouragement to come beyond the tent door,' he said, rising. With a glance to his timepiece, he said, 'The giantess will perform in ten minutes, and you may interview her after that if it is convenient?'

'Perfectly so,' Matilda said, and thanking him, they allowed Mr Burnham to return to the front of the tent before they walked down the makeshift hallway into the start of the exhibition.

Matilda was not easily frightened. Growing up the youngest with four brothers put an end to that, but she felt a level of anxiety rising at the thought of seeing these unfortunate people.

'Artists?' Daniel whispered, following closely.

'Indeed,' Matilda said, 'one big happy family.'

'I heard that some of these *artists* earned more in a year than the good folk viewing them,' Daniel said.

'I guess we all must do what we can to survive,' Matilda said, stepping into a large area where she found herself face-to-face with an exhibit.

Matilda stepped back straight into Daniel, who steadied her.

In front of them, frightening for the ill-prepared, was a poor creature – a man nonetheless covered in long hair and displayed for all to see.

Matilda nodded at the man, and he reciprocated but continued to pose and move as required for all to see his terrifying state of being.

Daniel read the sign so only Matilda and another nearby paying guest could hear. *'Jo-Jo, the Russian dog-faced man. A wonderful freak of nature, hairy all over.'*

'Come, let us not dally,' Matilda said. 'You may stay on when I leave if you like.'

Daniel nodded, intending to do so, his curiosity piqued.

Matilda kept close to the wall of the tent and made her way around with her eyes dipped, allowing herself the smallest of glances and to read the signs only – *Unzie, the Circassian youth from the Black Sea – white all over with pink eyes!*

Daniel's eyes were wide opened, his reactions audible. *The two-headed woman – meet sisters Ella and Elvira.*

'Oh, the poor, poor girls,' Matilda whispered. At last came the sign she was seeking – *The Giantess, Anna Tufton – A Marvel.*

'Here she is,' Matilda said, 'Mrs Tufton.'

'Mrs... I can't believe she's married,' Daniel muttered.

They stopped and were directed by another showman to two vacant seats in the front row. A show of some sort was about to start, and guests had taken the safety of the rows behind. The viewers were predominantly men, but there was a smattering of women.

A gentleman half-stood as Matilda went to sit beside him, nodded, and returned to his seat. Daniel sat beside her and opened the cover of his notebook, intending to illustrate the scene.

They were only waiting a few minutes before the showman made the announcement.

'Ladies and gentlemen, today you are in for a treat. Known to be the largest woman in the southern hemisphere, maybe even the world, I present on this stage, the giantess!'

It could hardly be called a stage, as it was on the same level, but it was roped off with a thick red coil of rope and hidden by a makeshift curtain that was pulled back for effect. A smattering of polite applause began, and then an enormous lady made her way to the centre of the area in front of them.

The audience gasped, and Matilda's breath hitched. Mrs Anna Tufton was indeed enormous in every respect.

The showman continued, 'Ladies and gentlemen, did I not tell you so? The giantess – Mrs Anna Tufton is a sight to behold, and light on her feet on the dance floor I'm told!'

The audience applauded again, and Mrs Tufton gave the showman a nod and smile. Daniel began sketching furiously and Matilda could not take her eyes off the woman who could not have been much older than herself. The giantess had shoulder-length, brown, tightly curled hair, and wore a fitted, sleeveless, knee-length gown of what appeared to be red satin. She didn't appear to be unhappy or happy, she was just present.

The showman continued. 'Isn't she the most marvellous woman of the age? Our giantess measures 90 inches around the body—' he waited for the gasps to subside before announcing what everyone wanted to know.

'—and weighs 42 stone, 10 pounds!'

'Heavens!' Matilda said, her mouth dropping open.

Daniel chuckled beside her.

'Why would she want to parade herself like this?' Matilda whispered to him. 'Does she really like the attention? She has a husband so surely she doesn't need to do this.'

'I'm guessing you'll be asking her that?' Daniel said.

Mrs Tufton walked around the stage in a circle as the showman continued his speech. 'Our giantess recently had a challenger from Victoria, but when both ladies presented themselves for weighing, our giantess was indeed the champion.'

Mrs Tufton gave a small bow to more applause, as though being a giantess was a feat one aspired to.

'Ladies and gentlemen, the giantess is seeking two gentlemen from the audience... be warned, she intends to lift you!' the showman announced.

There were gasps, claps and nervous laughter from the audience, and several men raised their hands.

Matilda looked at Daniel.

'No,' he said firmly.

She smiled. 'Fine then.' Matilda glanced to his drawing notebook. 'That's very good. You really are talented, Daniel.'

'Thank you. Thomas thinks he might be able to get me a position as one of the courtroom sketch artists. He knows someone through his position who owes him a favour. That should satisfy Father that I can make a living from my art.'

'Oh, that would be brilliant. Why had you not told me this before?' Matilda said, wincing as the giantess prepared to lift the two men simultaneously.

Daniel didn't answer as he hurriedly sketched the two men beside Mrs Tufton, ensuring to get the height perspective correct to accentuate her size. He drew her arms extended around the men, ready to lift and lift she did. The audience gasped and then applauded. Both men looked surprised and not at all embarrassed. The giantess placed them on the ground and soon her performance came to an end.

Matilda and Daniel remained behind. Unfortunately, so did the showman though Matilda had hoped for a private interview.

'Mrs Tufton, so good of you to speak with us,' Matilda said after introductions and polite talk about her show.

Matilda peppered her with a few questions and the giantess responded with the answers she had offered many times before, but sadly it was what people wanted to know.

'I was a normal-sized child until I was about eight, and then I just grew, and I kept growing,' the giantess said.

It amazed Matilda how girlish Mrs Tufton's voice was given her gigantic frame.

'Luckily my parents owned a farm and so my strength was useful,' she said, with a smile. 'No, none of my siblings are big. I have four brothers and a sister who are quite normal of build. But being large did come in handy living with my four brothers. I suspect my sister did not fare as well.'

Matilda laughed. 'I have four brothers, no sister. I understand completely.'

The giantess continued, 'I've been able to travel all around Australia and next year, I am touring England. It's an exciting opportunity.'

Matilda tried to read her for sincerity. Having now what she needed to write her article; Matilda looked to Daniel who indicated he had finished his work.

'Distract the showman,' Matilda whispered to her brother. Daniel understood. He rose and slapped the man on the back, offering praise and encouragement to the showman on his work and skills at creating an exciting atmosphere.

'Are you truly happy here, Mrs Tufton?' Matilda asked in a low voice.

Mrs Tufton, the giantess, shook her head, and with a glance to the showman, turned to Matilda and whispered, 'Help me.' She put out her hand to shake Matilda's, enveloping it completely, and pressed into Matilda's palm a folded piece of paper.

Matilda nodded, tucked it into her notebook and rose. On the way out she glanced back to see Anna Tufton take a deep breath, wipe a tear from her face and rise to prepare for her next appearance in the carnival.

*Chapter 2*

No one moved while the two detectives studied the room. Nearby, the coroner waited to instruct his staff to remove the body; a journalist hovered – a journalist who wasn't Miss Matilda Hayward the detective was pleased to note – and eagle-eyed witnesses impatient to tell their story waited outside the door, peering in as best they could around the constable who blocked the doorway.

Detective Thomas Ashdown hated the smell of blood first and foremost. Followed by – in no particular order – murderers who got away with it, wrongful hangings, warm beer, the disrepair of his current place of abode, and crying females. Three of those scenarios were currently playing out and he frowned at the wailing woman in the hallway. A young constable stepped in and led her away. Which made him think – he couldn't remember the last time he saw Matilda cry. He cleared his mind of her; this was the last place in the world he wanted to be thinking about a lady, but it's fair to say that he'd given Matilda and the list of things he despised some thought over the many hours he lay awake trying to work through a case.

Daniel had started the ridiculous list discussion when they had been well imbibed and had restricted the list to five, but Thomas found that a challenge.

Despite being the youngest detective at the city's new Roma Street Police Barracks, Thomas seemed to attract more of the most gruesome cases. Perhaps his willingness to work late and having no wife to go home to made him a favourite of the inspector's when it came to delegation. Maybe because he was partnered with an older, experienced detective who had a strong work ethic, they had become the first team to be called for duty. Or maybe his track record for solving cases might have had something to do with it as well. He had solved all but one case that had come over his desk in the last six months – a record unsurpassed amongst his peers. He hadn't given up on that unsolved case either.

Thomas recorded every detail of the room to memory before he turned his gaze to study the victim – another woman, dead. There had been a spate of assaults on women of late – up a third from the last year. After carefully studying the deceased young woman, Thomas glanced to the young constable who had returned and was standing in the doorway.

'What do you have on the victim?' he asked.

'Sir, she was a prostitute,' he said and stopped.

Thomas sighed. 'Aside from her line of work, Constable, what do we know of the victim?'

The constable cleared his throat, noting the rebuke from his superior officer.

'Mrs Florence Anderson, sir. She was thirty-and-two, five children, husband deserted some six months ago, but witnesses said they saw two men here this afternoon. One of them could have been the husband, as no one here knew what he looked like. Just before dusk, a gentleman who lived a few doors down the hallway heard screaming and when he opened his door to come and see, a man ran past him, and that's when he found Mrs Anderson.'

'Thank you,' Thomas said. 'Where are the children?'

'A neighbour has taken them to St Vincent's Orphanage, sir.'

Thomas nodded. 'I'll leave you to get statements from the witnesses, Constable, and I'll talk to the boarding house owner now,' he said with a glance around.

'He's next door, sir, he owns that one too.'

Thomas nodded and looked at his partner. 'Harry?'

'All done, Thom,' the older detective agreed, and proceeded to the door.

Thomas followed, not speaking until they arrived at street level. He breathed out through his nose with several large huffs, trying to clear away the smell, but it lingered.

'Aagh, that smell of death,' Harry agreed. 'I swear it seeps into my pores.'

'I can handle the smell of death and decay, it's the stench of blood that I can't stand.' Thomas grimaced.

'Blood?' Harry looked at his partner with raised eyebrows. 'Well, that's one I haven't heard before. You've got the best nose in the business. Ah well, let's be grateful we don't have to clean it up.'

Thomas smiled at the older man. He liked the old cop – Harry Dart. He was street smart, old-fashioned, polite, and tired, so he was happy for Thomas to be the young gun. Harry's ego didn't want to compete, and that made for a happy partnering. There had been the odd occasion that Thomas had to respect Harry's judgement and accept that his brash confidence at six-and-twenty may have needed checking, but Harry did it in his customary relaxed manner.

'Ah, that's probably the boarding house owner, leave it to me,' Harry said, identifying a man who appeared in possession of wealth alighting from the front entrance. He wandered off to speak with him.

The street was full of shadows as Thomas stood looking at the exterior of the boarding house, his face lit by the street gaslights. With his hands in the pockets of his trousers, he rocked back and forth. He must have stayed that way for some time thinking as Harry returned and interrupted his thoughts.

'Solved it yet?' Harry stirred him, and Thomas laughed.

'Yeah, I think so,' he scoffed. 'You should head home for dinner. I'll make a few notes and we'll talk in the morning, yes?'

'I can stay if need be,' Harry said as they hailed a hansom cab.

'No, she's dead, we're not saving any lives tonight,' Thomas said, stepping into the vehicle after Harry and giving the cabman the police station destination. Besides, I won't be working late. I've got a dinner invitation to the Haywards' tonight.'

'Ah, I saw those twin boys out the other night. They weren't short of refreshments.'

Thomas laughed at his partner's tact.

'It is time they settled down, I don't want to be seeing them in our cells,' Thomas agreed. 'Elijah's sensible enough, but Gideon will need a strong woman.'

'I could say the same of you, son,' Harry ribbed him. 'Find yourself a nice girl who can keep you in line, someone to go home to after you see these awful scenes who'll have a hot meal waiting for you and be dressed so pretty that your mind will forget the day and be rested for the night.'

Thomas sighed. 'That does sound good, but I can't say I've found one yet that I want to go home to every night or talk with in the morning for that matter.'

'I think there might be one just under your nose,' Harry suggested, and gave Thomas a wink, as he alighted from the hansom cab that had stopped outside the station. 'Perhaps that smell of blood won't let you smell her pretty perfume.'

Thomas offered his partner a wry look and Harry laughed.

'In the morning then,' Harry said and with a wave, he was gone, his home a brisk fifteen minutes' walk from the station, and tonic for Harry to remove the day from his conscience.

Thomas breathed out again, still trying to eliminate the smell and vision of poor Florence Anderson. He glanced at his timepiece – one hour until he was due at the Haywards' home. His mind broke that into segments – twenty minutes to make some notes for work, fifteen minutes to get freshened up before Daniel collected him as he passed the station. He stopped and mused that maybe he needed more than fifteen minutes to dress so that Matilda did not smell the crimes of the day on him. She would want to discuss the matter in detail. He also allowed fifteen minutes to get there, and ten minutes up his sleeve for the unexpected. His host, Mr Hayward, didn't care too much for punctuality but the cook did, and she was the best cook Thomas had ever encountered, so he would not get on her bad side.

*Chapter 3*

Matilda paced from one end of the drawing-room to the other – a considerable length in the Hayward family's Highgate Hill home. From the front windows was a fine view across the growing city – the river with its busy trade and in the distance, on a clear day – and most Brisbane days were just that – the mountains could be seen. This evening, dinner was not served for another fifteen minutes and Daniel and his best friend, Thomas, were expected to dine – they were late; Matilda assumed that was Daniel's fault. Her brothers, Elijah and Gideon, had made their excuses – they were spending way too much time at the club, and Matilda missed Elijah's calming influence. She suspected her father wasn't too worried about their absence as long as Elijah accompanied Gideon.

But for now, she had more important matters than Gideon's antics to think about. Mrs Tufton's plea had distressed her. What to do next?

*I'm a writer with some formal training and certainly no investigative skills,* she thought, but that would not stop her.

This was a story, and it might soon be a national front-page article she would deliver. And it all began in the *Women's Journal.* Her editor, Mrs Dora Lawson, would be thrilled and it would support Mrs Lawson's personal crusade to assist women in distress because of a disagreeable marriage, living standards, or lifestyle.

'Matilda, do stop pacing, dear. Either tell me what is on your mind, or pace elsewhere,' her father said with a sigh. 'While you up, perhaps you will refill my glass.'

'Sorry Pa, of course.' Matilda hastened to refill her father's brandy glass and, with a glance his way, poured a drop for herself.

'Do tell, my dear,' her father encouraged her and put down his newspaper, peering at Matilda through his thin wire-framed glasses.

'It's my next article, Pa, there's a complication and I have to do something above and beyond,' Matilda said, and then she began to tell her father about the giantess and the interview.

'What did the letter say?' he asked.

The door of the drawing-room swung open, and Daniel and Thomas barged in together.

'Good evening, Pa, Matilda, I need a drink,' Daniel proclaimed.

'Sir,' Thomas said, stopping and acknowledging Mr Hayward, who rose and extended his hand. The men shook.

'So glad you could join us, Thomas, we don't see you often enough these days, work commitments, I imagine,' he said. 'It's a standing invitation any evening and we expect your attendance on Sunday.'

'Thank you, sir, the invitation is always welcome.'

'How are you, son?' Mr Hayward asked of Daniel.

'Pa, never better.' He waved the bottle of scotch at Thomas, who nodded and turned to acknowledge the other guest in the room.

'Matilda,' he said with a small bow.

'Thomas,' she reciprocated with a smile that said she knew him, and his charm and good manners would not impress her. But she impressed him. Tonight, she looked beautiful. Her blonde hair was styled to expose her swan-like neck, a fitted blue dress highlighted her delicate figure, and her blue eyes, that looked far too clever for her sex, shone. Thomas's partner, Harry, was right. She had a way of distracting him so that all sensible thoughts left his head. He wasn't sure when this first began, as it was subtle and had crept up on him. It was once enough to compete against her, to be in her company and enjoy the teasing from Daniel's little sister, but now it was more. Daniel cut his vision stepping in front and offering him a glass of scotch.

'And you, Pa, everything okay?' Daniel asked.

'Well, Matilda was just about to fill me in on her latest story which has her most vexed,' Mr Hayward said.

'The giantess!' Daniel exclaimed. 'That was amazing today, you should have stayed and visited the other exhibits with me,' he said to his sister.

'You should not have, Matilda. I hope you didn't?' Thomas frowned at Daniel before turning his attention to Matilda.

'You're sounding like Amos now, Thomas. But no, I didn't stay, it was too distressing,' Matilda said. 'People as curiosities just doesn't feel right with me.'

'Rightly so,' Mr Hayward said. 'And Thomas is right, you are a young lady... we're prone to forget that in this manly household.'

Daniel laughed and turned to Thomas. 'I don't remember you being worried about Matilda's sensibilities when you threw a spider in her direction or tackled the ball from her to avoid Elijah's team winning, or—'

'We were very young.' Thomas cut him off, uncomfortably hot at the thought of tackling Matilda now.

'I'm still having nightmares about that spider,' Matilda teased him. 'I may never be the same.'

'Hmm, I doubt that,' Thomas said in good humour. 'But those freak shows are not a place for a lady. They can be quite alarming.'

The housekeeper, Harriet, made a clucking sound as she entered the room, indicating her agreement to the last comment spoken. She had earned herself an opinion, having been with the family long before Matilda was born. Widowed but five years ago, her security and comfort came from remaining within the welcoming breast of the Hayward family.

'Dinner is served, Mr Hayward,' she said, and on departure smiled at Thomas. She liked a young man with manners who enjoyed his food and she believed him to be a good influence on Daniel.

Mr Hayward rose and led the way. 'Come then, best we are not later for dinner; I for one don't wish to feel the wrath of Cook.' He offered his arm to Matilda, who slipped her hand through her father's and allowed him to escort her to dinner. Daniel and Thomas, nursing their drinks, followed.

The dining room was easily the loveliest room in the Hayward household with its pleasant fireplace, a cut-glass chandelier that had been lit earlier and the adorned plaster-of-Paris mouldings on the ceiling. Once seated and served, and praise given, Thomas addressed Matilda.

'So, what is vexing you, Matilda? Do share,' he said, in a voice that was part interest and part challenge. In truth, he was starving. He rarely ate during the working day, and as a bachelor with a pressing job, he never thought to have breakfast. Cook's roast lamb and vegetables deserved his full attention.

'Yes, my dear,' Mr Hayward said. 'As these two hooligans interrupted us when you were about to impart the contents of the letter, do continue,' he said with a fond glance at the young men.

Matilda finished a bite of her dinner and swallowed before starting.

'I think a woman is being exploited by her husband at the carnival – Mrs Anna Tufton, the giantess.'

Daniel scoffed. 'I can't believe she's married. Seriously, the giantess is an enormous lady and not meaning to be crude, but would her husband's interest be anything but financial?'

'Love comes in many forms,' Mr Hayward said with a shrug.

'Perhaps, Pa,' Matilda agreed, 'but Mrs Tufton whispered, "help me" to me as I left, and I think she is being made to work there.'

'She could pick her husband up and throw him away if she didn't want to stay,' Daniel said and chuckled, continuing to be irreverent.

Thomas did his best to repress a laugh, but Daniel had a way of making him forget he was a responsible adult these days.

'The letter she slipped you, what did it say?' Mr Hayward asked.

'It said that her husband was forcing her to work and threatened to sell her or have her institutionalised if she refused. Then it said, *please help.*'

Mr Hayward sighed. 'That poor woman is in a desperate situation.'

'I bet he's making a reasonable income from her,' Daniel said. 'When I stayed on, I spoke to the hairy guy—'

'—Daniel, really,' Matilda rolled her eyes at his lack of diplomacy as Thomas and Mr Hayward smiled.

'Sorry Tillie,' he said, using her nickname and giving her a most endearing look that he knew would make it impossible for Matilda to be angry with him. After all, they were best friends as well as sister and brother.

'Hmm, so what did Mr Jo-Jo say? I believe that was his name,' Matilda said, trying to sound stern.

Thomas smiled at the pair of them and their antics.

'Mr Hairy?' Daniel joked. 'He said he had bought two properties on the profits of his venture and would soon settle down, take a rental income for one and never be seen again.'

'Heavens!' Matilda exclaimed.

'I'm in the wrong job clearly. I need to come up with an act,' Thomas said.

'I could think of a few,' Matilda offered.

The men laughed.

'Thank you, Matilda, how helpful of you,' Thomas said, giving her a wry look which only made her laugh again.

'But you don't think they are acting, do you?' Matilda asked. 'Daniel, you were there, do you think it is an act? They seemed very real in their irregularities.'

Daniel nodded. 'I believe those two are genuine, but there are some that are fakes, I'm sure. Do you remember, Pa, that show that came through when we were boys with the real-life mermaid?'

Mr Hayward laughed. 'Yes, that was definitely a fake.'

Matilda looked from her father to Daniel. 'I didn't see the mermaid!' she said most indignantly.

'No, dear, that day you were with your mother, I believe taking tea with a friend,' her father answered. 'It was many years ago and you were young – about three or four.'

Matilda sighed. 'I would have liked to have seen the mermaid. But now, with Ma gone, I wish I remembered taking tea.'

'I know. But back to Mr Jo-Jo, before we become melancholy and ruin the evening,' Mr Hayward said. He finished his dinner and returned his attention to his brandy. 'Clearly he is a clever man who has made the most of his adversity.'

'What do you think, Thomas?' Matilda asked, startling him. Until now he had been enjoying eating and being on the periphery of the conversation, even if he knew that wouldn't last for long.

He put his eating utensils down and sighed. 'I suspect, Matilda, that the giantess's situation is quite common, sadly. I swear half my cases at the moment are female assault cases.'

Matilda's jaw tightened and she shook her head. 'What sort of world is this? It is 1888! We are about to enter a new decade, and we're close to a new millennium. How can our modern society be so backward when here in my hometown women are being manhandled? If I marry I cannot buy, keep or sell my own property; we cannot cast a federal vote; and if it were not for my small income, I would be quite dependant on you, Pa.'

'Which would be my pleasure and honour, Matilda,' he said, and she softened and smiled at him.

'Thank you, Pa.'

'Should you find the right husband, you won't be concerned about owning property separately,' Thomas added.

'Is that so, Thomas?' Matilda asked. 'I imagine I should be readily prepared to be in the family way too and fulfil my duties to my husband?'

Thomas shuffled uncomfortably, not averse to the idea.

Daniel came to the rescue. 'It is about time someone produced a grandchild for Pa, although we should expect one soon from Amos and Minnie, I imagine.'

'Yes,' Matilda agreed. 'Best Amos takes care of that and has a son so that the family name may continue. I will, after all, lose my name when I find the *right* husband,' Matilda said, paraphrasing Thomas and glancing his way with a look that could not be taken for kindness.

'Nevertheless, Matilda, the women's movement is gaining momentum and it is only a matter of time until you get the vote in our fair city. As for property ownership for married women, I've heard rumbles that is soon to change too,' Mr Hayward said. 'But to Mrs Tufton. What next then?'

'What indeed,' Matilda said. 'With Amos and Pa qualified in the law, and you, Thomas, in your police role, surely the resources available to me can provide some assistance?'

'What about me?' Daniel asked, his tone indicating offence.

'Your illustration of Mrs Tufton, once done, will create great sympathy for my cause, Daniel, I am sure,' Matilda appeased him, and he appeared satisfied.

Thomas inhaled and sat upright. 'If I can find time in between working on the many show acts you believe I could develop, I could see if her husband is known to us,' he teased, and was rewarded with a smile from Matilda.

'Thank you, Thomas, that would be appreciated.'

'And, my dear,' Mr Hayward started, 'before I offer any legal advice, may I suggest you talk to your editor and see what Mrs Lawson has to say. She has her own resources, trust me, and she is quite formidable. But failing that, if the giantess – Mrs Tufton – is in a position to pay, then I suggest you offer her the legal services of your brother Amos, to support his business, but I am at your disposal.'

'Yes, you are right, Pa, thank you. I shall do just that and you are most kind to offer yourself for our cause. Mrs Tufton cannot spend any longer than necessary in that horrible—'

'—Freak show,' Daniel supplied, saying the words with dramatic flair.

Matilda sighed, Mr Hayward shook his head and Thomas suppressed a laugh. The dinner plates were cleared.

*Chapter 4*

The noise of an office full of women absorbed in various tasks, all of which required regular communication, created an exciting atmosphere that Matilda loved being part of, especially just before the fortnightly print deadline. The mood in the editor's office was, however, quite the opposite.

'Appalling!' Mrs Dora Lawson, editor of the *Women's Journal*, exclaimed, rising from her desk and pacing up and down the large window that looked out at her working ladies.

She had a fine figure for a woman in her middle years and a forbidding pile of white hair atop, pinned and restrained to within an inch of its life. She liked order and the meeting of deadlines. Matilda admired her terribly.

'Matilda, you are on to something here. Something big,' she agreed after Matilda's summation of the giantess's situation.

Matilda opened her folder and passed Mrs Lawson the illustration of the giantess.

'This is Mrs Anna Tufton. The illustration is ours to use

should you wish to do so – my brother did it to accompany my story. I'm paying him from my fee, but he does not need to know that.'

'I prefer to pay women in my employment, but if the fee is reasonable, I will happily pay for this illustration,' Mrs Lawson said, admiring it. 'It's impressive and detailed. The resemblance?'

'Completely accurate and I say that without favour,' Matilda assured her editor. 'But now how to proceed? I can write a general story about the carnival and representation of women within it to meet this issue's deadline…'

'Yes, we have left space for that story and the owner, Mr Burnham, has expectations of it appearing,' Mrs Lawson said. 'Once published, that would give us the freedom to pursue Mrs Tufton's story in more detail while satisfying the exhibition owner that the article I promised has been printed while his carnival is in town – so distasteful!'

'Then I shall write a general piece now and include the illustration. Should I revisit the exhibition to alert Mrs Tufton that we are working on her behalf?'

Mrs Lawson turned from looking over her newsroom to face Matilda. 'Yes, I think that best. You could take two advance copies and offer them to the owner and Mrs Tufton as an excuse to get an audience. What do we know of the husband?'

'My friend, Detective Ashdown, came to dinner last night. He is an old family friend and my brother's closest ally,' Matilda explained, and Mrs Lawson cut her off.

'My dear, I may run a women's magazine and push for

women's rights, but I am not averse to men or appropriate relationships.' She raised her eyes to the ceiling, imagining heaven beyond, and continued, 'My Harold, God rest his soul, was not the role model for husbands, but he tried, and we produced some fine young citizens. Mind you, Harold had little to do with that, past the act of conception.' Mrs Lawson sighed and returned her attention to Matilda. 'Did you mention your concerns to the detective?'

'Under secrecy, yes. He said he would look to see if Mrs Tufton's husband is known to the police, and my father has offered his legal services should you need them.'

'Most kind. Please pass on my gratitude, but at this stage, the decision lies with Mrs Tufton should she wish to seek legal representation.'

Matilda nodded. 'I'd best get to work. I would value your feedback again on my work if you have time, Mrs Lawson.'

'Of course. Do keep me informed every step of the way with your investigation, Matilda, and should you need extra resources, I can pair some ladies with you.'

Matilda rose and left while Mrs Lawson, still holding the illustration of the giantess, returned to her desk, her lips pursed as she thought about all she had heard.

Matilda hurried to her desk. The sooner she wrote the piece, the sooner she could begin the story she wanted to write.

*Women's Journal*
Tuesday, 8 May 1888
Fortnightly edition
Vol.1, No.12. Price, 3d.

Special Feature, Burnham's Carnival in town for two weeks

A report by Matilda Hayward
Illustration by Daniel Hayward

Arriving in Brisbane from Sydney on Saturday morning was a collection of performers quite different to the theatre performers our readers may have recently celebrated.

Mr Alfred E. Burnham's Carnival has established its exhibition space on the Town Hall Reserve and has already attracted a sizeable crowd of visitors.

Reporting on behalf of the Women's Journal, it surprised me to find so many women in attendance to see what Mr Burnham refers to as "wonderful freaks of nature" or "medical marvels".

The kind and sympathetic face of Jo-Jo the Russian dog-faced young man accosts the viewer on entry. Jo-Jo's face is covered with a long wavy mass of silken, dark brown hair. I ventured past 'Unzie', a young man with hair and skin delicately fair and pure white, with eyes of pink.

Perhaps most fascinating to this writer was Mr Burnham's giantess, Mrs Anna Tufton, aged 23, from south-east Queensland. A woman of remarkable bearing and composure, her particulars include the weight of 42 st. 10 lb and 90 in. around the body. Her strength was such to lift two grown men – a show which I witnessed in person – with a man held under each arm and their combined weight totalled 26 st.

Mrs Tufton informed the writer that she was a normal-sized child until the age of eight, when she then grew at an incredible speed, overtaking her three brothers and finding herself most useful on the family farm where strength was an asset.

Mrs Tufton has toured Australia with the exhibition and will next travel to north Queensland, which she was looking forward to visiting.

Mr Burnham's show will continue until 20 May from 10.30am to 10pm. Admission is 6d.

*Chapter 5*

Detective Thomas Ashdown collapsed into the chair behind his desk and sighed at the collection of files that had emerged since his absence. He rifled through them, looking for one name in particular. There it was – Carl Tufton, husband of Anna, the giantess.

'What's that one then?' Harry asked, storming into the detective's office with a hungry look on his face.

'Not a crime yet, but one in the making,' Thomas said, sticking the file back in the pile and trying to divert his partner's attention.

'We've got enough to do without chasing down crimes that might never happen,' Harry said. 'It's well past the lunch hour and I'm betting you didn't breakfast either?'

'No, but I ate well last night at the Haywards. Their cook is the best in this town, I am sure of it.' Thomas sighed at the memory of it.

'I believe my wife has that title,' Harry was quick to tell him, and Thomas laughed.

Harry added, 'Shall we go to the dining room for lunch? I hear they've got some fancy German sausages today.'

Thomas needed no persuasion to go to lunch, but the thought of going to the police dining room didn't hold great appeal. 'How about the Prince Alfred instead? If we take these files we could call it a working lunch,' he suggested.

'Done then,' Harry agreed, his hat already in his hand.

Thomas scooped up the files, grabbed his hat, and followed his partner out the door and down the hallways of the police station. The nearby hotel served a decent sized lunch on a budget for the working man. Thomas and Harry were no strangers to its menu, and the Prince Alfred was no stranger to the clientele from the police department and the military officers stationed at the nearby barracks.

Once seated in a booth, the men ordered, and Thomas shared the folders with Harry and kept the file of Mr Tufton to himself.

Harry sighed as he opened their most recent case – the murder of prostitute and mother of five, Florence Anderson.

'Ah, the poor kiddies,' he said, and sighed. 'Let's hope they can rise above this and not end up on the wrong side of the law themselves.'

'I was mulling on that case late last night, running through the constable's notes and statements,' Thomas said, and ran a hand over his light beard as he thought.

'Of course you were,' Harry said. 'And what did you come up with?'

'The man who found her, the neighbour, killed her.'

Harry's eyes widened with surprise and then they narrowed as he studied the younger detective to see if he was having a joke at Harry's expense. He waded through the paperwork in the file until he found the statement of the neighbour.

'Herbert Poolman,' he said and sat back to accept the lager placed in front of him with a nod of thanks to the waitress.

'That's him,' Thomas said.

'Go on then, tell me your theory and we'll have Herbert Poolman arrested,' Harry invited him.

Thomas took an appreciative gulp of the cool amber fluid and righting the glass began.

'At first it looks as if it would fit any of the usual scenarios – a client didn't pay, Florence's pimp arrived and cleaned him up; or a lover, husband or client walks in on another and kills him in a rage of passion. But no. The other neighbours said Herbert Poolman was always hanging around Florence's door, especially when he had a bit under the skin. Florence's friend who lived a few doors down the hallway said he'd never show his money, just expect Florence to open the door to his charms. Poolman's got a history of drunken and lewd behaviour, and it was interesting that he heard the screams and was first on the scene. I recall his neck had scratches on it that he had attempted to hide by pulling his collar up high. His trousers had some dark stains on them which might have been blood and might have been fresh.'

Harry nodded, impressed. 'He's probably washed them by now but go on.'

'My theory is that he didn't get what he wanted and heard she was having some fun with someone else, so he barged in and threatened Florence and her client. The client's run down the hall, Poolman has stabbed Florence in a fit of rage, she's scratched and clawed to get him away and once he'd realised what he had done, he's hidden the knife, raced out into the hallway and yelled for help. The tenant on the bottom floor saw the client running out a bit earlier and Poolman claims to have found Florence that way thus pinning it on her last client.'

'One of the witnesses said they saw two men.' Harry fished around in the file for the relevant statement.

'Yes, but a tenant was coming home around that time according to the building manager and the milkman had just been, so either of those might have been the second sighting.'

'Right you are then,' Harry said. 'I'll get a senior constable with me, and we'll go and visit Mr Poolman this afternoon then. We'll take a look at his wardrobe too.'

'Be careful,' Thomas warned, remembering Harry was only a few years short from hanging up his badge. He wanted to see Harry get the gold watch and farewell party so Harry and Mrs Dart could do the exploring they wanted to do – birdwatching trips. No crime there. Thomas continued, 'If my theory is right, there's a knife somewhere still in that room or thereabouts, and he's not afraid of violence. Get the doctor to check out those scratches he's sporting, too.'

Harry nodded as he wrote a few notes on the file and closed it. 'You obviously think well in those late hours of the night.'

'I've done some of my best work then,' Thomas said with a hint of innuendo and a sly grin. He cleared the thought from his mind and moved his files to allow for the first of two courses – a bowl of thickened chicken soup – delivered to him with a fresh bread roll. The two men need not worry about table manners in the company of each other and proceeded to eat their soup like two starving men and read at their leisure. Harry moved onto another file while Thomas opened that of the giantess's husband, Carl Tufton.

When they had finished their soup, Harry said, 'Tell me about the crime yet to happen.'

Thomas smiled; he couldn't get much past his partner. 'It's between us for now?' he asked.

'Got that, isn't everything?' Harry asked.

Thomas looked at the older detective with admiration; he was the best of partners and Thomas knew he was lucky.

Thomas took a large gulp of his lager, which he realised would have tasted better if he finished it before the soup, placed it down and said, 'The Freak Show's in town.'

'I heard it was. I went to one when I was a young man, never again. I felt as if I was in a human zoological garden,' Harry said with a shake of his head.

'Indeed,' Thomas agreed. 'However, Matilda – Miss Hayward – visited with the purpose of writing an article for that newspaper she works for,' he said with obvious disdain. 'While there, the giantess slipped her a note relaying that she was being forced to appear at the exhibition by her husband.' Thomas tapped on the outside of the file bearing the name Carl Tufton.

'She's married, the big woman?' Harry said.

'Apparently so,' Thomas said. Like Daniel, he could not imagine bedding such a large woman.

'Oh well, there's no accounting for taste and what some men might find appealing. In all my years of policing, I'm rarely surprised by human nature, but I prefer a more feminine figure of a woman,' Harry said and stopped to admire the waitress who brought them their cutlery, salt and pepper and the promise of steak and kidney pie.

Yes, me too, Thomas thought. Someone like Miss Matilda Hayward.

He continued, 'Just as I thought, this Tufton character has a record as long as my arm – petty theft, drunkenness and attempted murder.'

'Attempted?' Harry asked.

'He was acquitted.'

'Then making his wife work in such a place is not beneath him,' Harry said.

'I agree. I'll alert Matilda and confer with her father on a course of action for Mrs Tufton.'

'Did you want me to do that for you?' Harry asked, and laughed when he saw Thomas's face. 'Just teasing you, my boy,' he said. 'I would never deprive you of a bona fide opportunity to meet with Miss Hayward.'

Thomas cleared his throat, uncomfortable with the topic. He had made no advances to Matilda, and he did not believe they would be welcomed.

'It's not like that,' he assured his partner.

'Because she's your best friend's sister?' Harry asked.

'Maybe, although I don't think Daniel would object, he appears to think I'm all right.' Thomas smiled. 'But I've known Matilda since we were children, we're friends.'

'But she's a woman now, and a beautiful one at that. I suspect a few men have noticed.'

Thomas stiffened; he had noticed too. After all, detecting was his business.

He took a deep breath. 'If I were to court her and then we fell out, it could ruin my relationship with the family.'

'But if it worked out, imagine the relations you will have. They are already family, are they not?' Harry asked. Before Thomas could reply, Harry glanced at the file. 'But let's win Miss Hayward's favour by saving Mrs Tufton before it is too late.'

'Yes,' Thomas agreed. 'I'll call on Matilda this evening.'

Harry's endorsement was like approval for Thomas to follow through with the lead; the young gun wasn't averse to taking the recommendation of his colleague when it best suited him.

*Chapter 6*

The ink was barely dry from Mrs Lawson's printing press when, armed with two copies of the latest edition of *The Women's Journal*, Matilda made her way back to the carnival, but first, a quick stop at her home. The evening was falling, and she thought it best to let Harriet know that she needed to run an errand and might be late for dinner.

'Really Matilda, it's dangerous for you to be going to that place on your own at the best of times, let alone in the evening,' Harriet scolded her. 'I shall keep your dinner warm, but I'm telling you that your father won't be pleased, and I won't be keeping it from him.'

Matilda grimaced. 'Thank you, Harriet. I hardly need an escort, but because it is getting dark, I won't go alone.'

'Well, none of your brothers is home yet so unless you intend to engage Mr Hayward to take you and he is busy in his study, who did you have in mind?' Harriet asked, overstepping the mark which she had done for years and was expected, given her good intentions.

'I'll ask Thomas – Detective Ashdown – to accompany me.'

Harriet breathed a sigh of relief. 'Good. That does set my mind at ease,' she said. 'Make haste then and don't be any later than you need to be.' Harriet put her hand to her chest as though calamity was inevitable. 'Be careful.'

Matilda nodded. 'Don't worry, I shall be fine and home before you know it.' She gave Harriet a quick kiss on the cheek, hiding her frustration – she had no choice now but to drop into the constabulary and see if Thomas could escort her, not that she felt she needed an escort. She would be home before the clock struck seven.

'Your hat!' Harriet called behind her, and with a roll of her eyes, Matilda hurried back, snatched the straw sailor hat from Harriet and plonking it unceremoniously on her head, hurried on again hearing Harriet's mutterings of, *'you must be bonneted, booted and gloved to attract a man,'* ringing in her ears.

In truth, Matilda didn't want Thomas coming with her. There was no point wasting his time when she was merely dropping off the newspaper copies and privately assuring Mrs Tufton, the giantess, that she was investigating further on her behalf.

Fortunately, the matter of Thomas escorting her was quickly resolved.

'He's not in, miss,' the young constable at the front desk advised her. 'Can I leave a message?'

'No, that's fine, thank you,' Matilda said, relieved, and she hurried to catch the omnibus that would take her to the exhibition which ran nightly until 10pm. If it were daytime, she would have comfortably walked the distance at her leisure.

When she arrived, there was a small queue waiting for their turn to enter – most people were probably at home having dinner and bound to come after for the evening shows. The owner, Alfred E. Burnham, recognised her immediately.

He bowed low. 'Ah, already?' His eyes widened at seeing an edition of the newspaper in her hand.

'Hot off the print press, Mr Burnham,' Matilda said, handing him a copy. 'I knew you would be keen to see it. May I go through and give Mrs Tufton her copy?'

'Of course,' he said, standing aside and ushering her through.

Matilda thanked him and continued. She avoided looking at the troubled souls on display, where possible, and if there were no people to obstruct her view, she glanced only enough to give them a small nod of recognition and to move on. Arriving at the giantess's area, Matilda found the stage empty, as she expected. A sign indicated the next show was in fifteen minutes, and a few people sat in the gallery resting until the show. Matilda moved closer to the stage curtain.

'Mrs Tufton, it's Matilda Hayward from *The Women's Journal*. May I enter?' She felt oddly nervous, and then the curtain opened slightly. Matilda stepped through.

'You've come back, Miss Hayward,' said the woman, towering over her.

'Matilda, please.'

'Anna,' Mrs Tufton reciprocated. She stepped back, understanding how imposing her size may be to a more delicate person. 'Please take a seat.'

'Thank you,' Matilda said, and both ladies sat. Matilda noted Anna wore a duplicate of the last satin dress she saw her in, only this time it was bright blue. Perhaps they were made for the show.

'May I speak freely?' Matilda asked.

Anna shook her head in the negative, but played along. 'Of course, and it's good to see you again. Did you have more questions?'

'No, in fact, I brought you a copy of the newspaper, just printed. I thought you might be keen to see it.' Matilda handed it over. She paused at the sound of a scream, but Anna did not seem at all surprised.

'Some of the ladies get a little overwrought on seeing some of our artists,' she explained. 'Thank you for bringing me a copy, how wonderful.'

They continued the charade; Matilda unaware of who might be listening in, but respecting Mrs Tufton's wishes.

'I'm glad you caught me,' Anna said. 'In a week I'll be heading off to our next venue, most exciting and across the country. I arrive in Perth just in time to celebrate my twenty-fourth birthday.'

Matilda smiled and nodded her understanding. 'I am glad I caught you too and many happy returns for when the day arrives. As well as bringing you one of the first copies off the press, my visit has another purpose. I wanted to assure you that your story will remain with me.'

Matilda glanced around and returned her attention to Anna. For just a moment they stared at each other, their gaze saying volumes, and Anna nodded.

'That's very kind of you.'

'I'd love to stay in touch. You know I enjoy writing, so perhaps we could correspond,' Matilda suggested.

'Indeed, that would be my pleasure,' Anna said. 'If you provide your address, I'll advise of my forwarding addresses as I tour.'

Matilda scribbled her address and on the back of her note wrote, 'non perdet fidem' – *don't lose faith*. She wasn't sure if Anna's education would afford her understanding of the line, but she could research it. Matilda was quickly rewarded as Anna read it, nodded and mouthed the words, 'thank you.'

'Will Mr Tufton be touring with you?' Matilda asked.

'Yes, he manages my appearances, makes the bookings, collects and manages our household purse.'

'Lovely. How did you meet, if you don't mind me being too familiar?' Matilda asked, attempting to make her question sound friendly, as if two ladies were speaking over tea and scones. The thought made her hungry, as it was, after all, dinner time.

'Mr Tufton, Carl, was known to my family. We are a farming family, and his family had a mercantile store in the nearby town. Carl asked my father for permission, he consented, and we had a short courtship. We both love the country and like to travel.'

'Yes, I see, and how fortunate to find love nearby and to share things in common,' Matilda said, and both women hid their smiles from their shared secret. Matilda continued talking in riddles that Anna would understand: 'I have four brothers and no suitor in sight. Most of us are single, but my eldest brother, Amos, is a solicitor and recently married. Like my editor, Mrs Lawson, he is a quick study on all legal matters pertaining to marriage, separation, home purchasing...'

Anna nodded that she understood. 'I imagine that with four brothers, you would be spoiled for suitors should you express interest.'

Matilda smiled. 'One of my brothers' childhood friends, Detective Thomas Ashdown, is a close friend of mine. Perhaps one day... but at the moment he is busy on cases and working his way through people's history and past offences.'

'Must be terribly time consuming but I expect it shows the character of those involved or suspected to be involved.'

'I imagine so,' Matilda said and gave her a brief nod and smile. She had succeeded in getting all her information across to Mrs Tufton and advising that she had the two men working on her behalf. 'I'd best not keep you; I imagine you want to prepare before your next show.'

'Thank you,' Anna said. 'It was good of you to remember me, Matilda.'

'You are unforgettable, Anna, and not for the reason you may think,' Matilda said and rising, the ladies shook hands, Matilda's engulfed in Anna's meaty hand. The desperate look on Anna's face touched Matilda's heart and she left feeling most despondent.

As she moved through the small crowd that had now queued to enter the tented exhibition and accepted the thanks yet again from Mr Burnham who seemed pleased with the article and free promotion of his event, she made her way towards the road. The crowds were swelling, particularly in the tent serving beverages, which was a little too close to the carnival for her liking. Several men had a skinful as her father would say.

'Evening miss.' A man tipped his hat to her.

She nodded and gave him a small smile, while increasing her pace as best she could in her corset and fashionably tight skirt. She avoided eye contact and continued away from the crowd but not before she overheard several lewd and complimentary remarks made in her direction.

'Goodness,' Matilda said, jumping back a step as a man appeared and stumbled before her. She moved away, well past his reach and attempt to accost her. Then she felt a hand on her shoulder and wheeled around, startled to find another stranger, who was no stranger to the bottle.

'Ma'am would you like to join me for a drink and a little company?' he said, slurring his words and squeezing her shoulder. It was hard to distinguish whether the alcohol or tobacco was the strongest scent emanating from him.

'No, she would not care to join you,' a man said, giving the large, inebriated stranger a firm push away.

Matilda turned to find Detective Thomas Ashdown beside her.

'Thomas!' she exclaimed with relief at seeing the detective.

'Matilda,' he said, in a voice far from happy.

The man came back at Thomas, angry and fuelled with alcohol.

'I'll take you on. I saw her first,' he said and made a wild swing at the detective.

Matilda yelped as Thomas pushed her behind him with one hand and ducked the blow. He fired back one of his own and then straightened his hat as the man stumbled to the ground. He shook out his fist; the man had a jaw of iron.

Thomas stood over him. 'I suggest you don't rise until we are out of sight, or you'll spend the night in the lockup,' he said and flashed the police badge clipped inside his coat.

'Right you are then,' the fallen man said, slurring his words and staying on the ground. 'Sorry, I didn't know she was spoken, for especially by a policeman.'

'She's… never mind,' Thomas said as Matilda appeared from behind him. His mouth was drawn in a thin line, and he steered her away from the tent.

'Take my arm, Matilda,' he said. 'You are quite safe now.'

Matilda put her arm through his offered crooked arm and they walked towards the street to hail a ride.

Thomas felt the weight of her arm on him, a familiar ache returned, wanting this to be the future, her arm always through his.

'Thank you, Thomas. How did you know I was here?' she asked.

'I came by your house to speak with you about Mr Tufton—'

'—ooh, did you?' she interrupted him. 'What did you find out?' she asked, looking up at him with admiration.

Thomas cleared his throat, trying to maintain his displeasure with her.

'And that is when Harriet informed me that you were here, with me, apparently. But obviously, that is not the case,' he said, continuing to walk at a pace too fast for Matilda.

'Stop, Thomas.' She pulled him up. 'I can't keep your pace with this skirt on, otherwise I'm sure I should outpace you.'

He was just about to challenge that notion when he realised that was absurd, they were all grown up now.

'I apologise,' he said, altering his step and slowing for her.

'And I was not telling an untruth to Harriet,' Matilda said defensively. 'I went by your station to ask if you could accompany me at this hour of the night and only because Harriet insisted, but the young constable said you had departed. I only intended to drop off two copies of our latest edition and return home. Really Thomas, it is not as though I was entering a brothel!'

He snapped to look at her. 'And how would you know what that might be like?'

'Well, I don't, not as you and Daniel do, but I don't believe it is a secret what goes on there.'

He made a huffing sound. They arrived roadside, just as an omnibus pulled in. It would stop conveniently close to Matilda's Highgate Hill home. Thomas offered her his hand as she stepped up. Once en route she asked again, her voice lowered, 'What did you find out about Carl Tufton?'

'Never mind that, what might have happened if I hadn't arrived?' he asked her, conscious of her proximity to him and her blue eyes studying him with affection.

She lifted her small bag. 'I could have swung this at him.' Matilda concealed her smile at Thomas's reaction. 'You are right Thomas, you're my hero, thank you,' she said.

'You need not tease me, Matilda, I was only concerned for your welfare,' he said, haughtily. 'It's a man's business to look after himself and the women he is responsible for through marriage or contact.'

Matilda laughed. 'Is that so?'

'Yes it is so,' he said, his frustration rising. 'And I am always willing to render my services to you, but when you put yourself in these dangerous situations—'

Matilda cut off his lecture. 'Well, indeed I am grateful, Thomas. Will that suffice?' she asked, and he huffed again. 'So tell me, please, Carl Tufton, what did you learn?' she begged, her clever countenance and bright eyes assessing him.

'That he is a shady character, and you need to step away from this story,' Thomas said, sternly.

Matilda dismissed his comment. 'Oh Thomas, sadly I know you so well and for so long that your fearsome detective act does not deter me. Quite the opposite. So what now?'

## Chapter 7

Aunt Audrey – Mrs Samuel Bloomfield – was generous of bosom and opinion. She had a particular fondness for her brother, Mr Hayward, and as they were both widowed and she was her brother's only surviving sister, Aunt Audrey felt it was her duty to accept the role of matriarch when visiting the Hayward household. Thus, she took pride of place at Sunday lunch, looking at the faces around the table of her nephews and niece, Matilda, along with Amos's wife Minnie and Daniel's childhood friend, Thomas – a regular guest for so many years that no one thought to invite him anymore.

Today, as always, she was dressed in her mourning black, despite Mr Bloomfield having passed away some fifteen years prior. A wealthy woman and handsome with her white hair piled atop her head and startling blue eyes, she was not without her suitors. Audrey wore black to deter them.

'At my age, all they want is a nursemaid or a household manager,' she would respond should anyone encourage or inflict a suitor upon her. She was perfectly happy with her life and the company she sought. However, she was always on the lookout for good household staff and making offers to them was not beneath her.

'You have the best cook in Brisbane, brother, I don't know how you manage it,' she said, admiring the Sunday spread before them. 'I have tried to poach her several times I am not ashamed to say.'

'As to have I,' said Mrs Amos Hayward – Minnie – sitting opposite Audrey. Amos looked at her, shocked. 'You need not look at me like that, Amos. Your career is important and as your father is kindly putting more business your way, entertaining is paramount to your success.'

'Absolutely correct,' Aunt Audrey decreed, making Minnie squirm with pleasure. Audrey's fortune was worth winning and her good opinion most sought after by Minnie.

'Sorry Pa,' Amos muttered under his breath.

'Not at all,' Mr Hayward said and grinned. 'Cook is free to go wherever she pleases but for some reason the dear soul stays here. For that, I am most grateful even though my dull meal requests must leave her frustrated sometimes.' He did not know that Cook was listening on the other side of the door and was touched by his words and consideration.

'Probably because you are too generous with her wages and you never check her menus or the hours she keeps,' Aunt Audrey said.

The twins – Gideon and Elijah – glanced at each other and smiled. Cook was going nowhere; the household was safe for now.

'And you two need not smirk,' Aunt Audrey said to them. 'Soon you will be married and running your own households and you will know what it is like to have an inferior meal. And as for you, Thomas, you are getting way too thin and must mind your diet.'

'I promise you, Aunt, I shan't be marrying anytime soon,' Gideon responded quickly, saving Thomas from making excuses for his lifestyle. Gideon continued, 'A man must sow his wild oats and enjoy all the city has to offer.' No one needed that comment elaborated upon.

'Nor am I rushing to the altar, Aunt,' Elijah concurred. 'But should I do so, I'll be sure to remind you of this conversation and tell you that you were indeed right.'

Mr Hayward gave his son a grateful smile. Elijah, ever the peacemaker and sensible one.

Aunt Audrey patted his hand. He was her second favourite Hayward boy, Amos being the first. She continued, 'Speaking of which, not married yet, Matilda?'

'Not since last Sunday, Aunt Audrey.' Matilda smiled. 'But how is your annual fair committee coming along with their preparations?'

'Don't try and change the subject, young lady. I'm sure your father could arrange something if you can't find a suitable suitor,' she said, with a glance to her brother.

Matilda laughed. 'No doubt he could, Aunt Audrey, but I am not currently seeking a husband.' She cleared her throat and requested the gravy boat.

'I know several young men who would be very suitable if you were to give up your writing hobby,' Minnie offered. 'Ouch,' she exclaimed as Amos bumped her and subtly shook his head.

'Don't tell me you are still writing for that women's paper!' Aunt Audrey exclaimed. 'No wonder you don't have any suitors.'

Matilda sighed and her shoulders slumped. 'I do have—'

Gideon cut her off. 'Matilda has many suitors. Why, just last week two of our friends from the club, William Datt and George Kille, both asked about her situation and said they would call to visit.'

Matilda grimaced. Across the table, Thomas's eyes narrowed, and he sat upright.

'Is that not the George Kille who lost a fortune playing poker recently?' Thomas asked.

'Strike him from the list immediately,' Aunt Audrey said even before Gideon could defend his friend. 'One does not need a man who gambles away the family's fortune.'

Matilda glanced to her father for rescue. He gave her a sympathetic look; there was no stopping Audrey, he knew that from experience.

'What's this William Datt character like then?' Aunt Audrey asked haughtily.

'Respectable. A fellow doctor, new at it like me,' Elijah said, defending his friend and his twin's selection. 'I believe the ladies find him attractive as well.'

Thomas had no recourse and could think of nothing to dislodge this contender.

'It would be lovely if you found love, Matilda,' Daniel teased her.

'Do shut up,' she said, giving him a warning look.

'Love? You're not waiting to fall in love, surely?' Aunt

Audrey continued, sitting back and allowing Harriet to remove her first course. 'Matilda, love is not necessary.'

A round of laughs, shuffles and sideway glances greeted her comment.

'Nevertheless, Aunt, I want it,' Matilda said. 'I believe it can exist and that couples genuinely have love and affection in their relationship, like Pa and Mother, Amos and Minnie, and yourself and Uncle Samuel.'

'True,' Aunt Audrey conceded, 'but your father and I were both fortunate and unfortunate. To lose our partners early in life means the eternal love continues to bloom without fault or favour,' she said, and sighed. The reprieve was short-lived for Matilda and Aunt Audrey continued, 'Find yourself a presentable man with a fortune, get a capable housekeeper, oversee the running of his household and then you are free to do as you please, even if it is writing for that newspaper.'

Minnie, sitting opposite Aunt Audrey, gasped, surprised at the acceptance of Matilda's occupation.

Aunt Audrey turned her attention to the end of the table, where Thomas had enjoyed his first course of lunch and was congratulating himself on remaining on the periphery of the discussion.

'What about you, Thomas? You are quiet today, young man, have you nothing to say about Matilda's situation? I believe you are a handsome, single man, with a suitable occupation and income,' Aunt Audrey said. 'And of marriageable age, if I am not mistaken.'

Thomas heard Daniel chuckle beside him, and the amused looks of the brothers and Mr Hayward turned towards him. Matilda gazed at him with an expectant look on her face and raised eyebrows. Thomas cleared his throat, hoping for someone to intercede. They did not.

'Well madam,' he said, constructing his answer, 'I think it would be a very lucky, brave and ambitious man who would ask for the hand of Miss Hayward.'

The men erupted in laughter and Matilda frowned at Thomas before giving into a smile herself.

Aunt Audrey made a humph sound and turned to Mr Hayward. 'And that would be your fault, brother, for forgetting she was a girl in those impressionable years.'

'Ah, I wondered when it would come back to me,' he said and chuckled. Aunt Audrey smiled at him with good grace. Mr Hayward raised his glass. 'To our Matilda.'

'To our Matilda,' the table guests responded, and raising her glass, Matilda acknowledged the toast with a sip and allowed Thomas to give her the quickest of winks.

## Chapter 8

Thomas was long overdue at the club; it had been a few weeks since he had made his way there for a drink with colleagues and to indulge in the offer of female companionship. Even so, his heart was only half in it. He attributed this to the additional time spent in the company of the Hayward family over the past week, and in particular Miss Matilda Hayward.

His walking pace picked up as frustration boiled to the surface and he fumed to himself; she should not have gone out alone in the evening to that carnival with the shady characters that were inebriated and wouldn't hesitate to take advantage should the opportunity arise. On the other hand, he liked to come to her rescue. That's how he wanted her to see him – dependable, strong, a provider. As for this Dr William Datt – Gideon's friend – if he knew when and if Dr Datt intended to call, he'd make sure he was there at the time.

She was infuriating. Many women and their mothers had been only too happy to make themselves known to him, keen on a match with a hard-working, well-established young man. As for Matilda, she appeared to think of him as one of her brothers; he wondered if she had ever looked at him with a romantic notion.

He pushed open the door to the club and entered the loud, smoky and comfortingly familiar surroundings.

'Ashdown, over here,' he heard a voice yell as he wandered towards the bar.

Familiar faces from the office – other ranks and brother detectives – were well ensconced, lagers in their hands, women draped around them. There were eleven detectives on the payroll across the entire state, and Thomas was one of seven in Brisbane. Three were here tonight and he acknowledged the men as they gave a cheer on seeing one from their ranks.

'Long time no see; where have you been, Ashdown?' Burton, a colleague from his training days asked him, cuffing him roughly around the shoulders. 'Look who's back from the dead, boys!'

'I've been working, Burton, you should try it sometime,' Thomas said, giving his mate a good digging.

Burton laughed. 'You'll keep. I'll shout you your first round since you've been so dedicated.'

Thomas nodded. 'Fitting, thanks.'

He wore the jibes from colleagues and settled comfortably amongst them. He'd forgotten how much he needed this, to not think about the dead bodies he'd seen this week or the pressure of solving cases to keep the inspector happy. Daniel might be his best friend, but he'd never understand the headspace that was required for a detective day-in and day-out. Sometimes, he needed to be among his own.

'So, getting any romantic action lately?' Burton asked irreverently, placing a decent sized serving of whiskey in front of his friend.

Thomas raised his glass to his friend and took a mouthful. He shook his head. 'Can't boast of any victories, but I could do with the distraction.'

'Plenty of nice ladies here,' Burton said looking around, 'except for the blonde near the door. I'm working my magic on her.' He glanced that way with a look that said ready to pounce.

Thomas checked her out. She was nowhere near as attractive as another blonde that occupied his thoughts.

'I think I prefer a brunette,' he said.

'Sure you do,' Burton grinned. 'I hear you've got yourself one of those women liberator types, writing for that paper. She'll keep you in line... we'll be expecting to see more of you here then.'

Thomas scowled at him, but played along as expected. 'Don't start giving me a hard time, I've come in here to be free of worry for a while.'

Burton held up his hands in retreat. 'Wouldn't dream of it. So keeping yourself for her are you?'

Thomas grinned and shook his head. 'Shut up.'

'As I thought.' Burton laughed. 'Mary, get yourself over here and meet my friend, Thomas.'

The detective groaned as a scantily dressed brunette smiled at him and sashayed towards him with her assets on display, her face well-powdered and lips stained deep red. There was no doubting she was attractive and the thought of some relief and a brief time off the clock appealed to him given his standard hours of six days a week had been 9am to 9pm with a dinner break.

'My friend here is suffering from unrequited love,' Burton said, and Mary gave Thomas a sympathetic look.

'Poor you,' she said, and touched his face.

'And my friend is exaggerating,' Thomas said, with a sigh and a less appreciate glance in Burton's direction.

'How could any girl say no to this handsome face?' Mary asked, draping herself over Thomas and pressing herself against him.

'Hard to imagine,' Burton agreed, and laughed.

'She hasn't said no—' Thomas explained and then stopped. He had no business to be telling his story to these two.

'So you haven't even asked her out then!' Mary exclaimed. 'Well, how you goin' to know? If you be asking me out, I promise to say yes. What's wrong with her then?'

Thomas smiled despite himself. 'Nothing's wrong with her but she's made it quite clear that she's not interested in being shackled or having her possessions claimed by a man.'

'Well, la-di-da, how nice it'd be to have some possessions,' Mary said. 'Mine are all natural gifts.'

'And mighty fine they are, Mary,' Burton assured her and raised his eyebrows in Thomas's direction. 'Take the night off from ruffians and ladies out of your reach, Thomas, and enjoy the bounty in front of you.'

Thomas had to agree, Mary was as tempting as the large glass of whiskey in front of him and he was a man who needed a distraction, be it ever so fleeting. He had little else to spend his earnings on.

*****

The sharp rap on his front door woke Thomas before seven the next morning. He rolled on his side and leaned up enough to glance to the hallway at the clock; seeing the hour, he groaned. He was usually up well before now, but too much of everything last night had been his downfall.

The next rap came on his window.

'Coming,' he yelled and winced. He raised himself from his bed, ran a hand through his hair and, making sure he was presentable to open the door, made his way down the musty hallway of his timber home. It was coming up to two years since he had bought his modest family home from his father who wanted to retire to the country and intended to sell it. The sale proceeded at a good price, but he had done nothing to the house since the day his father handed him the key.

Thomas opened the door a crack to find his partner, Harry, on the doorstep.

The sight of Harry woke him up quickly. 'What's happened?' he asked, knowing there would be no reason for a social visit.

'You'd be looking the worse for wear,' Harry said. 'There's been a murder.'

Thomas sighed. 'Another. A lady of the night?'

'Not this time, praise the Lord.'

Thomas frowned and stood back to allow Harry in. He closed the door and passed him to lead the way to the kitchen, filling a glass on the sink with tank water. 'I'd offer you some tea but—' Thomas waved his hand around to show the barren state of affairs.

'You're living here, yes?' Harry frowned.

Thomas grimaced at him. 'It's a roof over my head. I've been meaning to do some work on it.' He glanced around, seeing it from Harry's eyes. His mother's feminine touches were long gone except for the faded curtains, and the only sign of his father was the furniture he chose not to take with him to his new abode. At least that included a decent mahogany bureau and a respectable chintz sofa that would improve with new upholstering.

'My nephew is moving in next week. He lost his job down south – he's a handy lad. Free board in exchange for doing some work around the place while he's looking for a job,' Thomas said, and winced. The sunlight and even talking was causing him pain.

'Well, that's the best idea you've had for a long while,' Harry said.

Thomas looked out his kitchen window to his dishevelled garden and the district view beyond as he filled another glass with water. 'So, who's dead?'

'Alfred Burnham.'

He cricked his neck and after gulping the water down, turned to Harry. 'Who's Alfred Burnham when he's at home?'

'The owner of the carnival,' Harry said.

Thomas's eyes widened and he slapped the glass down. 'Why didn't you say so? Give me a minute.' He rushed past his partner to get dressed. He wasn't a man who usually rushed his toileting as he had learned early in his career that appearance matters – dress, shoes, small touches – especially to the police hierarchy of old school gents. But this morning he hurriedly put on his attire and with a glance to his mirror, conceded he could not be on call and expect to look the part all the time. He splashed some cold water on his face and ran a brush through his hair and light beard. He preferred to be clean-shaven, but it was easier in this job with its late nights and early starts to maintain a beard.

In the meantime, Harry opened a few of the kitchen cupboards and shook his head. He'd have to get his missus to help the detective out. A sorry state of affairs, it was. The man needed a wife, not another young man living with him.

*Chapter 9*

Amos instructed his sister, Matilda: 'Tell Mrs Tufton not to say a thing.' He read the couple of lines again that Mrs Tufton had somehow managed to get to Matilda at her place of work this morning:

*Dear Miss Hayward, Mr Burnham has met an untimely end.*

*I may need your assistance please and that of your brother should he be willing. I assure you I am in a position to pay and above reproach in this matter.*

*Please visit at your earliest convenience, I have information.*
*Mrs A. Tufton, c/- Burnham's Exhibition.*

Matilda informed her editor of the contents and with Mrs Lawson's permission, abruptly left to visit her solicitor brother, Amos, who would know what to do.

Now, he sat across from Matilda and looked very much the part of the young solicitor about town. Since his father's retirement from the firm that he established decades ago, Amos seemed to have grown into the role quickly, standing on his own two feet.

'Not a word to the police or anyone else,' he reiterated.

'But won't that make her look as if she knows something?' Matilda asked.

'It would be worse if she said the wrong thing. We don't need the police sentencing her and asking questions later, which has happened on many occasions.' He saw Matilda's expression. 'I'm sure your detective wouldn't do that though.'

'He's not my detective, Amos.' Matilda blushed. 'I believe you were with us when we grew up… remember him?'

Amos smiled. 'Old teasing habits die hard, I'm afraid.'

'Well, that works both ways. Now Father said—'

'You took this to Father first?' he asked, stiffening and looking affronted.

'Yes, he offered his services for free – he does take on a few charity cases in his retirement – but he said as Mrs Tufton has indicated she can pay, and her husband may also pay for legal services, I'd best give you the business first.'

Amos nodded. 'Good, rightly so.'

Matilda studied him; he was once so confident – the eldest and most like her and their mother. Quiet, considerate and not needing to be as demonstrative as the other boys by his position of being eldest which came with its rewards. She wondered if Minnie was expecting too much from Amos or if he was putting undue pressure on himself to meet her standards, imaginary or real. Amos would never admit that, so she determined to rectify it as best she could.

'Besides, Amos,' she said, 'you are the most diplomatic and influential person I know, and Mrs Tufton needs you.'

His lips betrayed a small smile of pleasure and he read the note again before pronouncing, 'Let us go then and hear what she has to say,' and rising from his chair.

Matilda retrieved her hat from Amos's desk and waited while he briefed his clerk. They descended the stairs from his office together and Amos hailed a hansom cab. He gave Matilda his hand and helped her into a seat; she allowed it as they were in public near his workplace.

Settling next to her, he said, 'I am impressed, Matilda. Don't tell me you are becoming a lady at last.'

'I do know when to play the part, especially for your sake, Amos. That would impress Minnie, wouldn't it?' Matilda said with a smile. 'I am quite capable of getting in and out of a cab without the assistance of a man's hand… don't forget I was always a much better climber than you and should the opportunity present itself, I am sure you will find I still am.'

'Heaven help us,' he said, rolling his eyes and Matilda laughed.

She reached for his hand. 'Thank you, Amos, for helping me.'

'Don't thank me yet. It might all be over before we begin, or her information may not be of any value. When we arrive, if there are police present, leave me to talk with them and you go in and see Mrs Tufton. Remember…'

'Tell her to say nothing,' Matilda said and nodded.

'Precisely.'

*****

A sizeable crowd was milling around the grounds of the carnival, held back only by a rope draped across the entrance path stopping public entry. A sign hung from it reading 'Closed today. Management apologises for any inconvenience.'

Thomas glanced around, concerned about the encroaching crowd.

'Death can be inconvenient,' Harry agreed as he caught his breath; his partner's stride far exceeded his own at this time in his life.

A young constable stood near the marquee, preventing anyone unofficial from entering. He drew himself up straighter on seeing Detective Thomas Ashdown and his partner, Detective Harry Dart, approaching.

'Sir,' the young constable said.

'What have we got, Constable?' Thomas asked.

'A dead body, sir, a man in his forties identified as the owner of this show, Alfred Burnham. He appears to be bludgeoned to death, around the head. The coroner is in there now. Mr Burnham was last seen alive around 11pm and was dead when found at 6am.'

Thomas nodded. 'Any witnesses?'

'Yes, sir, Constable Robinson is talking with a few of the, um—'

'Artists in the carnival, Constable?' Harry helped him out.

'Yes, that's it, sir. He's getting statements now if they saw or heard anything.'

'Good work,' Thomas said, remembering how little

encouragement he received in his early days before making detective rank and being partnered with Harry.

A swelling crowd of curious locals was getting closer to the tent and Harry put an end to it.

'Nothing to see here, ladies and gentlemen. I suggest you get on your way, or we may need to detain and talk with you,' he bellowed, and the crowd dispersed.

A man appeared through the marquee flaps and ventured to the three police colleagues.

'Morris Wilks, at your service,' he said. 'I'm afraid Mr Burnham is not available this morning, he's had an… accident.'

Thomas flashed the man his identification.

'Yes, a nasty one,' Harry agreed. 'Let's see the body and talk with the coroner then.'

'Right. Best you come in,' Mr Wilks said, standing straighter and glancing around uncomfortably as if he were the obvious suspect. 'The show—' Mr Wilks asked.

'May go on,' Thomas informed him, 'once we no longer need the premises and we've spoken to everyone on-site, including yourself, Mr Wilks.'

Mr Wilks nodded. 'Some of the artists will not wish to speak with your people; you have to understand they are not all comfortable talking with people.'

'I'm sure that feeling is mutual,' Thomas said.

## Chapter 10

Detective Thomas Ashdown left Harry to finish talking with the front man, Morris Wilks, and entered the tent. He couldn't be counted as amongst the curious – he had seen plenty of freak shows in his everyday investigations – murders, assaults, wife and husband bashing, abandoned children, industrial accidents – the sights inside this tent were some of the least freaky sights he'd encountered thus far. But he understood those in the police force who were new and green and who may not feel as comfortable in these surroundings.

He moved along the internal corridor of the tent until he came upon a large area with several rows of chairs – a private exhibition area perhaps, he thought. There he encountered Constable Douglas Robinson whom he noted was waiting, pencil and notebook in hand, his shoulders back and chin up.

Good man, Thomas thought, best to look confident even if you don't feel it and he could tell the constable was not comfortable; his breathing gave him away.

'Constable Robinson?' Thomas asked.

The constable eyed him suspiciously until Thomas opened his suit jacket to show his badge.

'Sir,' he said nervously. 'I'm waiting on the first frea–uh–subject to interview.'

Thomas nodded. 'I'll observe, you ask your questions.' He moved several of the front rows of chairs and turned them so that they faced the row behind with a comfortable gap in between, to create a makeshift interview room. Thomas then took a seat and suggested the young police officer do the same.

The young constable left the middle seat between them, sat and swallowed, nervously.

'Don't worry,' Thomas assured him, 'we'll cover for each other.'

'Sir.' He nodded and took a deep breath.

They waited and Thomas looked around, taking in the area until his eyes rested back on the constable, who sat perfectly erect and still as if at attention.

'At ease, Constable. Are you stationed in the city then?' Thomas asked, attempting to relax the young man.

'Yes, sir, I graduated three months ago.' He ventured a smile. 'They told me during training that I'd see some odd sights and meet all types, but I wasn't expecting this.'

Thomas smiled. 'No, well you wouldn't be, that's for sure. Who is first up?'

Constable Robinson glanced at his notes. 'Jo-Jo, the Russian dog-faced man. The manager said that some of the exhibitors didn't speak English, so they'd be escorted to see us with a translator.'

'Good.' Thomas nodded, and they both turned as a couple entered – a middle-aged blonde woman, hard of features but attractive nevertheless, accompanied by a smaller person, a man, completely covered in hair. The small man walked with a limp and was supported by a cane.

'Mr Jo-Jo doesn't speak English,' the woman said in a strong Russian accent, 'so I'll translate for you.'

'Thank you, Ma'am,' Constable Robinson said. He gave Mr Jo-Jo a nod of greeting which was reciprocated. 'This is Inspector—' he stumbled on Thomas's surname.

'Ashdown,' Thomas said, and offered his hand to the woman and Mr Jo-Jo.

Constable Robinson's eyes widened in surprise, and Mr Jo-Jo offered a small smile as he took the detective's hand to shake. It was not often Mr Jo-Jo received human contact; people feared touching him as if the hair growth would be contagious.

'Shall we sit?' Thomas asked, indicating the row of chairs.

The four people each took a seat.

Thomas and Constable Robinson sat opposite the interview subjects.

'Who might you be, madam?' Thomas addressed the woman with Mr Jo-Jo.

'Irina Wilks, Mrs Irina Wilks. My husband is the manager.'

'Ah yes, we met Mr Wilks on the way in.' Thomas nodded, and then looked at the constable, inviting him to start the interview.

'Right.' The constable looked to the translator. 'Could you ask Mr Jo… uh, Mr Jo-Jo where he was between 11pm and 6am last night, this morning?'

While Irina translated, Thomas glanced up at a sound to his left and saw a woman, or rather, two women conjoined, watching them from the doorway. She or they entered the room and took a chair or two in this case, in the corner as far away from the interview as possible. The translator turned and addressed them in English.

'Ella, Elvira, the police will be with you soon.' One lady nodded to show that she understood.

Thomas tried not to stare; he noticed now that Constable Robinson shuffled uncomfortably. Thomas didn't like the ladies being close enough to hear the questions and formulate answers in advance, but he doubted, given the small stature of the ladies and balance difficulties, that they could have bludgeoned Alfred E. Burnham to death.

He returned his attention to the subjects in front of him as Irina's gravelly voice cut into his thoughts. 'Mr Jo-Jo said he was asleep in his caravan and never left the premises. And before you ask, he said he had no witness to his activity.'

Thomas nodded; Irina was clearly no stranger to police investigations and her answer was a lot shorter than what Mr Jo-Jo had said. He wondered if he was getting the full translation or the version that management wanted him to hear.

Constable Robinson asked his next question. 'Could you ask Mr Jo-Jo if he noticed anything suspicious in the last few days or anyone loitering around other than paying spectators, uh, public?'

Thomas's partner, Harry, interrupted. 'The coroner is ready to see us, he's waiting at the entrance,' he said to

Thomas. 'Why don't you meet with him, and I'll see this through with the young constable.'

Thomas gave his partner a grateful nod. He rose. 'Thank you. Constable Robinson, I think you've got this in hand, but Detective Dart will be here. Send us your report when you are finished.'

'Yes, thank you, sir,' he said, looking fleetingly pleased until his gaze travelled to the ladies in the corner waiting.

'Meet me outside when you're done?' Thomas asked, securing a nod from Harry. Thomas excused himself and made his way out through the tent corridor to the entrance, where he saw more people had now gathered as word of the murder spread.

As he engaged the coroner's eye, he saw a familiar figure disappearing into the exhibitor's caravan area – Matilda, and in front of her, just a fleeting glimpse of a tall man, his face obscured.

Thomas let out a frustrated sigh. As soon as he was done with the coroner, he'd be finding out exactly what Miss Matilda Hayward was doing here, how she knew to come, and most importantly, who that man was accompanying her.

## Chapter 11

According to Mr Wilks, manager of Burnham's Carnival, the giantesses' caravan was second from the end of the row with a red stripe upon it. Matilda followed Amos, tentatively looking around him in search of the van, aware that they were in a private area and tensions were running high.

'Over here,' Amos announced, indicating the caravan with the door ajar. He stood back to let Matilda make the first contact less he should frighten the lady within, regardless of her size and capability.

Matilda stood outside the ajar door and cleared her throat with a delicate cough. 'Mrs Tufton, it's Matilda Hayward. My brother, Amos, accompanies me.'

She waited a moment and, to her relief, footsteps approached.

'Matilda, please come in, both of you,' the giantess said, peering through the door, her smile genuine and a look of relief on her countenance.

'Thank goodness you are all right,' Matilda said. 'Such a terrible affair.' She took the two steps up and entered the caravan. 'May I introduce my brother, Amos Hayward of Hayward & Bruce Solicitors.' The Bruce had long since departed but the name remained out of respect.

Amos lifted his hat and bowed. 'At your service, madam.'

Despite her imposing figure, somehow Mrs Anna Tufton, the giantess, came across as vulnerable.

'It was so kind of you to come. Please take a seat. Can I offer you tea?' she asked.

The caravan was small, but at one end was a large bed and at the other a table with two bench seats. Opposite was a small sink, kettle and a large jug of water. A small milk jug sat covered with a lace top.

'Thank you, we would love tea,' Matilda said, taking off her hat. 'Allow me to help.'

Amos seated himself to get out of the way while the ladies prepared tea and the giantess placed a plate of biscuits on the table. Amos thanked her and happily accepted one. Minnie would not allow him treats for fear of him gaining a married man's figure.

'This is delicious!' Amos declared of the Florentine biscuit and received a genuine smile of pleasure from Anna.

'In an interview some time ago, I mentioned my favourite biscuits were Florentine. Whenever I come to a new town, I often receive a gift from the local bakery. It's a kind thought.'

'And good for them, I suspect,' Matilda said with a sly smile, 'especially should you thank them during your show.' Matilda put the sugar bowl, spoon, and teacups on the table as directed by Anna and then sat out of the way.

'I do that a couple of times during our stay,' she conceded. 'It seems only fair.'

Anna placed the teapot on the table along with a small, hand-painted milk jug. Her size made everything seem more delicate. She took a seat, and Matilda and Amos sat opposite, the two of them comfortably fitting on the one bench.

Matilda got down to business. 'The police are here. I'm sure you know that.'

Anna nodded. 'Yes. Mrs Wilks told me she would come for me when it was my turn to speak with them.' She poured the tea, passing the cups to her guest.

Matilda took the lace from the top of the milk jug and poured a little in her and Amos's cup, offering the same to Anna, who accepted.

'Who is Mrs Wilks?' Amos asked.

'She's the wife of the general manager. Mr Burnham was master of ceremonies and owner, but Mr Wilks was his right-hand man. Mrs Wilks is Russian, but he is not.'

'Is she an artist?' Matilda asked diplomatically.

Anna shook her head. 'No, but she's involved with obtaining artists and negotiating the contracts.'

Matilda explained how Amos might assist and his basic fee, finishing by advising, 'But if you are not in a position to afford that fee, Amos can discuss that, or if you would like to interview several lawyers before making your choice, please don't hesitate.'

'I can afford that rate, thank you, and I would like to retain your services, please,' she said to Amos.

He nodded. 'Then my first piece of advice is to say nothing. You mentioned in your note to Matilda that you had information, so can you share that?'

She nodded, glanced at the door before returning her attention to the Haywards and took a deep breath. 'My husband is in town. He always comes with me to each location where we perform, but he rarely stays on site with me. He has business to attend to in town and it is more convenient for him to remain there.'

Matilda and Amos read between the lines and understood the delicate situation. The carnival was well positioned near the town centre, so they understood the couple to be separated.

'Last evening,' she continued, 'he paid the owner, Mr Burnham, a visit to discuss my contract and payment.'

'I see,' Amos said. 'Were you present?'

'Yes, and my husband, Carl, insisted I be paid more. It became quite heated, so I left the men to their negotiations and returned here to my caravan.'

'About what time was this?' Matilda asked, knowing that Detective Ashdown would soon have a time of death for Mr Burnham.

'Carl arrived around 10pm and I returned here around 10.30pm. I didn't see Carl or Mr Burnham after that, and I don't know the result of the negotiations as yet.'

'You haven't seen your husband this morning then?' Amos confirmed.

'No.'

'So, you want us to ensure that your husband is not incriminated?' Matilda asked.

'No, that is not the legal representation I am seeking,' Anna said, and looked from Matilda to Amos. She explained to Amos, 'It is not my choice to be part of this exhibition. I don't want to do this; I don't want to be entertainment for the masses.'

'I understand,' Amos said.

'Of course you don't,' Matilda empathised with her.

'I want a divorce, my freedom, and as I have been the major earner for our family for the last ten years, I want a pension or any money I can retrieve from Carl so I can live modestly and have my freedom. What happens to my husband is of little concern to me,' Anna said in the softest of voices, as though she were discussing the weather.

Matilda's eyes widened. She turned to Amos.

He nodded and swallowed. 'Then first and foremost, Mrs Tufton, let's work out what you will say to the police in your interview now, shall we, and then from there we will work out the best way to proceed with a divorce.'

'Thank you, Mr Hayward,' the giantess said, and visibly relaxed.

The fact was not lost on Matilda or Amos that Mrs Anna Tufton's husband might be the killer. Or for that matter, she may have killed the showman herself.

*Chapter 12*

Detective Thomas Ashdown studied the prone body of Mr Burnham. Thomas wished he hadn't had such a big night; his head thumped, and the sun was far too bright this morning. Exhaustion crept over him and he was hungry now that he was sober.

The coroner, Dr Patrick Nevins, joined him as he stared at the deceased. Dr Nevins was neat, slim, in his fifties and greying. He was polite enough not to mention the living looked as bad as the dead this morning; he recalled being a younger man and enjoying the pleasures that came with it. He gave his brief and initial thoughts.

'I can't tell you much until I complete the post-mortem examination,' he said, knowing every detective hoped he would have all the answers immediately. 'There's a significant wound to the throat and also many blows to the body. My first thought would be that your victim was bludgeoned to death with something resembling the shape of a cricket ball, a steel cricket ball.'

Thomas frowned. 'Well, that is one I haven't heard before.'

The doctor elaborated, 'It is the best way I can think of to describe it. The shape is like a ball imprint, round, quite distinct and as if it were a cricket ball made of hard metal and repeatedly used to hit the victim. Some blows don't have that imprint – they are more like a stick.'

'Anything come to mind other than a steel cricket ball or a stick? Perhaps a golf stick?' Thomas asked.

'Perhaps. I saw a trophy like that once with a ball bottom and a thin base. The head of a golf stick is too cylindrical… sorry, that's the best I can do,' the coroner said. He moved around the body as he spoke. 'I suspect he was dead by the third or fourth blow, but it appears he was hit more than a dozen times. I'll know more soon.'

'Good grief,' Thomas said, studying the doctor. 'Any refinement on the original time of death?'

Nevins smiled. 'What did I tell you previously – 11pm to 6am?'

Thomas nodded.

'Well, it was a cool last night, so the body didn't deteriorate at a great rate. I'll grace you a few hours,' he joked, and Thomas gave him a grin. 'Make it 11pm to 4am.'

'That makes all the difference,' Thomas joined in the joke. He thought aloud, welcoming the doctor's input. 'So, it would take someone of reasonable physical strength to inflict the blows?'

'I'd say,' Nevins agreed. 'The rest of the blows were either delivered in anger, or fear that the man might still arise, or delivered by many hands.'

Thomas looked surprised. 'Hmm, imagine a death

surrounded by—' His words fell off, as he thought of the oddities in the carnival, each of them bearing a weapon of attack.

'Live by the sword and all that,' Nevins said. 'Of course, it might have been just one hand that held the weapon.'

'Handy if we could find it,' Thomas agreed.

'Don't disregard the bruising to the throat, that might yet be our cause of death.'

'You'll send for me when you are ready?' Thomas asked.

'I shall,' he agreed.

The men bade each other farewell and after Nevins' departure, Thomas continued studying the corpse and the surroundings. His partner, Harry, soon joined him.

'Ah good, I need your eyes,' Thomas said. 'I've studied the area and the body, but it would be good if you could commit it to memory too.'

'Of course,' Harry said, his eyes noting the blood and violence in front of him.

'Anything of note in the interviews?' Thomas asked.

'We've still got a few to do, but so far, nothing worthy of mention. I've given the constable and Mrs Wilks a rest break; she insists on accompanying everyone. In time there may prove to be some little detail that will be useful when I check consistencies across all statements and run each of the exhibitors for criminal records.'

Thomas chuckled. 'Do you think they'll have criminal backgrounds? Poor bastards probably wouldn't be exhibited if they were criminally minded.'

'True, but you never know,' Harry said, studying the body.

'You never know,' Thomas concurred.

'I saw your lady friend, Miss Matilda Hayward, arrive.'

Thomas didn't bother to correct the misconception. 'Where did she go?' he asked, trying to make his voice sound casual.

'I believe she's talking with the big lady,' Harry said. 'She's got her brother with her. The blond one who looks like her. What's his story?'

'Amos.' Thomas breathed a sigh of relief. 'He's a solicitor.'

The two detectives looked at each other.

'And why would the big lady need one of those?' Harry asked.

*****

Constable Robinson joined the detectives as they watched the body of Mr Burnham being removed; the white sheet covering the brutality of the attack.

'Sirs, I've interviewed everyone now except for the big lady who calls herself the giantess. She insists on having her solicitor with her and will only speak with you two detectives. She's on her way to the tent now. She doesn't want Mrs Wilks present.'

Thomas nodded. 'You've done a good job, Constable, thank you. Detective Dart and I will see her now. You may let Mrs Wilks know her services are no longer required.'

'Right, sir, I'll do that and then head off to do my report,' he said.

Thomas turned to his partner, Harry, and rubbing his temples said, 'Let's see what she has to say and then I've got to eat.'

'See, if you got yourself a lovely wife like mine, you'd be fit and fine. Bacon, eggs, and thick toast was served up at my place this morning,' Harry said, ribbing his partner. 'Can that nephew of yours cook?'

'I live in hope,' Thomas said. 'But I'm not sure I could have handled that breakfast this morning. Now, I could do it justice.'

The men left the area cordoned off and re-entered the tent to interview Mrs Anna Tufton. As he entered the room, the sight of the giantess momentarily shocked Thomas, as most people were in her presence. He heard Harry mutter, 'Strewth' under his breath.

Seated on one side of the giant lady was the delicate Miss Matilda Hayward, and her brother sat on the other side of Mrs Tufton. A most forbidding scene, almost rehearsed, Thomas mused.

Amos rose and offered his hand.

'Thomas, I mean, detective,' he said, correcting himself given the business nature of their meeting.

'Mr Hayward, Miss Hayward, Mrs Tufton I believe?' Thomas gave a small nod. 'My partner, Detective Harry Dart,' he said by way of introduction.

Once everyone was seated, Amos began.

'With your permission, Detective, Mrs Tufton would like the following known…' He read out where she was before the death of Mr Burnham, and where her husband was. He detailed the circumstances of the meeting between the exhibition owner and her husband, the tension that arose, and what time she returned to her caravan. Amos also added to be on the front foot, that Mr and Mrs Tufton led separate personal lives and might make that legally binding. Amos didn't want that coming up later and looking suspicious.

'And did you see anything peculiar or anyone you didn't recognise on the grounds at that time?' Harry asked.

Anna looked at Amos, who nodded. She answered negatively to the question.

'No, Detective. I saw no one else. My path was directly from my caravan to meet with Mr Burnham and my husband, and then back. I heard movement in some of the caravans as I passed and returned to mine, but I am not sure I could recall accurately which caravans for the purpose of confirming the whereabouts of my fellow artists.'

'Did anyone see you return to your caravan?' Thomas asked.

'Not that I am aware of, but it might be so,' Mrs Tufton said.

Thomas's glance shifted to Matilda as Mrs Tufton spoke, and then he addressed Matilda directly.

'You were here yesterday, and you interviewed Mr Burnham previously. Did you notice anything that now in context might have been threatening or unusual?'

As Matilda was about to answer, Amos answered on her behalf.

Thomas noted the flash of impatience across Matilda's face, but she tolerated it given the current situation.

'Matilda was here quite some time before the unfortunate death of Mr Burnham to secure the interview, and again recently to provide a copy of her publication. But on that last occasion, she saw Mr Burnham alive and well. As you arrived to escort her home, Detective, you would have noticed how many people were milling around at the exhibition and enjoying the nearby hospitality.'

Thomas nodded, unimpressed with Amos's inference. Thomas returned his attention to the giantess. 'If I may speak candidly, Mrs Tufton, if I am to understand that you and Mr Tufton may seek to make your separation legally binding,' he paraphrased Amos, 'why would your husband be negotiating your fee structure if you were intending to leave him and the exhibition, or were you going to remain and manage your own payment?'

Again, Mrs Tufton looked to Amos, who responded on her behalf to Thomas's great frustration.

'Mr and Mrs Tufton have been living in separate quarters, but Mrs Tufton had not yet made her desire to legally separate known to Mr Tufton. His negotiations were on the basis that life would proceed as usual and Mrs Tufton would continue with the exhibition,' Amos said, and the giantess nodded her agreement.

Thomas noticed Matilda gave him a sympathetic look.

Harry stepped in. 'Did Mr Burnham know, or could he have heard what your plans were? I am wondering if he told your husband which provoked a fight.'

Mrs Tufton responded on her own. 'I spoke of it to no one except Miss and Mr Hayward.'

Thomas soon wound up the interview; Amos saw his client back to her caravan and Harry went to advise Mr and Mrs Wilks – the manager and manageress – that they were departing for now.

Thomas turned to Matilda once they were alone. 'How did you come to hear of the murder?'

'Mrs Tufton, Anna, sent me a note asking me to come.'

'I'll need that note,' Thomas said.

'I'll let Amos know.'

They looked at each other; Thomas annoyed that Matilda was ingrained into his investigation, Matilda frustrated by his attitude.

'What's got into you, Thomas?'

'Nothing, I am trying to do my job.'

'Your job? Have you not been home since last night?' she asked.

'Of course I have.'

'You have rouge on your collar, and you smell like...' She wrinkled her nose on inhaling sharply. 'I'm guessing that is an abundance of whiskey? I hope you and your lady had an enjoyable night.'

He cleared his throat. 'A night out with fellow detectives,' he said.

'Yes, necessary for some relief, I imagine, amongst other things,' she said, her small smile far from genuine. Matilda was not fooled that Thomas, along with Daniel and her twin brothers, were enjoying the company of women as need be.

Amos re-entered the room. 'Shall we go, Matilda? Let me know if you need anything further from Mrs Tufton, Detective.'

Thomas nodded and smiled at him. Before Amos got to the exit, Thomas asked, 'Why did Mrs Tufton feel she needed a solicitor?'

Amos held his gaze. 'She didn't, not concerning Mr Burnham's death. She sought my help to start divorce proceedings and a pension from her husband; they've lived separate lives for some time, as discussed. But as I was here, I offered my services for the interview.'

'I see,' Thomas said, his mind working overtime. He bade them goodbye, dipped his hat slightly, and watched Matilda's shapely figure as she departed. Not once did she look back. He imagined waking up next to her every morning and ran a finger around his collar. Rouge. Damn it.

## Chapter 13

Mrs Lawson shook her head. 'That poor woman,' she said. 'While her husband has been her manager, she has been publicly humiliated and providing an income for both of them. Shameful!' She looked out at the ladies working in the print room outside the large glass walls of her office.

Matilda nodded in agreement with her editor. The office was a hive of activity as the ladies wrote, edited, illustrated, and met the required deadlines. Matilda turned back to Mrs Lawson. 'Mrs Tufton has hired my brother, Amos, a solicitor, to start divorce proceedings and secure her a pension from her husband.'

'Hmm, I'm not sure she'll get both. I know of women who have stayed married and received a pension or divorced but had to show fault in their husband to get any kind of security. Of course, if her husband murdered Mr Burnham, that would serve as a fault,' she said with the hint of a smile.

Matilda returned her smile. 'Yes, I imagine it would. I guess it is a blessing they have no children.'

'Indeed,' Mrs Lawson agreed. 'He could ensure she never sees them again. Filing for a divorce is going to be difficult.'

Matilda lowered her voice. 'Confidentially, as they have been separated for some time – rarely sharing the marital bed and not always in the same city, Amos thinks Mrs Tufton might have a better case for abandonment. She is already working to support herself, and him, so she may be entitled to a pension from him if he is gainfully employed elsewhere.'

'Well, I guess that is a small relief and an option,' Mrs Lawson said. 'To your story then…'

'Yes, I was thinking as the daily paper is carrying the story of Mr Burnham's demise, would you like me to step away from an insider story on Mrs Tufton until the dust settles?'

'I was pondering that myself.' She walked across the front of the glass windows and back again, thinking. Matilda did not dare interrupt.

Mrs Lawson clicked her fingers and looked up at Matilda. 'I think your next article needs to be more intimate. Something sympathetic and emotional, and a little broader so we don't interfere with the investigation – what life is like for the ladies of the carnival.'

Matilda's breath hitched, and she tried not to show her reaction. Interviewing Mrs Tufton was easy, but the conjoined ladies…

'Only if you feel you can do it?' Mrs Lawson said – a red rag to a bull.

'Of course, it is a brilliant idea. Shall I include management too?' Matilda asked. 'The manager's wife, Mrs Wilks is Russian and involved in the day-to-day running.'

'Excellent, yes!' Mrs Lawson clapped her hands together with enthusiasm. 'It will fascinate our readers learning what these ladies must contend with. You may even find some relevant information to share with that detective of yours,' she said and gave Matilda an affectionate smile.

'Ah, he is not mine, but he was someone's last night – he had rouge on his collar,' Matilda said, still smarting.

'He is a single man with no obligation,' Mrs Lawson reminded Matilda. 'Unlike poor Mrs Tufton. To have the misfortune of being linked to a deceitful or neglectful man for life from an agreement formed in the helpless innocence of girlhood, that is a great tragedy, and I suspect your Mrs Tufton and many other women find themselves in the same situation.'

Mrs Lawson's compassion inspired Matilda.

'I'll seek the interviews tomorrow and begin,' she said.

Mrs Lawson nodded. 'Excellent. I'll hold space for you in the next fortnight's edition. I have another consideration for you...'

'Yes?' Matilda asked as Mrs Lawson moved towards the door of her office.

Mrs Lawson leaned out and motioned to a young lady busily scribbling in a book. 'Alice, do you have a moment?'

Alice rose quickly, grabbed her notebook and pencil, and hurried into the office.

Mrs Lawson did the introductions. 'Miss Matilda Hayward, this is Miss Alice Doran.'

'How do you do, Miss Hayward,' Alice said with a clipped English accent.

'Lovely to meet you, Miss Doran,' Matilda acknowledged.

Mrs Lawson smiled her pleasure at the two ambitious young ladies before her. 'Miss Doran has just joined us. She is keen to report on the efforts of the newly formed Queensland Women's Suffrage League.'

'Indeed,' Matilda said enthusiastically.

'However, it would be a good experience for Alice to write some profile pieces and helpful to you, Matilda, to have support. Could you work on these profile stories together?'

'Of course,' Matilda said, and Alice beamed with pleasure.

Mrs Lawson glanced out the window at an empty desk and then back to the two ladies. 'Given we are one artist short this week, I would be willing to commission your brother again at the same rate to do another illustration or two for your piece.'

'That is wonderful, thank you, Mrs Lawson,' Matilda said, delighted.

'I have an ulterior motive,' she confessed. 'He can escort you both and illustrate while you undertake the interviews. There is, after all, a murderer on the loose.'

Matilda and Alice sobered at the thought.

'Has your brother some stature?' Alice asked.

'Oh yes, he's tall and strong,' Matilda said, reassuring Alice.

'Can I leave you to discuss what needs to be done and deliver by the deadline?'

'Of course, Mrs Lawson,' Matilda agreed, moving to evacuate the editor's office.

Alice looked thrilled. 'Thank you, I'm sure we shall achieve a great deal.'

Matilda laughed. 'Let's start.'

One hour later, as Matilda departed from *The Women's Journal* office with a firm plan in place, she felt a little more relieved that she did not have to face the ladies of the carnival by herself. One other small thought nagged at her – Mrs Lawsons' reminder that indeed Thomas could do as he pleased as a single man. Not that she had a right to be, but she felt just a little envious of the applicant of the rouge on the detective's collar.

*****

'What have we got?' Harry asked bearing two large cups of tea, the contents the colour of dishwater, as he joined Thomas in his office.

Thomas grimaced, but thanked his partner. After all, it was the thought that counted, he conceded, even if Harry couldn't make a cup of tea to save himself. Thomas seated himself on the edge of the desk while Harry grabbed a piece of chalk in readiness to fill in their blackboard, which still had two other current cases on it.

Thomas gulped the weak but hot tea and began. 'Mr Alfred E. Burnham, carnival proprietor, bludgeoned to death by one or several hands – the blows inflicted multiple times to the body and throat. Exhibitors of his show that we interviewed say they are happy with their wages and touring conditions, but that requires some further digging and once we find out if any of the exhibitors have criminal records, I'd like to speak to them with our translator and without Mrs Wilks present.'

Harry agreed. 'Speaking of which, we have a manager and his wife who is second-in-charge – Morris and Irina Wilks – now running the show. Perhaps they thought they could do a better job of running it and it is now convenient that Mr Burnham is out of the way.'

'Yes, indeed,' Thomas mused. He waited while Harry caught up on scribbling the names and motives. Checking the pages of transcript from the constable and his own scribbled notes, Thomas continued. 'We've got the giantess's husband, Carl Tufton, who saw Mr Burnham that night to discuss an increase in his wife's wages or a share in the profit; he probably thinks his wife is the major attraction. We've got the giantess herself, Anna Tufton, who says she wants a divorce and nothing more to do with her husband. She might have thought getting rid of Burnham would close the circus down and she'd be free of obligation.'

'Or the giantess could have agreed with her husband that she was worth more, they could be in on it together,' Harry mused, putting chalk dust on his suit as he crossed his arms to view the board. 'It's a little odd that she hired legal help before speaking with us.'

'Yes, although Amos says that was about her potential divorce and it was just opportune, in his opinion, that he was there,' Thomas agreed. 'But it is odd that she should request his services that very morning when Burnham is found dead... or was it a coincidence?'

'I think she knows something for sure,' Harry said and, finishing his tea, thumped his large cup down on the table.

Thomas continued on that train of thought. 'And I'd like

to know exactly what the giantess said to get Matilda and Amos there to see her before we questioned her. Why the urgency if it was just a divorce query and was she surprised Burnham was dead or did she know?'

'Or, it might have been an uprising and every member of the carnival surrounded Burnham and took a turn at delivering a blow,' Harry said, and visibly shuddered.

'Maybe he was cruel or miserly,' Thomas added.

'Well, we've got plenty to keep us busy then.' Harry sighed. 'By the way, did you want me to have a word with Miss Matilda Hayward about her timely arrival at the carnival this morning and how that came about?' Harry asked, teasing Thomas.

Thomas snapped to look at him at the mention of Matilda's name and saw him smiling.

'You'll keep,' he said with a wince.

Harry laughed. 'It's a shame you didn't look your best this morning; Miss Hayward looked lovely.'

'Yes, she pointed out to me I looked below her standards.' Thomas scowled at the memory.

'Let's start at the top and work our way down then,' Harry said, looking at the names on the board.

Thomas agreed. He thought about interrogating Matilda, and the thought secretly thrilled him. He decided it was best to leave that for a day or two and approach her with a fresh shirt and no smell of liquor upon his breath.

## Chapter 14

Mrs Samuel Bloomfield – Aunt Audrey – peered over the Hayward family cook's shoulder to personally inspect the roast for tonight's birthday dinner. It glistened with juices, was perfectly browned, and the smell was mouth-watering.

Cook held the roast out for inspection. Years of cooking and many offers to move to grander households had never swayed her and mainly for that reason – Audrey might poke her nose into the kitchen a few times a year, but Mr Hayward gave Cook complete free rein and now in her fifties, she did not feel the need to cower to a family matron. Besides, several nights a week Mr Hayward liked cold roast meats and salads, so that was what the entire family ate. It was wonderfully easy, and Cook could finish early for the day. It also allowed Cook to use leftovers, and with her spare time to bake some sweets as a treat for the boys – she refused to acknowledge they were grown men able to feed themselves. Daniel's favourite was her jam roly-poly, while the twins loved Cook's lemon meringue pie. She thought of dear, sweet Amos and his fondness for her bread-and-butter pudding. As for Mr Hayward, he loved a good sponge cake – a man most easy to please. Matilda never had a sweet tooth, even as a child – most unusual in a young lady.

'Ma'am?' Cook asked, waiting for the verdict.

'It's perfect,' Aunt Audrey said with a sigh. 'I wish you would consider my offer to join my household. If you were worried for Mr Hayward, I assure you I could recommend an accomplished cook to meet the family's needs,' Audrey said, full of her own self-importance. 'I do have to entertain the mayor, the minister and several town committee members regularly.'

The cook put the roast back into the cooking stove and straightened up. 'I'm flattered, Mrs Bloomfield, but I've become attached to the family and the household, and it's my home.'

Audrey sighed. 'I understand.' She frowned at the sound of rowdiness coming down the Hayward family hallway and followed the noise, leaving the cook in peace.

Audrey entered the drawing-room.

'Aunt Audrey, you're here,' her favourite Hayward, Amos, said, breaking away from his brothers who were raiding their father's bar.

'I am, dear boy.' She accepted a kiss from him on the cheek. 'How are you, Minnie?'

'Very well, thank you, Aunt,' Minnie said, giving a brief nod and a demure smile.

'A charming shade of blue.' Audrey commended Minnie's gown.

Mr Hayward entered the drawing-room with Daniel, who appeared slightly out of breath as he rushed to make the required time.

'Hello Audrey.' Mr Hayward addressed his sister. 'Ah, we are almost all here.' He glanced around and did a quick head count. All boys, no girl. 'And here are the birthday boys,' he said, accepting a brandy from Elijah, the elder twin by twelve minutes.

'Goodness, three-and-twenty today,' Matilda said as she entered the room and was greeted by her rowdy family.

'Yes, your days of sowing your wild oats are over, surely,' Audrey said with a glance to Gideon. Elijah was eminently more sensible.

Gideon sighed and looked at his twin. 'I guess, brother, we should soon take ourselves off the market and make two lovely ladies very lucky.'

Elijah chuckled. 'I'll begin the process immediately. I'm sure Matilda, Minnie and Aunt Audrey would welcome some more ladies around the table.'

'Did someone say table?' Harriet asked, entering the room. 'Dinner is ready, sir,' she said to Mr Hayward.

'Thank you, Harriet. Shall we move into the dining room?' Mr Hayward suggested and offered Audrey his arm.

Daniel did the same for Matilda.

'That's the birthday boy's honour.' Gideon sidestepped Daniel and offered his arm to his little sister.

Daniel stepped back and offered his crooked arm to Elijah, as Matilda laughed at their antics and happily accepted.

Audrey glanced back at the pair. 'So, Matilda—'

'Still not married, Aunt Audrey,' Matilda cut her off, and Audrey had the good grace to smile.

'Then I shall challenge your brothers to get motivated and bring home a range of suitable suitors for you.'

'Quite so,' Mr Hayward agreed and turned to give Matilda a wink.

'More importantly,' Gideon cut in, waiting until the ladies were seated at the dining table and then taking his seat, 'Matilda should bring home suitable acquaintances for her brothers to meet.'

'Well,' Audrey pondered Gideon's suggestion, 'that is actually a good idea.'

Gideon beamed and kicked Matilda under the table.

'Yes, perhaps you are right. The sooner you move out the better,' she teased him.

Mr Hayward sided with his sister. 'Audrey has a point; you don't want to miss out on all the best catches. Look at your brother – Amos has led the way with a fortunate marriage to a beautiful young lady.'

Minnie beamed and smiled at Amos, who returned the favour; Gideon rolled his eyes and his father continued, 'as Daniel is dragging the chain, then Elijah, Gideon, I believe you should both step up to bring this family some marital joy.'

Matilda smiled. For once she was happy to have the marital spotlight off herself. That changed quickly.

'I don't see why Daniel gets off so lightly,' Gideon complained. 'He's three years older and next to go. Surely there's someone desperate enough to marry him.'

'Because it is your birthday and the focus is off me for tonight,' Daniel reminded him. 'If I'm lucky, I may marry before my next birthday, so we won't need to revisit this discussion.'

'Really? Do you have a young lady in mind, Daniel?' Aunt Audrey asked with renewed interest in the conversation.

'I am sorry to say, Aunt, that I have not met the future Mrs Daniel Hayward yet.'

Aunt Audrey sighed. She wasn't one for frivolous conversations, she wanted action and an outcome.

'So, sister, do you have any respectable friends that you can introduce to your twin brothers?' Gideon asked.

Matilda smiled. 'It depends. The last time you deigned to take one of my friends out for tea, you behaved most despicably, Gideon,' she teased him. 'She never heard from you again.'

'I'm sure that was Elijah,' Gideon said, 'we're hard to tell apart.'

Elijah grimaced, no stranger to his twin's antics. Minnie laughed; she had a soft spot for Gideon, being so silly to Amos's sensible nature.

'Actually,' Matilda continued, 'I have a new writing partner and we're doing several profile pieces together – her name is Miss Alice Doran, and she is quite lovely. But Daniel will meet her first.'

'Excellent news,' Daniel said. 'Since I'm dragging the chain and all. Regardless, she's bound to go for me as most handsome of all the brothers.'

'Speaking of handsome and eligible suitors, where is

Thomas tonight?' Aunt Audrey asked abruptly. 'I can't remember a family event he hasn't been at for a long time.'

'Working.' Daniel spoke for his friend. 'There's been a spate of murders and assaults and he's behind his case closure rate.'

'I heard that there had been an increase in assaults against women,' Elijah added.

Mr Hayward nodded. 'Amos and I have heard as much in our legal circles.'

'Dreadful and hardly dinner conversation.' Aunt Audrey shook her head. 'This push for the vote would not be helping.'

'It's inevitable,' Amos said. 'South Australian women can now vote and stand for parliament.'

'I don't understand why you would want to,' Minnie said, believing her beauty and accomplishments far superior to engaging in politics and having to make decisions not related to house and home. She continued, 'It's so boring and I don't want to have to learn about the parties so I can cast a vote. I'll just vote the same as you, Amos,' she said, looking to her husband.

Daniel jumped in, seeing Matilda about to speak. 'Well, the good thing is, Minnie, you can do that if you want to, or you can vote if you have your own preference. Let's say the birthday boys decided to run for office, well you could vote for them.'

Gideon laughed, but Elijah seemed to consider the idea eminently sensible. Matilda turned to her aunt.

'Do you support it, Aunt Audrey, the vote I mean?' She

never really knew which way her aunt might sway – she was an astute and clever woman but also traditional in many ways.

'Indeed I do, Matilda. If a woman can run a household, I suspect she can run the country or at least should have a say in it,' she said most firmly.

Matilda's eyes widened with surprise.

'You need not look so surprised, Matilda. You know I am involved in many areas of the community and the right people in office can make all the difference. However,' she raised her eyebrows at her niece, 'as a poet said, "the hand that rocks the cradle is the hand that rules the world," so you my girl will have more power with motherhood.'

Matilda's face fell and her brothers around her smiled.

'To motherhood then, eventually for Matilda and Minnie if they so choose,' Gideon said, holding up his glass for a toast.

'You are just lucky it is your birthday,' Matilda said, joining in the toast, 'but tomorrow it isn't!'

## Chapter 15

It was after nine that evening when Thomas walked up the front path. He never thought he'd admit it, but returning to a home with someone inside, the lamps lit, and the smell of cooking wafting out, made for a welcome change – even if it was his nephew. Edward had arrived several days ago but up until now; Thomas had barely been home to set eyes upon him. He sighed, remembering the last time he had a day off and enjoyed some company that wasn't work-related or a drink at the club with his colleagues. It was last Sunday's lunch at the Haywards'. Which got him thinking… that doctor friend of Elijah's better not have bloody well gone to the twins' birthday dinner. He imagined some toffee-nosed snob charming Matilda. His partner, Harry, was right. She was beautiful, she was of marriageable age, and she wouldn't go unnoticed by the men of the town. For once he was pleased that she was headstrong and not seeking a husband. However, should she fall in love…

He closed the front door behind him, hung his hat over

the hook near the front door, and proceeded down the hallway, treading a well-worn path to the living areas.

'Teddy?'

'In here, Uncle, I'm glad you're in. I've cooked us up some dinner and kept your serve warm,' he said, looking pleased with himself. 'Have you eaten?'

'No, I'm starving, thanks.' Thomas smiled at his tall, rough, red-haired nephew, who looked too large for the kitchen; he would be more at home in the lumberyard. Teddy rose from the table where he had been working his way through the daily *Brisbane Courier*.

'Smells fantastic, where did you learn to cook?' Thomas looked in at the large pot of stew and inhaled the aroma from its steam.

'I was an apprentice cook for a while, but that fell through. Sit down then and I'll serve you up a bowl.'

Thomas grinned; his wild nephew was known to speak before he thought, and he didn't have to ask what became of that job.

'I'm thinking of trying for it again though, I enjoy cooking.'

'How far did you get along?' Thomas asked.

'My apprenticeship is half done; the references won't be great though.' He shrugged.

'Well, if you partner with another hothead, he'll understand. I'll ask around,' Thomas said, throwing his coat over a nearby chair. 'Someone must owe me a favour.'

Teddy chuckled. He placed the bowl of stew in front of his uncle.

'This is excellent,' Thomas said and picking up his fork, he dug in, giving an appreciative groan.

'I'm making a cup of tea; will you have one?'

'Yes, please. You know you don't have to cook just because you're staying here. You can focus on finding some work.'

'I did that today too.' He gave a nod to the newspaper on the table near his uncle. 'Speaking of staying here, I saw some tools out the back. I was thinking your place could do with a bit of work and a lick of paint would not go astray. I like to keep busy.'

Thomas looked around. 'It could do with a lot of things. I confess I haven't touched it since Dad left; he'd be disappointed if he visited. I welcome all improvements.'

'The curtains should go immediately,' Teddy said. 'I never saw you as a pink-chequered type of bloke.'

'I picked those myself,' Thomas joked as Teddy sat down with two cups of tea and joined his uncle.

'Have you been working on that freak show murder today? I heard about it… everyone around town was talking about it.'

'What are they saying?' Thomas stopped eating long enough to have a mouthful of tea.

'That the inmates got fed up and murdered the master of ceremonies, the owner,' Teddy said.

Thomas made a humph sound. 'Any reason they got fed up? The deceased had previously boasted about them all being one big happy family.'

Teddy shrugged. 'The guy in the butcher shop when I went in to talk about a job and get a cut for tonight's dinner said that the owner and manager were making big profits and the freaks were getting paid next to nothing. He said that one cook at the carnival came in to get some meat and got quality cuts for the management and cheap offcuts for the rest. He said that the meals for the freaks were full of bread to make them go further.'

'Not surprising, that,' Thomas said.

Teddy continued. 'The fellow at the hair-cutter and dresser store was having a smoke outside, so I stopped to talk to him. He said he was told by a crew member who put the tent up, that the crew and the freaks were supposed to get their board as part of their rate, but the rent for their board kept getting hiked up and no one is happy.'

Thomas considered his nephew's comments and thought about them for a few moments. 'Anything else?'

'The lady who worked behind the counter at the bakery said she'd sent some biscuits to the huge lady and some other goodies to the owners, and was told not to expect anything in return. That was rude – certainly doesn't make for goodwill in the town you're visiting.'

'Yeah, it was rude and stupid,' Thomas agreed. He finished his bowl and pushed it away. 'Good job, I should put you on commission; you got around a bit today.'

'Yeah, well, I told them all I was looking for work and would do anything. I'll show my face every few days, so they remember. People love to talk, don't they?' He shook his head and smiled, adding, 'even to a stranger.'

'Thank God they do,' Thomas agreed. 'But you have a charm about you, Teddy. They don't naturally talk to me.'

'That's because you look like a gruff bastard.' Teddy nudged his uncle and laughed.

'It comes with the job. That dinner was great, thanks, stay as long as you want,' Thomas joked. 'But now you've got me thinking…'

'The stew did? Gee, didn't see that coming,' Teddy said, and Thomas chuckled.

'Yeah, you take after my brother, smart-aleck,' he said with a grin, thinking of Teddy's father, Sewell. 'I'm wondering if there might be a temporary job going as a cook or assistant cook or handyman with the carnival while it is in town.'

Teddy's eyes widened. 'That'd be great. I could spy for you and earn a crust, so to speak.'

'You'd have to be careful, there's a murderer on the loose,' Thomas said, and Teddy just shrugged.

'Yeah, I don't believe that either,' Thomas added. 'I think it was a crime of passion, but someone knows something and if anyone wanted to talk with you, well that'd be welcome.'

'It'd be great, meeting those people and getting to hear their stories. That'd be something,' Teddy said and shook his head.

'Yeah, well let me see what's going on with staff and who hires them. I don't know who to ask or trust just yet.'

'It might be better if I just wander in and seek a job,' Teddy suggested.

'You might be right. But no one can know who you are for your safety, and so that you can earn trust. You can't be an Ashdown,' Thomas said.

'I can use Mum's maiden name – Clements,' Teddy suggested.

'That might just work. Don't tell your parents though, they'd kill me.'

'Maybe I'd make a good copper!'

'Long hours, dealing with criminals and ne'er-do-wells… cooking sounds better. Regardless, the carnival's only got another week left in town, so if it is going to happen, it'll have to happen fast.' Thomas sighed. 'Just when I get a decent meal, I give away the cook!'

## Chapter 16

Alice placed her hand on Matilda's arm to halt their progress, her bravado barely covering her trepidation. She took a deep breath. 'I confess, I'm nervous.'

'As am I,' Matilda assured her. 'This is my fourth time here and I'm always so uncomfortable. I feel I am...' she searched for words, 'exploiting their misery.'

'Yes!' Alice agreed, 'as do I. But we are not coming here to stare or to shame them. We want to present them as real women, to give them a voice as Mrs Lawson always says.'

Matilda nodded. 'It's our duty.'

They smiled, rejoicing in the bond of a new and soon to be firm friendship, and continued towards the tent. They were, without doubt, the most stylish of guests that morning in their fashionably fitted skirts, crisp dress blouses, hats and gloves. They both held their skirts a little higher off the ground as they avoided puddles and muddy ground on their walk across the green. The ropes were gone, and the exhibition was open for business again, so soon after Mr Burnham's demise. Even mid-morning there was a decent crowd willing to pay their money to enter the odd exhibition.

Matilda recognised the manager, Mr Wilks, wandering around the exterior of the tent and, catching his attention, she gave him a small wave.

He hastened towards them.

'Ah, the ladies from *The Women's Journal*, I presume? Welcome to you both,' he said, lifting his hat.

'Mr Wilks,' Matilda returned his greeting. 'We weren't formally introduced before. I am Matilda Hayward and may I introduce Miss Alice Doran.'

'The two most beautiful ladies I have set eyes on in a long time,' Mr Wilks said in an attempt to flatter. Sadly, his stature, age, and not to mention his married state, did little to make him appealing to the ladies. His gift of shrewdness ascertained that right away and he got down to business. 'My wife tells me you are keen to write a feature on the lives and adventures of our female artists and of Mrs Wilks herself.'

'Indeed we are, sir,' Alice said in her British accent, which some might describe as posh. 'I imagine you all work so hard to bring entertainment to the towns you visit, so I'm sure there's a tale or two to tell from such an unconventional life.'

Alice had won him over; Mr Wilks had quite forgotten himself as he studied her pale skin, blue eyes, and charming smile.

Matilda refrained from giggling at her friend's performance; Alice was quite captivating.

'It is a life out of the ordinary,' Mr Wilks agreed. 'Please allow me to show you to the sitting area. Who were you hoping to speak with first?'

'The conjoined ladies, if that is suitable please, Mr Wilks?' Matilda asked.

'Ah, yes, our two-headed woman – Ella and Elvira. Come this way, and I'll fetch them or her...' He chuckled at his own joke.

Matilda and Alice followed and once seated, set themselves up with their notepads and pencils ready to undertake the interview. They agreed to ask a question apiece, so they had time to make notes after each answer while the other pursued their next question.

Matilda straightened her red skirt and glanced at Alice. 'How are you feeling?'

Alice nodded. 'I'm fine. I suspect the ladies are more nervous than us.'

Matilda nodded. 'That might be a good way to start the interview,' she said, but before she could explain, the ladies entered. They moved at ease despite being joined from the shoulder and down their torso.

Ella and Elvira were not identical in appearance, and Ella seemed more comfortable, her head at a better angle, her body less strained.

Matilda and Alice stood to greet them and once they were all seated, there was an awkward pause.

Matilda cleared her throat. 'Before you entered, we were saying how nervous we were.'

The ladies laughed and Ella on the left of the body answered, her voice soft and husky. 'We were saying the same thing.'

Elvira smiled and gave a small nod, as much as her

head and neck might allow. 'We're used to performing,' Elvira said, her voice stronger than her sister's, 'but being interviewed is more personal.'

'Of course,' Alice said, 'and we don't want to ask anything that may offend you, or to reveal in our article anything that you don't wish us to write.'

The two ladies visibly relaxed. 'Thank you,' Ella said.

Matilda began. 'So do you like the same things?'

The twins laughed. 'We're fortunate that we do most of the time because it would be hard to escape each other if we didn't,' Elvira said, 'but I have to put up with some things.'

Ella's eyes widened and she laughed. 'Do tell, sister?'

'I'm a better singer than Ella but I have no choice but to listen to her,' she teased her sister.

The interview continued comfortably, and Matilda and Alice soon found themselves having fun. The ladies were so different – Ella was sweet and quiet; Elvira was funny and sharp.

'Thank you. It has been so much fun meeting you both,' Alice said, at the end of the interview.

'May I ask one more question that isn't for the interview and won't be published?' Matilda asked. She saw the curious look Alice gave her and the twins' eyes widened. 'It's not of a personal nature,' Matilda assured them, 'and if you prefer not to answer, I'll understand.'

'Go ahead, please,' Elvira invited her.

Matilda swallowed; she had planned her question so that it was not intrusive but might glean her some answers. 'I've been talking with Mrs Tufton – Anna, the giantess – and she was one of the last people to see Mr Burnham alive. I know you've spoken with the police, but are you frightened?'

'You talk, sister,' Ella said, inviting her twin to answer.

'I'm not frightened, though Ella is a little. We are no strangers to violence; we spent some time in an asylum because of our oddity and before joining with Mr Burnham. But we don't know why someone would do that to him. We all relied on him, and he was a good person.' Elvira lowered her voice and awkwardly looked over her shoulder.

'We're alone,' Alice ensured her.

'I'd understand if it was Mr Wilks who was killed.'

'Elvira!' her sister hissed.

'Well, it's true, sister,' she continued in a whisper. 'Since he joined the Exhibition as the manager everything has changed. We earn less profit, the food is terrible, and the hours are longer.'

'Mr Burnham was so lovely and kind,' Ella whispered and blinked away tears.

'He was our friend,' Elvira agreed.

'I am so sorry,' Matilda said.

'Did Mr Burnham not know what was going on, what Mr Wilks was doing?' Alice asked.

'I don't know. We didn't tell him, it's not our place to do so,' Elvira said. 'I can't say if any of the other artists did, but we're not in a position of power and Mr Wilks can get quite angry.'

'Perhaps he never knew,' Ella said, thinking of Mr Burnham. 'Mr Wilks seemed to be very nice to Mr Burnham whenever they were together, so he might have thought Mr Wilks was like that with everyone.'

'May I share this information in confidence with my friend, Detective Ashdown?' Matilda asked. 'He will be discreet, I promise you, and it will help the investigation for him to know that Mr Burnham was genuinely respected by his artists, I'm sure. Unless you told the police that already?'

The ladies thought about it, then Ella gave a subtle nod and Elvira agreed. 'You may share. We didn't say a great deal in our police interviews. Mrs Wilks was there, and we were still feeling shocked by the news. So, yes, if it will help do tell him.'

'It's exciting what you do,' Ella said shyly, glancing from Matilda to Alice. 'Writing for a newspaper.'

'Our editor is amazing,' Alice gushed, 'so brave, and her goal is to inform and help women. I hope to be as strong and useful as she is in due course.'

'I've no doubt you will,' Matilda assured Alice, and then turned to the twins. 'I'm so glad we met you both, thank you. Please stay safe.'

Ella flushed slightly and Elvira smiled. 'We have our own protector,' Elvira said, and Ella gave a girlish giggle.

Ella explained. 'We never thought love was possible for us. Our parents never thought so when they left us in the asylum. But it seems it may be. Two men who work with our exhibition as part of the assembly team, well, we have all become close.'

'I think you are both very loveable!' Alice blurted out, and the ladies laughed.

'If only we were all so lucky,' Matilda said. 'I'd love to have a protector.'

'From what I heard, you have a gentleman keen to be so.' Alice nudged Matilda and Ella's eyes widened – she was the romantic out of the two.

Matilda flushed and Elvira teased her like an old friend. 'That is the blush of a woman in love.'

'I have much to do before I want to be shackled to a man,' Matilda said, 'as handsome as that man might be.'

'Then you need a man who will let you do your work and be married,' Alice said. 'Here's to finding a progressive man.'

They all turned as a person rushed into their seating area.

'Was someone looking for a man?' Daniel asked upon overhearing the last of the conversation. 'I'm so sorry I'm late, Matilda. There are a few excuses but none of them is good.'

Ella giggled, Alice's eyes widened in appreciation of the new guest, and Elvira studied him with suspicion. Daniel seemed unfazed by the conjoined ladies; he had seen them now a few times. He sat beside his sister so as to not appear too imposing.

'Oh, Daniel,' Matilda sighed at her handsome and ruffled brother. 'This is my brother, Daniel Hayward, the perpetually late,' she began as a way of formal introduction. 'He was to do an illustration for our story today, if there were no objections? Daniel, may I introduce Miss Ella Hove, Miss Elvira Hove and Miss Alice Doran.'

Daniel stood again and bowed to each, 'Misses Hove, Miss Doran.'

He had charmed them. When his eyes locked with Alice, Daniel temporarily forgot time. Matilda pulled at his jacket, and he sat back down beside her and cleared his throat.

'Forgive my tardiness,' he said again. 'Would you be comfortable with me doing a quick sketch of you both, Miss Ella, Miss Elvira, for the article? I can return another time to show you my finished result, or to fill in detail if time is limited?'

Ella waited for Elvira to respond as seemed her practice.

'Will you make us look like freaks or attractive young ladies bonded for life?' Elvira asked, her voice more curious than cold.

'It would be impossible not to draw you as attractive young ladies, even for an artist of my calibre,' he said to Elvira and gave her a wink.

She laughed. 'Well, best to it then,' she agreed, and Matilda relaxed beside Daniel. The small party bantered during the sketching and Daniel, with his frankness, shocked Matilda but had quite the opposite effect on the twins.

'We have twins in our family, did Matilda tell you?' Daniel asked. 'They arrived twelve minutes apart. I suspect you two didn't have that problem.'

'Daniel!' Matilda declared, but the twins just laughed.

'Perhaps that is why we are joined,' Ella told him. 'We were both trying to rush out at the same time.'

'Bravo you, Ella,' Alice laughed, 'what a clever comeback. That will be hard to beat,' she said with a glance at Daniel. She had been studying him subtly since he arrived, but now had permission to glance at him with her challenge.

He looked away from his drawing momentarily to smile at her, and then returned to his work again.

'I know when I'm beaten,' he said and smiled at Ella. 'Do you eat for one or two?'

'Oh, that's a good question. I wish I had asked that,' Matilda said with a sigh and Alice grinned.

'We're learning,' Alice said, making excuses for them both.

Elvira answered. 'You are quite different, Mr Daniel Hayward, refreshing.'

He gave her a smile and a nod of thanks as he continued drawing as fast as he could get the strokes down.

'To answer your question, we both have our favourite foods,' she continued, 'but we need very little to fill us, so I guess we eat the same as Matilda or Alice in quantity.'

'Are they alike, your twin brothers?' Ella asked Matilda.

'They look alike, but Elijah is sensible, and Gideon is a rascal, well that's what Harriet our housekeeper calls him, and he's never grown out of it.'

'Neither of them is as clever or good looking as Matilda and me,' Daniel jested, as his hand continued to move freely, capturing their likeness on his notepad. 'At least if no one will have them, they have each other I guess.'

'Exactly so,' Ella said. 'Elvira and I will never be lonely.'

'So true, sister,' Elvira agreed and lowered her eyes.

Matilda saw Elvira blink away tears, she was not all bravado after all.

'That is very good,' Alice said, glancing over at Daniel's drawing.

'It will suffice for now and I will continue on it in my own time,' he said, just as Mrs Wilks came in. 'Thank you, Miss Ella, Miss Elvira.'

'The ladies need to get back to work. Have you all you

need?' Mrs Wilks asked, and with that, she hustled the sisters from the room and Matilda, Alice and Daniel were alone.

Matilda rose. 'Thank you, Daniel. We are seeing Mrs Wilks in two days at 2pm if that suits you to illustrate? But now I must go to see Mrs Tufton and then Thomas with some information. I am sorry to leave you, Alice. Daniel, perhaps you could escort Miss Doran out?'

'Ah that won't be necessary. I am quite capable of walking, but thank you,' Alice said, ever independent but not averse to having Daniel walk beside her.

'I felt the same just recently when Thomas berated me for being here alone,' Matilda said, 'but there are some rough sorts around here, especially with the alcoholic beverages served nearby.'

'Allow me to offer this small service,' Daniel said to Alice. 'Or failing that, you can protect me.'

Alice laughed. 'All right then, since you put it like that, we shall look out for each other.'

As Matilda watched them leave, secretly satisfied with her matchmaking effort that fooled no one, she was left wondering how Ella and Elvira's lives would be now with their new manager and their dear friend gone. At least they had love, she thought.

*Chapter 17*

Carl Tufton stood, arms crossed over his singlet-clad chest and blocking the entrance to his lodgings. He was a solid man of ordinary height, balding on top, with tufts of grey and brown hair for sideburns. His face was weathered from years of farming before he determined that a lady of abnormal size should be his wife and thus could handsomely provide for him if he took on the role of business manager.

'I've been expecting you; I thought I would be your first port of call,' he said, looking from Detective Ashdown to Detective Dart with a scowl.

'Can we step inside?' Thomas asked, flashing his badge for good measure.

Tufton moved aside. His breakfast tray was still on the table as they entered, and he shoved it out in the hallway to be collected. He preferred not to eat with the other lodgers, too much small talk required, and he found himself to be by far the most interesting of the guests.

'Not staying with the wife in her caravan then?' Harry asked, knowing the answer.

'You've met her, haven't you?' Tufton snickered. 'Not much room left in that caravan. And before you ask, she's better off staying there and not here so she's got access to the exhibition if she gets any special requests. Private visits can make us a lot of money.'

Thomas sniffed his displeasure. He pulled out a chair from under a small table near the door of the boarding house room as Tufton lowered himself on the edge of the bed, and Harry took the only decent lounge seat.

'Tell us about your visit to Mr Burnham that evening,' Thomas began.

'You read what I said to the young cop?'

'We did. So, colour it in for us,' Harry responded. 'Be as detailed as you can, it all helps.'

Tufton sighed. 'The Mrs, Anna, has been working for Burnham now for four years and she's his biggest draw card. But since he got that new manager, her expenses have increased but her wages haven't risen. I went to put that right.'

Thomas nodded. 'So why do you think Mrs Tufton is the biggest draw card?'

'She is. He featured her in all his advertising. The other exhibitors are freaks of nature. Big deal, born unlucky. Anna is a giantess,' he said, emphasising the word. 'Remember when you were a kid and you read about giants, dragons, fairies, all the mysteries of the world? Anna is not a freak, she's part of mythology. She's a real giant.'

He had the gift of selling; he was so good that Thomas almost believed him.

'So that's why you fell in love with her and asked her to be your wife?' Harry asked, drily.

Tufton gave Harry a scowl that changed his countenance and made him look like the kind of man who could give even the biggest woman a good beating or injure a man, for that matter.

'I've known Anna for years. We grew up in the same community, and we went to the same church. It was a natural progression,' he said.

'Why didn't you negotiate with Wilks if he was the new manager?' Thomas asked.

'Wilks! I don't like the man, and Burnham was still the owner. I've always negotiated with him. He's a fair man, he was a fair man.'

'So, he agreed to pay more then?' Harry asked.

Tufton shook his head. 'No. But he wasn't opposed outright to the idea, and he agreed Anna was their best attraction, but he said he'd have to look at the books. He complained about costs going up – costs to rent the ground, put advertising in the newspaper, even the food bill. He said everything had gone up but if he put up the price of entry, fewer people would come.'

'What happened in your last ten minutes together?' Thomas asked, keen for Tufton's version of events.

Tufton frowned as he thought about it. 'Well, he promised he would look at the books and get back to me. He said if I wanted to come up with some other ideas to promote Anna, he'd be open to it, and then I thanked him and left. He was alive and about to turn in for the night when I left.'

Neither Thomas nor Harry spoke for a moment, hoping Tufton might add more but he didn't. He knew his way around a police interview.

'That it then?' Tufton asked.

Thomas drew himself up in his seat. 'We heard the meeting involved Mrs Tufton but she left because there was some tension.'

'Tension? That's an outright lie, there was never any tension,' he added indignantly.

'You've got a bit of a history of getting hot under the collar,' Harry said.

'I know what you're doing here.' Tufton rose.

Harry rose as well, ready to subdue him if necessary; he was fairly confident he could still land a good right hook.

Tufton snapped at them, 'You're trying to pin this on me. I can see how I'd fit it neatly for you, but I'm telling you, there was no tension. Why would I kill the man who provided our living? I might have been frustrated but I'm not a bloody idiot.'

'Did you see anyone else around or hear anything unusual?' Thomas asked, his voice moderate, not rising to Tufton's anger.

Tufton strode to the window, looked out, and then turned and leaned back against the sill. Harry sat in the chair he had abandoned.

'I saw Wilks and his wife hovering around, as always. They were walking back from the kitchen tent, probably giving the chef a hard time for something.'

'Did they join you and Mr Burnham during the discussion at any time?' Harry asked.

'No. I just saw them as I was leaving, and they were walking towards their caravan. She's an attractive woman, and I heard he doesn't let her out of his sight.'

Thomas stored that detail and rose to leave.

'What's my wife been saying?' Tufton asked.

'Nothing to us and nothing that incriminates you,' Harry assured him.

'She's been talking with that woman from the newspaper. Probably getting ideas of independence. Are you sure she didn't tell you something?'

'Like what?' Harry asked.

Tufton shrugged.

'No. Nobody told us anything pertaining to you that you don't already know,' Thomas assured him and sighed. 'Right then. Don't leave town before the exhibition does.'

Thomas opened the door and departed with Harry close behind. They headed down the stairs of the boarding lodge, and as they walked past the front of the building, Thomas looked up to see Tufton watching them from his room window.

'What's your thoughts on him?' Thomas asked Harry.

'A bastard of a husband, a shrewd businessman, and way too greedy to kill the source of his income,' Harry muttered.

'Yeah, couldn't agree more.'

*****

'Someone to see you, sir,' the young desk clerk said as Thomas and Harry entered the police station twenty minutes later.

123

'She has been waiting for about ten minutes and said she'd leave if you weren't back by the top of the hour.'

'Thank you,' Thomas said and headed down the hallway to his office with Harry close behind.

Thomas cast around in his mind for victims or relatives who may be waiting to speak with him – he hated this part of the job, as it required empathy and time and he felt short on both. And then he stopped on hearing the sound of her voice coming from his office. A young police officer came out of that very room, smiling, and sobered at seeing the detectives. Thomas quickened his step and ignored the officer who acknowledged the detectives as he passed.

Taking a deep breath, Thomas entered his office and his eyes searched her out. Matilda was standing near the window, peering out. He stopped suddenly, Harry nearly ran into his back, as his emotions went from delight to concern.

'Matilda! Is everything all right?' He took in her fine figure in her beautifully fitted red skirt and a white blouse, not a hair out of place beneath her straw sailor hat trimmed with a black ribbon. By her feet rested a small basket, the contents covered by a white cloth. Harry stepped around him.

'Yes, yes, fine, thank you, Thomas. Hello Detective Dart, lovely to see you again,' Matilda said with a smile for Harry.

'And you, Miss Hayward,' Detective Dart removed his hat. 'Well, I'll leave you to it then,' Harry said.

'It's a business call,' she assured Detective Dart. 'I have some information which you may or may not know concerning the character of Mr Burnham and Mr Wilks,' Matilda said. 'If now is convenient?'

'Of course,' Thomas said, inviting Matilda to sit and indicating a chair for Harry. He returned to the other side of his desk. 'Would you like tea or a glass of water?'

'No, I won't detain you any longer than necessary, but thank you.'

'I would like tea,' Harry said, and Thomas grinned at him.

'You would care for tea, Detective Dart?' Thomas asked, reissuing the invitation.

'Yes, I'll organise it.' Harry grinned and rose.

'Well, if you two are going to partake, so shall I,' Matilda said.

Harry collared a young constable passing by to organise tea for three. He returned to his seat, and they made the customary polite small talk, asking after family and discussing the weather.

Once the tea had arrived and been served, Matilda began.

'Alice and I were interviewing the Siamese twin ladies today at the Exhibition,' she said.

'You went to that place again by yourself?' Thomas grimaced.

Matilda sighed. 'Really Thomas, it was mid-morning, and we are not made of glass. Besides, Daniel came with us to illustrate the ladies for our story.' She failed to mention that Daniel came quite a bit later, but the element of truth was present.

Thomas visibly relaxed. 'Good. Who is Alice?'

'Miss Alice Doran; she has just started work at *The Women's Journal* and is sharing the writing of the profile pieces with me.'

Thomas muttered, 'Another one, Lord help us.'

Harry was about to chuckle but seeing Matilda's expression took stock of his behaviour.

'Thomas, you are being most objectionable today. Perhaps I should just speak with Detective Dart and let you return to your business if this is how you are when you are not playing the gentleman at my household.'

'Yes Miss Hayward, this is exactly what he is like all the time, and I have to put up with it,' Harry added with a smile, extracting the same from Matilda who was quick to temper and just as quick to forget once the moment had passed.

'I unreservedly apologise, Matilda,' Thomas said, reining in his shortness and opinions. 'I have been going around in circles on a few cases and I am—'

'Hungry perhaps?' she suggested, cutting him off mid-speech. 'I have four brothers and they are all more obnoxious when they are hungry.'

'It is way past lunch,' Harry agreed.

'Obnoxious is a little strong.' Thomas bucked up.

'You are most fortunate because I have some bakery items that should tide you over,' she said, reaching for the small basket that she had placed at her feet. 'Mrs Tufton gave them to me this morning. Apparently, the nearby bakery keeps sending her little gifts and she claims to not have a sweet tooth except for a particular biscuit.' She pulled back the towel covering to reveal pastries and offered it to Harry, who was closest.

'Ooh, don't mind if I do. Thank you, Miss Hayward,' he said.

'Take two at least,' she insisted, and he needed no encouragement. She offered the basket to Thomas.

'You were taking these home for your family, I imagine?' he asked, and Harry froze just as he went to bite.

'No,' she assured them, and Harry resumed his bite. 'As you know my family has an exceptional cook and she would be most insulted if I brought home someone else's baking. I was going to leave them with the front desk if you weren't in.'

'That would have been a tragedy,' Harry said, licking the dusting from his lips.

Thomas chuckled at Harry and accepted two pastries; he encouraged Matilda to continue while he made quick work of them.

'As I said, Alice and I were interviewing Ella and Elvira Hove, who were most agreeable by the way. After we spoke about their lives, I asked permission to discuss what happened the night of Mr Burnham's murder and promised we wouldn't include it in our story. I then asked could I tell you if you were the soul of discretion.'

'Well done, Matilda,' Thomas said, trying not to sound too condescending. 'Harry and I will be just that.'

She nodded. 'I asked them about Mr Burnham, and they said he was their friend, and that it was very much like a family environment at the exhibition. The ladies held him in high regard, and they were visibly upset and not able to comprehend who would do such a thing. But then Elvira said it was a shame it hadn't been Mr Wilks who was killed instead.'

Thomas and Harry exchanged looks and Thomas nodded for Matilda to continue.

'Elvira said Mr Wilks was prone to anger, had driven up their boarding cost, was working them for longer hours and that the quality of the meals had declined terribly. She didn't think Mr Burnham knew because Mr Wilks was always so nice to him.'

Harry and Thomas accepted a third pastry and, brushing crumbs off his facial hair, Thomas remarked, 'this is most interesting and very helpful. We didn't get any of this in the constable's report.'

'I asked them what they told the constable,' Matilda said. 'Apparently, Mrs Wilks was with them throughout the interview which restricted them, and they were also distressed having just heard the news of Mr Burnham's death.'

Harry shook his head. 'We didn't even think about that. I knew the ladies spoke English but I let Mrs Wilks stay because she said the artists were fearful of the police.' He made a hmph sound.

Matilda continued, 'There was one last thing – something that Anna, that is Mrs Tufton, said to me when I dropped in on her after interviewing the twins. She said Mr Jo-Jo – you know the—'

'Super hairy man,' Harry cut in.

'Yes, that's him,' Matilda said. 'Anna said something strange is going on… petty thefts from around the exhibition.'

'Such as?' Harry asked, brushing down his suit front and feeling happily sated after the pastries.

'Mr Jo-Jo and Mr Burnham's walking canes have gone missing and Mr Jo-Jo is quite upset about it, because, unlike Mr Burnham – who had his cane for show and twirling – Mr Jo-Jo needs his cane according to Mrs Tufton.'

'Odd, but probably no chance of getting those back given the people that pour through that place,' Harry said, missing the point.

Thomas was frowning. 'Did she say what these canes looked like?'

'Not exactly, but Anna said Mr Jo-Jo is quite upset because his cane was of sentimental value. Anna said it was quite beautiful and featured an engraved, ornate brass knob on the end that was a gift from his grandfather before his death and before Mr Jo-Jo was forced to make his own way in the world.'

'Like a steel cricket ball perhaps?' Thomas said with a glance to Harry, who caught up.

'I couldn't say,' Matilda said, and finished her tea. 'Well, I best get off and leave you to it. I have an interview to write.' She rose and lifted her now empty basket.

'I will see you out,' Thomas said, standing. 'Matilda, you have been immensely helpful.'

'Have I?' she smiled, pleased with herself. 'Good. I shall remind you of that.'

'I have no doubt you will.' He smiled.

*Chapter 18*

Amos Hayward preferred to see clients in his offices – they were neat rooms, spacious, clean, and well-appointed. Sadly, he had no choice but to go to Mrs Tufton's caravan, given the impossibility of her visiting without causing much curiosity and discomfort. After hailing a hansom, he collected Matilda on the way, and they were at the grounds in time for their half-past-two appointment with the giantess and her husband to discuss their legal separation.

'I feel I have been here more than I've been at home lately.' Matilda sighed as Amos offered her his hand to descend the cab.

Amos's expression of distaste said volumes. 'I can't stand meeting in that small caravan, but it is better than entering the exhibition tent.'

'You are good to come, Amos,' Matilda soothed him as they walked towards the exhibition and to the row at the back where Anna Tufton's caravan stood at the far end. 'We'll be as quick as we can, but you will have to take tea and observe the hostess's niceties.'

'If we must,' he agreed and stood back as Matilda knocked on the caravan door and announced her arrival.

The door was opened with a great deal of force, and Carl Tufton stood in the doorway.

'Miss Hayward and Mr Hayward, I assume?' he said in a rough manner.

'Good morning, Mr Tufton,' Matilda said, and Amos offered his hand.

The men shook briefly. Tufton moved away from the door and the Haywards entered the now tight space with four bodies in it. The table was set with a milk jug, sugar bowl and four cups, plus a plate of biscuits, and Anna remained seated.

'Forgive me for not rising,' she greeted them, 'but space does not permit it.'

'Of course,' Amos said, and took the offered seat.

'I shall make tea since you have prepared it, shall I?' Matilda asked, allowing Mr Tufton to sit opposite his wife and next to Amos.

'Thank you, Matilda, yes please.' Anna gave her a grateful smile. No one appeared comfortable with the arrangement. The scene, while reflecting the traditions and manners of a gathering for tea, was reminiscent of no such gathering – instead, a giantess looked meek in the corner, her husband angry and defiant, a solicitor most uncomfortable and a temporary hostess looked out of place.

After tea was served, Amos began.

'Mr Tufton, as I am acting on behalf of your wife, you of course will need your own representation.'

'I am using the services of Milford and McDonald, and as I intend to run for my local council this year, a divorce does not suit me,' he said and glared at Amos as if that would settle the matter.

Anna could not have looked more surprised, and Amos stepped in before she spoke.

'My client, Mrs Tufton, is seeking a decree of nullity. Should the court grant this, then there is no legal marriage and that should not hinder your proposed career if the court deems the marriage was never legal.'

Tufton thought about this for a moment.

'On what grounds?' he finally asked. He was no fool. 'We have consummated the marriage, we've lived together, I have never raised my hand to Anna, and we were compatible in our early years.'

Matilda avoided looking at Anna as the discussion became indiscreet. Instead, she studied Tufton – an imposing figure of restrained anger.

'Mrs Tufton seeks a decree of nullity for misunderstanding that the marriage would require her to be exhibited and to be the family breadwinner,' Amos said, and Tufton scoffed. 'I am not saying it will be an easy case to win on this basis, but it will be a sympathetic case to present to a judge. Failing that, Mrs Tufton will file for divorce.'

'That doesn't suit me,' Tufton said.

Anna's lips narrowed with frustration and Matilda rose to open the door to let some more fresh air into the caravan than the two small windows afforded.

'I've got a solution and my legal representatives will deliver the papers to you if you are in agreement, Anna,' he said curtly, addressing her directly. 'If you are not, then the divorce will take a very long time as I am not consenting to it.'

Anna sat straight and her face flushed, but Amos held up his hand.

'Mrs Tufton, do not be distressed. Let us first hear what Mr Tufton proposes as it may suit both of you.'

Tufton nodded. 'I will agree to a mutual deed of separation. You continue as you wish, Anna, and so will I. For the purposes of my career, I have a legal wife and am not divorced.'

Anna turned to Amos. 'I need to understand what that means for me in the long-term,' she said. 'I am not averse to a formal separation, and I don't wish to harm your future career options, Carl, if you do not wish to interfere with mine,' she added to her husband.

'He'll explain it,' Tufton said rudely, with a nod to Amos.

Amos addressed Anna. 'In essence, it states that it is a mutual decision to live separately, but neither party is ready for pursuing divorce proceedings. It entitles you to similar claims as a divorce, such as access to matrimonial assets and you are free to permanently live apart.'

'And if I want to proceed with a divorce in due course?' Anna asked Amos.

'Then you can do so after three years if you both agree, or four years if Mr Tufton does not agree,' Amos informed her.

'It doesn't seem any different to what we are doing now, only I have a four-year wait if you don't agree to divorce,' Anna said. 'Why would that interest me?'

Tufton scowled. 'It gives you respectability to be married and it is not as if there'll be a queue waiting to put a ring on your finger.'

Matilda cleared her throat. 'Would you like us to leave and give you some time to think about it, Anna? No decision needs to be made today does it, brother?'

'I'd like it over as soon as possible without a public scandal,' Tufton answered before Anna had a chance to speak.

Matilda wondered how Anna ever fell for this charmless man. He continued, 'Then we needn't see each other again unless I choose to remarry and seek a divorce.'

'If I am fortunate, you might pass away in those three or four years and save us both from the indignity of divorce,' Anna snapped back.

Matilda inhaled sharply and sat back. It was the first time she had seen Anna in anger or capable of anger. Her thoughts went to the investigation and the deceased, Mr Burnham. Could Anna have harmed him as a way out of this life? Did she think the carnival would shut down and she could stop travelling?

Amos held up his hand to stop the warring between the Tuftons. 'I think the only benefit for Mrs Tufton in agreeing to a mutual deed of separation is if she receives a small payment of alimony. It would be an honourable thing to support your wife, especially as you are still legally married and if you are in office. It would be unfortunate if we made it public that your wife supported you or that you abandoned her to a Freak Show to support herself.'

Matilda gave her brother an admiring glance.

'Oh, I knew it would get to the money,' Tufton snarled.

'No doubt your legal team suggested that,' Amos said, not fooled by Tufton's front and bluff. Amos turned to his client, Anna. 'My recommendation, Mrs Tufton is that if you do not intend to remarry in the near future, you accept the mutual deed of separation so as not to hinder your husband's career, in exchange for an alimony payment each week.' Amos suggested a figure he knew would be acceptable to the court, manageable for a working man, and would see Mrs Tufton comfortable. It would allow her to leave the carnival and it was high time that Mr Tufton got to work in Amos's opinion.

Anna looked very pleased and Tufton did not seem surprised at the figure or the discussion outcome.

'Of course, if that is not suitable, I understand you inherited a farm from your parents. We could file for divorce and halve your marital assets, but as you said, that would not reflect well on your budding career and it would be tied up for some time during the sale and legalities,' Amos finished.

'The farm is worthless, it's costing me more to own and run then it brings in,' he said.

'I am aware it is no longer a working farm, but the land will fetch a reasonable price in good time,' Amos said, and Anna visibly relaxed. He had well and truly done his homework. 'Did you both want to think about it, and we shall meet again?' Amos said, unhappy at the thought of returning.

'I would be prepared to accept that offer,' Anna said.

Tufton rose. 'I'll talk to my lawyers and get the paperwork sent to you.' He departed without any polite exchange.

The party did not say a word until they believed he was gone from the site and then Anna threw her hands over her face and began to cry. Amos stood up and removed a white handkerchief from his pocket, offering it to her.

'I am free,' she said, accepting it with thanks. 'I could not have achieved that outcome without you, Mr Hayward, thank you. Once that is done, I am free to leave here. I can get a comfortable abode away from the city and see only who I wish to see, run my own home, and be private.'

Matilda reached for Anna's large hand and squeezed it.

'I am so happy for you, Anna,' she said, and turned to her brother. 'Amos, you were brilliant.'

He gave her an affectionate smile and thanked her modestly.

Anna dried her eyes and smiled. 'Thank you both, thank you. You will never know how you have changed my life.'

'I shall wait for the papers and return to get your signature. I must get back to work, but know that I am pleased you are happy with that compromise, Mrs Tufton,' he said, formally. 'Matilda, shall I give you a ride?'

'Please stay and have another tea with me?' Anna asked. 'I feel I need to talk and celebrate.'

'Of course,' Matilda said, sensing the woman needed someone to share her relief with. But for the first time, she was just a little fearful. Anna Tufton was getting exactly what she wanted… was this how it all started?

*Chapter 19*

T homas's nephew, Edward Ashdown – or rather Teddy Clements as he chose to be identified as the new assistant cook for the remaining seven days that the carnival was in town – finished up creating the evening's meals and left them to be reheated closer to the dinner hour. The rumours he had heard at the butcher shop were true, the artists were eating the fatty leftovers and terrible cuts, but he did his best to make them appealing. He whipped up his Irish Stew recipe using offcuts, then ground and minced what he could to make shepherd's pie. Teddy missed not having a Sunday roast since he'd been on the road, and he could put money on the fact that a roast never saw the light of day at the exhibition.

A big man who looked like someone who knew his way around a pot and pan peered over Teddy's shoulder. He dusted the flour off his hands and onto his apron.

'You've done all right, Teddy, or should I call you Blue?' he asked, attempting to ruffle the new redheaded cook.

'Yeah, Teddy'll do, thanks Mr Secker,' Teddy replied and got a laugh.

'You can call me Chas,' he said good-humouredly. 'A good day's work indeed. You'll have Sunday off as we just do cold fare on that day, and I'll have Mondays off so cook whatever you like with what you can find on hand. Four major dishes and two large desserts tends to feed the lot, and we have a special meal for management but that's small fare. You can make the desserts early in the day to give yourself plenty of time.'

Teddy nodded. 'Thanks, Chas. Do any of the crew or—' he searched for the best word to describe the other residents.

'Freaks?' Chas asked. 'I hear they like to be called artists.'

Teddy nodded. 'Yeah, do any of them do a bit of hunting? I could cook up some good meals with a bit of game.'

'Ooh, you've got me mouth-watering now,' Chas said. 'When I think of my mother's baked rabbit and Nan's roo stew...' he sighed. 'But you're right there... that kind of meat will only be got from hunting, lad, because I can tell you right now this lot isn't spending money on anything that resembles a reasonable cut.'

Teddy gave him a grin. 'I hear you loud and clear.' He began cleaning up and decided to work in a little conversation about the recently deceased, Mr Burnham. 'So, did you like the poor man who met his end, and dare I ask if my cooking's bad, should I expect the same?' He wanted to have something to tell his uncle, Detective Ashdown, that night.

Chas chuckled. 'You're as safe as me, if that's any consolation. But, as bosses go, I did like him. Never said a bad word, appreciated every mouthful he ate and told me so. He was a good man, and that's as much as I hope someone says about me one day,' Chas said.

'I guess it is good that the show goes on, for the artists' sake.'

Chas shook his head. 'It's going to get worse from here on in.' He looked around and lowered his voice for just the two of them in the kitchen. 'He's a miserable sod that Wilks and his wife is as tough as nails. I'm telling you that this exhibition won't be the same this time next year if it still exists at all. Can't say I'll be here that long.'

Teddy nodded. He wasn't one for gossiping or small talk and he didn't want to come across as too inquisitive, so he continued with his work for a little while saying nothing. Once he had cleaned up, he looked to help Chas.

'I'm all right here, Teddy. You've done enough and a good day's work, so get going while you can or else I'll find something else for you to do,' he joked.

'It was a great first day, thanks Chas.' Teddy took off his large coverall and hung it up. 'I'll take the rubbish out as I depart and see you in the morning.'

'Worth your weight in lager,' Chas said, slapping the young cook on the back as he left Teddy to empty the bins while he started preparing the different menu for the managers' meals.

*****

It was nearing four o'clock when Matilda stepped from Anna's caravan feeling relieved and rather proud of herself.

From the first moment the giantess had slipped a note into her hand asking for her help, to now with her brother securing an independent income for Anna to live her life with dignity, she could not have foreseen such a positive outcome. Plus, she had made a new friend in Alice Doran – her writing partner. They were due to interview and write Mrs Wilks' story tomorrow afternoon, and she hoped the spark of interest between Alice and Daniel would ignite.

Matilda made her way through the corridor of caravans and as she turned the corner past the last of the temporary living quarters, she heard fast thumping footsteps on the grass behind her. She turned, feeling a presence close by. Suddenly she was pushed hard against a caravan and before she could scream, two large hands wrapped around her throat, choking her. Inches from her face was Carl Tufton.

Matilda choked and struggled, and he tightened his grip, a leer on his face, his breath upon her.

'I could snap your neck in a second, you meddling cow. It's you that's been putting independent ideas in my stupid wife's head. She wouldn't come up with them by herself.'

Matilda struggled to breathe; she thumped her fists against his body, but it did little to deter him. He left one hand in a stranglehold around her throat and moved the other lower, pressing his knuckles into her chest and moving towards the buttons on her blouse.

She gasped, her eyes watered with pain, and the more Matilda struggled, the tighter he gripped. And then he laughed.

'Hey, what are you doing there?' a loud male voice asked. A tall redheaded man appeared, dropping a bin of rubbish.

Tufton pushed away from Matilda, glaring at her.

'Get lost, we're talking.'

Matilda hurriedly moved away from Tufton, grasping her neck and panting.

Teddy Clements guided Matilda behind him and stood a head taller and wider, looming over Carl Tufton.

'It doesn't look like much talking is going on,' Teddy said. 'Are you all right, miss?' he asked, glancing back at Matilda.

'I am now, thank you,' she said, staying well behind him, her words soft, pained.

'Bugger off. This has nothing to do with you,' Tufton said.

'I work here and as far as I know, you don't, do you? So I can call the police, or you can *bugger off*,' Teddy suggested, imitating him.

Tufton glared at him, and, deciding he most likely would come off the worse, he grunted, turned, and strode off.

Matilda collapsed against the caravan and choked back tears.

'You're safe now, miss, I assure you. Teddy A—' he stopped himself from nearly revealing the wrong surname, '—Clements at your service.' He gave a small bow, conscious that he smelled like the kitchen and was wearing no hat.

'Matilda Hayward, Miss, thank you, Mr Clements,' Matilda said, offering her name while straightening her straw hat, and checking her attire. 'I'm not sure what might have happened if you hadn't intervened,' she said, regaining her strength.

'Do you have business here, or may I see you somewhere?' he asked.

'I had business. I was meeting with Mrs Tufton – the giantess,' she added, seeing Teddy's confused expression. 'But I am heading home if you could see me to a cab or the omnibus.'

'Of course. Allow me one minute to return the bin and I'll join you promptly. Please stand here where I can see you should you need me,' he said and directed her to a more visible spot.

While she waited for Teddy, Matilda straightened the blouse tie around her neck, patted down her skirt and her hair and checked she was still in one piece. Her throat was sore, and her chest ached from the force of Tufton's knuckles against her skin.

Teddy hurried over to pick up his bin, empty and return it, before wiping his hands and returning with a hat in his hand.

'Forgive my appearance, I've been in a kitchen for hours.'

'Not at all.'

He offered his arm, which Matilda accepted.

'You have a friendship with the giantess?' Teddy asked as they walked.

'Yes, confidentially, she is conducting business with my brother and seeking separation from her husband. That was the very husband that you chased away. He holds me responsible.' Matilda saw him study her and added, 'it's not true, of course.'

'Of course,' he said and grinned.

She couldn't help smiling in response.

'Allow me to see you home since you have had a bit of a shock,' he said.

'That would be most kind, but I don't want to take you out of your way.'

'I'm sure we are going in the same direction. Where is your residence?'

Matilda told him.

'Ah, right near mine,' he said and the look of disbelief she gave him made Teddy laugh.

'Well, near enough,' he assured her.

'Thank you,' Matilda said.

'The pleasure is all mine.' He gave a tip of his hat and Matilda relaxed in the knowledge she would get safely home despite the ache around her throat and the fear Tufton's threat instilled in her that he could snap out her life easily, and she was by no means ready to leave this world yet.

*Chapter 20*

Matilda thanked her protector. 'This is my home, or rather my father's,' she said as they arrived outside the gates of a palatial home on the rise of Highgate Hill. The autumn evening was closing in and the street was in shadowy darkness now with only the lamps shining from inside the windows to guide the way up the path.

'May I offer you a cup of tea before you depart?' She hoped her new friend would not accept; she felt raw and emotional and needed to get herself together, but yet manners dictated she issued the invitation.

'Thank you, but I'm not appropriately dressed for calling. Should you wish to return to the Exhibition, I am there most days except Sunday, so please seek me out if I can be of service,' Teddy said.

'I can't thank you enough, Mr Clements,' Matilda said.

She entered the gate, closing it behind her, and was relieved to be in the safety of her residence. She was conscious that he was gallantly ensuring she safely reached her front door, so she increased the pace of her walk up the path and took the few stairs to the front door, turned and smiled before disappearing within.

'Oh good,' Harriet said, bustling out to assist with taking Matilda's hat and gloves. The familiar sight of her in a dark grey gown with lace collar, hair neatly back in a bun, caused a wave of emotion in Matilda. 'It is getting dark, and I like you home well before the evening crowds venture out.'

'Thank you, Harriet,' Matilda said. 'I am rather exhausted, though. I think I will just lie down for a while. If I'm awake, I'll join Pa for dinner, but otherwise please give my apologies.'

She felt Harriet's eyes upon her and hurriedly made her way up the stairs, supporting herself on the banister. Once inside, she lowered herself onto her bed. Then she turned and cried miserably into her pillow, ashamed of her weakness. But in those moments when the breath was being withheld from her throat, as Tufton glared and sneered at her, she'd thought of her family; fleeting thoughts that she might never see her pa again and the grief it would cause him to have her body returned to the home, lifeless. The faces of her brothers, and Harriet and Cook, and Minnie, all the people in her life that she might never see again, appeared in her mind. It terrified her.

She felt deep affection for Thomas and knew how disappointed he would be in her being there without protection.

Yes, she was strong and independent, but the man's world she had grown up in had been a kind one, civilised and protective. She was encouraged to be free thinking and to have an opinion and even to write and support that independence. Mr Tufton's attack had frightened her to the core.

*****

Harriet watched Matilda make her way up the staircase to her room. Behind Harriet, Daniel appeared and grabbed for his hat to head out.

'Just a quick drink at the club. I'll be back for dinner unless Pa wants to dine earlier, then if Cook could keep me a plate? I'll attempt to bring Elijah and Gideon home with me,' he said, and planted a kiss on Harriet's cheek. 'Or I might drop in and see if Thomas is home...' He was still talking as the door closed behind him.

'Goodness, the comings and goings in this house, I can't keep up,' Harriet said, talking to herself. 'I'll tell Cook to just cook then and whatever is left over can be eaten another time.' She sighed. Harriet glanced back at the stairs again where Matilda had just departed and then to the study where Mr Hayward worked inside, his door closed. She could not hear a noise from inside Matilda's room, but if she could have seen through walls, she would have found Matilda weeping miserably.

Moments later, Harriet returned with a cup of tea and made her way up the stairs to Matilda's room. She knocked gently and received no reply.

'It's just me,' she said.

'Come in.'

Harriet entered to find Matilda sitting on the edge of the bed and wiping her face. It was clear she had been crying – most out of character.

'Tea will fix everything,' Harriet said, offering her the cup, and Matilda smiled as she accepted it.

'It does seem to, thank you,' she agreed, and took a welcomed sip.

Harriet sat in a chair near the window and studied the young woman she had raised since Mrs Hayward had died when Matilda was four. She often thought it was a great shame Mr Hayward had not remarried and provided a motherly role model.

'Now tell me what happened. Do you have a broken heart?' Harriet asked.

Matilda looked confused. 'Oh no, nothing like that,' she said, dismissing the idea as though it were preposterous. 'If I tell you, Harriet, you must not scold me or tell a soul until I choose to do so.'

Harriet thought about it. 'If it is not a matter of life or death, I suppose I could be bound to that agreement.'

Matilda smiled. 'The matter of life and death is over. I was… attacked.'

Harried gasped. 'Oh Matilda. Do we need a doctor? I can fetch Elijah home immediately.' She rose and came to sit beside her, taking Matilda's hand in hers.

'No, no, nothing like that,' Matilda assured her and told her the story, her hand close to her throat as she recounted it.

'How terribly frightening. How could we live without you?' she said, and now Harriet was dabbing a few tears from her eyes with a handkerchief removed from the sleeve of her dress.

'I don't think he ever intended to kill me,' Matilda soothed her.

'We don't know that. He might have killed that other man who died there and not hesitated for you to follow that fate.'

Harriet realised she wasn't helping the situation. 'But you are probably right,' she agreed, stiffening with resolve. She was never one for *what-ifs*. 'He sounds like an angry husband who doesn't like his business interfered in.'

Matilda nodded. 'Yes.' She looked at Harriet. 'I was so scared that I would never see all of you again. But you can't tell until I am ready to do so,' Matilda reminded her.

'Why ever not? That man needs to be brought to justice.'

'I will tell Thomas, I promise. But if we tell Father it will distress him, Amos will be consumed with guilt that I did not leave with him and will insist I be accompanied everywhere, Daniel will want to go to Thomas immediately and demand action, Elijah will want to give that man a piece of his mind and Gideon will do just that, knock him out and get himself in trouble.'

They looked at each other and laughed.

'Yes, well that does sum up the likely reactions,' Harriet agreed. 'Shall we call for Detective Ashdown in an official capacity?'

Matilda shook her head. 'No. I just need tonight to think about it and regain my strength. I am getting angrier now, so I am feeling better and stronger. I'll drop in and see Thomas first thing in the morning.'

'Do you promise me?' Harriet asked.

'I promise.'

'You shouldn't return to that awful place.'

'I have an interview there tomorrow. Alice and I.'

'Oh Matilda, no, it is too dangerous,' Harriet said, alarmed.

'Daniel will be with us, and a lovely man who works there – Mr Teddy Clements – a cook I believe, came to my aid. He will be there tomorrow too.'

'I don't like it.'

Matilda took her hand. 'I know. I will be much more careful now that my eyes are opened. I will ensure someone is with me at all times.'

Harriet nodded. 'Come down then when you are ready. Later, when it is quieter after dinner, I want to see where he grabbed you. We'll see if I can reduce the pain a little with one of my home remedies – I have a very good salve.'

'Don't I know,' Matilda teased. Harriet had applied it for years to every injury in the Hayward family. 'I make a vow to never be so vulnerable again.'

'That's the spirit,' Harriet said, departing with an ache in her own heart. Sometimes bravery and determination were not enough to counter physical strength and intent.

## Chapter 21

Thomas walked up his front stairs and through the front door not long after 7pm. He would rarely be home at this time, preferring to go to the club rather than return to an empty house or to stay at his desk and get some work done when everyone had gone, and it was quiet – except for the night shift on the front desk but they rarely interrupted him unless it was murder calling. But now that Teddy was likely to be home, and the possibility of a dinner on the table, the house felt more like home. If the young man hadn't already cooked, Thomas decided he would take his nephew out and introduce him to a few of the better establishments for a lager and meal.

Light emitted from the rooms down the hall. 'Teddy,' he called, taking off his hat and hanging it near the door.

A head appeared around the dining-room door. 'Ah, good, you'd ruin the dinner if you were much later,' Teddy said, seeing his uncle. He disappeared just as quickly, and Thomas went to join him.

'I didn't expect you'd be cooking tonight as you've spent

the day cooking,' Thomas said with a smile, 'not that I am unhappy in the least. I was going to suggest we eat out.'

'Next time for sure,' Teddy said.

Thomas offered his nephew a drink and poured for two. 'It's nice to be home,' he said with a sip and sigh.

'Even if I'm invading your space?' Teddy asked.

'I wouldn't be home otherwise. The house would be dark and cold and nothing to welcome a man after a long day at work.'

Teddy gave his uncle a grin. 'Glad to earn my place. Shall we eat?'

'That would be great,' Thomas said, moving to the already set table to share a meal. 'How was your first day?' he asked, dying to know but not expecting too much insider news. He cut the bread on the table and slathered a generous serving of butter onto a piece.

'The first day was interesting and confirmed that the rumours I heard at the grocer and butcher were true.'

They heard two loud knocks at the door and Thomas sighed, expecting to be called back to work. But the door opened before he had to make his way down the hallway and Daniel's voice called, 'Are you in?'

'In the dining room, come through,' Thomas called back.

Daniel swanned in, hat in hand. 'Ah, you must be the nephew,' he said, offering his hand.

'Daniel, my nephew Teddy,' Thomas said, and returned to his bread. 'Staying for dinner? Teddy's a bloody excellent cook.'

'There's plenty,' Teddy said, carrying a large pie to the centre of the table, placing it down and taking a seat.

'Wow, smells great. I'll be in, thanks,' Daniel said and grabbed his own cutlery. He sat at the table as Thomas placed a large slab of bread on Teddy and Daniel's plates and pushed the butter closer to them.

'That looks bloody amazing,' Thomas said like a man who rarely got a good feed.

'Steak and kidney pudding, one of my favourites,' Teddy told them, dishing them both up a hearty sized serve.

'I tell you what, if I could afford you, I'd hire you to work as a cook for me full-time,' Thomas said, and Teddy laughed. 'It'd be boring, I concede, but you'd have plenty of time on your hands.'

'You wouldn't get your money's worth given the few meals you get home for,' Teddy said. 'Dig in then.' He was clever enough not to discuss his work in front of Daniel without the all-clear from his uncle. He glanced his way and raised an eyebrow.

Thomas nodded and addressed his best friend. 'Speaking of work, I've got Teddy doing an odd job for me. You can know about it if you keep it between us. His safety depends on it.'

'Have I ever divulged any of our secrets?' Daniel asked. 'I even took the cane for you once.'

Thomas grinned. 'That's the truth, but it was your plan, I was just the one caught. There was that time you told Matilda that I took her ribbon because I liked her.'

Daniel chuckled and turned his attention to Teddy. 'We were thirteen, so it was a while ago. Thom has had his eye on my sister for many years.'

Thomas flushed slightly, and Teddy laughed.

'So why haven't you made good on that, Uncle Thom? You're not getting any younger and I won't be here to keep house for you forever. Where's this lovely lady then?'

'I've been busy,' Thomas answered, 'and Matilda had made it quite clear that she is not interested in binding herself to any man. Yet.' He changed the subject before Teddy had a chance to tell them about his meeting with a lady by the name of Matilda at work today. Thomas informed Daniel of Teddy's undercover job.

'I'm glad you told me,' Daniel said. 'I'll be at the carnival tomorrow with Matilda. She works for one of those women's newspapers and is interviewing the ladies of the Freak Show,' he explained to Teddy. 'I'm earning my keep as her illustrator. Odd little job but interesting.'

'Ah illustrating… the court job, I have news,' Thomas cut in, remembering he promised to make enquiries on Daniel's behalf to be a court illustrator. 'You've got an appointment next week to make your case.'

Daniel grinned. 'That's bloody fantastic, thanks, Thom.'

Thomas gave a small shrug. 'It was nothing. You still have to get it. So, Teddy, what did you learn today?'

Teddy filled his uncle in on the chef's dislike of both Mr and Mrs Wilks and his kind words for the victim, Mr Burnham.

'That seems to be universal,' Thomas agreed, accepting a second helping.

Daniel knocked back the offer. 'I told Cook to keep me a plate, but thanks. You'll be getting fat, Thomas, if you keep this up every night.'

'Plenty of room on these svelte bones for some meat,' Thomas said with a smile, brushing his hand down his thin front frame. 'Any other observations, Teddy?'

'Yes, I got the impression that the Wilks' wanted to run the show, but Chef doesn't think it'll last the year now under their rule.' Teddy elaborated on the conversation.

When they finished their meal and discussion, Thomas rose and poured the men a small glass of port, congratulating his nephew on a sterling meal. They stayed at the table, relaxed.

'There was one other incident,' Teddy said. 'It's something that I imagine didn't concern anyone who worked there, but it certainly gave a young lady a fright.'

'What's that?' Thomas asked.

Teddy accepted a cigarette from Daniel's cigarette case and a light. He smoked and exhaled before continuing.

'I was taking out the bin, just before leaving for the day, when I saw this ruffian holding a lady by the throat between the caravans. I suspect he'd come from the ale tent.'

Thomas sat upright. 'Did you intervene?'

'Of course, and I had a foot on him in height and width. He was a rude bugger. I don't know what it was about, but he removed his hands from around her throat and told me to mind my own business. I told him I was making this my business and he strode off. She said she was all right, but I saw her home nevertheless.'

'What was it about, did you find out?' Daniel asked.

'Yes. The lady was seeing a friend, the giantess, so she said.'

Thomas's port glass hit the table hard enough to shatter. 'Did she tell you her name?'

'Yes, and I was going to say earlier that I'd met a Matilda today – a Miss Matilda Hayward. A great beauty too and brave. She didn't shed a tear and she was putting up a good fight.'

'My sister!' Daniel exclaimed.

'Wait, Miss Hayward is your sister? The very sister you have feelings for, Uncle?' Teddy looked from Thomas to the guest.

'The same,' Daniel answered.

'You saw her home and she was fine?' Thomas clarified.

'She was.'

'Did you not see her before you came out tonight?' he asked Daniel. Thomas was now on his feet.

'No, I heard her come in, but she went straight to her room. Shall we check on her?' He rose.

'Absolutely. Teddy, do you wish to accompany us?'

'No, I don't think you need me there, Uncle, I'll clean up.' His voice was laced with disappointment. He had hoped to have made an impression on Miss Matilda Hayward, but she might already have her heart spoken for and if not, it would not put him in his uncle's favour if she reciprocated Teddy's feeling.

'Thank God you were there and thanks for this.' Thomas slapped his nephew on the back and nodded at empty dinner plates. He grabbed his hat on the way out and followed Daniel up the street until they hailed a hansom cab and took it to the house he knew so well, as well as his own. To Matilda.

On the way over Thomas – no stranger to drama – coached his closest and oldest friend, who sat agitated and working himself up more with every minute.

'Just still for a moment, Dan. Take a deep breath and relax. Matilda is home safely, and if she needed assistance, she would have sought one of us,' he said. 'I'm sure Harriet would have noticed too.'

Daniel's jaw was locked in anger, which was how Thomas felt, but he was better at masking it. He gave Thomas a brisk nod.

'I'm going to kill—'

'No!' Thomas cut him off. 'I'm going to kill Tufton and then arrest him or not quite in that order. You are going to be the strong brotherly shoulder she needs.'

He exhaled and turned to face Thomas. 'You are right. Thank you.'

'It's all right, I deal with it every day. I'm not saying I'm not angry, I could kill Tufton with my bare hands and I still might.'

Plus, he thought, I want to see Matilda again, and losing my temper might be the quickest way to push her away.

'I won't be responsible for my actions if I see him.' Daniel spat the words.

'Well, I'd rather arrest him than arrest you, so do your best not to see him too soon,' Thomas warned him. Their cab pulled up at the Hayward residence, Thomas paid the cabman and they rushed up the stairs and inside, removing their hats as they entered the residence.

'She's not in her room,' Daniel said with a glance up the

stairs and seeing the open door of Matilda's bedroom. He continued walking straight ahead.

Thomas followed him into the kitchen area. Matilda sat, her neck tie undone, along with the first few buttons of her blouse, revealing her neck and all the bruising. Harriet sat next to her, dabbing a salve onto the raw area.

'Matilda!' Thomas exclaimed, sorting through a range of emotions – shock, anger, and concern.

'We heard what happened.' Daniel dropped into the chair next to her.

She stared at Thomas with wide eyes and hurried to close the fabric of her blouse around the exposed flesh of her neck and chest just as he realised the impropriety of the situation.

'Forgive me,' he said, turned and exited the room.

'Leave, Daniel,' Harriet ordered, and he stood with a sigh and followed his best friend.

Thomas paced up and down the hallway. 'I'm going to bring him into the station tonight. Let Matilda know he'll pay for this,' he said and, placing his hat back on his head, he stormed out and into the night.

## Chapter 22

By mid-morning, Carl Tufton's legal team had secured his release. Courtesy of the constabulary, one detective in particular, Tufton sported a few more bruises than he might have had before entering the station. Matilda did not wish to take the matter further, and Detective Thomas Ashdown was more frustrated than ever.

'I was hoping we could keep him in here a little longer,' his partner, Harry, grumbled as he paced around Thomas's office.

'That makes both of us,' Thomas agreed. 'You should have seen the bruising around Matilda's neck.'

'You saw that?' Harry asked, surprised, his eyebrows raised.

'Yes, no, accidentally. Harriet was applying a salve when Daniel and I burst in to see if she was all right.'

'Did you tell her about the amazing coincidence with Teddy being her rescuer and your nephew?'

Thomas shook his head. 'I didn't stay. As soon as I saw the bruises I pursued Tufton. But Daniel dropped by this morning to invite Teddy to Sunday lunch as well, so Matilda could offer her gratitude again.'

'Good on him,' Harry said and smiled.

Thomas did not want to talk about Matilda; he was coming to the point of no return – it was too painful to be around her and not have a promised future with her, and too painful to be without her. He was pleased when a constable knocked on the door, putting an end to the conversation and the inevitable lecture from Harry about there being no time like the present.

'Sirs, there's someone to see you at the desk. They want to report a murder and they've asked for you!'

'I'll see to it,' Harry said, and wandered off.

Thomas sighed, but not about the murder – he was thinking about his nephew, Teddy, who was a few years younger than Matilda but still a worthy candidate for her hand. Handsome, strong, hardworking – although he imagined Mr Hayward held the hope of Matilda securing a more fortunate marriage. But maybe not, he was eccentric and took little interest in class order and the rules of society. If Mrs Hayward – Matilda's mother – had been alive, the suitor scrutiny most likely would have been different. Thomas had stayed as near as he could to Matilda so when the time was right for her to want marriage, he would be on hand, willing, affectionate, with good prospects and a home to offer. He didn't mind waiting; the time not spent in a relationship allowed him to sow his wild oats, focus on his career and get his life in order. Besides, she was annoying, and a few years of maturity might take away that competitive edge she still sported with him. But what if she should fall in love – what if Teddy was now her hero and her feelings were for him?

He needed to see Matilda for no other reason than he didn't sleep all night thinking of her with her hair loose around her shoulders and her neck bare. How beautiful and vulnerable she looked at that moment; he wanted to hold her; to love her and to provide for her comfort. To have that honour.

Thomas thought of her movements and realised she would be at the *Women's Journal* office this morning and, to his annoyance, Daniel advised that Matilda intended to go to the carnival in the early afternoon for her interview with Mrs Wilks. He decided to go to the offices and see her there. He just needed to find a reason to do so. Perhaps he could officially offer a friendly warning to Mrs Lawson to ensure her lady writers always travelled in pairs at the moment while a killer was on the loose – that might just do the trick. He could go on the way to the recent murder case if in the same direction.

A loud rap on the door snapped him to attention as his partner, Harry Dart strode in, interrupting his train of thought.

'We've got to go, it's Carl Tufton,' he announced.

Thomas waved away the concern. 'Whatever he's done now, it can wait. There's somewhere I want to go before we follow him up.'

'No—' Harry started again, but Thomas rose and cut him off.

'Let's go and collect the warrant. I want to search that carnival top to bottom. We need to find that cane or the weapon with a globe hard enough to bash a skull in.'

Harry blocked the door. 'The murder... it's Carl Tufton, he's dead.'

## Chapter 23

It wasn't unheard of for men to enter the premises of the *Women's Journal*, but it was a rare sighting. Even more so when the man leading the way was tall, handsome, and confident. A titter ran through the floor, but the women kept working, after all, it was a professional organisation. As Thomas reminded Harry, Tufton was already dead, so another fifteen minutes getting to the scene would make little difference and it would give the younger police officers a chance to get statements. Harry saw right through him.

'May I help you gentlemen?' a mature lady of good size girth and small spectacles enquired.

'Thank you, yes.' Harry stepped in while Thomas scanned the heads on the floor for Matilda. She wasn't hard to miss – her back was to him, her golden hair tied in a neat bun and the back of her neck visible.

'Detectives Ashdown and Dart for Mrs Lawson if she could spare us five minutes, please,' Harry asked, but it wasn't a request. He wasn't averse to turning on the charm when needed and the mature man with the salt-and-pepper hair, well-maintained figure and pale blue eyes held a definite appeal to a mature woman.

Before the receptionist could announce the gentlemen, Mrs Lawson appeared at the door of her office and beckoned them in.

Thomas strode down the centre of the room towards her office, the heads of the younger girls turning towards him like sunflowers. Except for Matilda. Finally, she looked up at the last minute just as he was about to enter, and her eyes widened in surprise and then narrowed. He realised she might think he was going to tell of her incident, of which he had no intention of doing.

'Mrs Lawson, I'm Detective Thomas Ashdown, and this is my partner, Detective Harry Dart. Could we have a moment with you and the two ladies assigned to the carnival profile stories?'

'Of course,' Mrs Lawson said, indicating they should step further into her office. She moved around them and called for Matilda and Alice. Mrs Lawson did introductions where necessary, and the men noted Alice's beauty accordingly and privately.

Thomas's gaze travelled to Matilda's throat, which was well hidden by the fabric of her high-necked blouse. He turned to Mrs Lawson.

'Mrs Lawson, as you know the proprietor of the carnival Exhibition was murdered recently, and this morning, we found the husband of one of the exhibitors dead.'

Matilda gasped at hearing the news.

Harry stepped in. 'Mr Carl Tufton, husband of the giantess.'

'Anna's husband! How? Why?' Matilda asked.

'He has been found dead on the grounds of the Exhibition in much the same area as where Mr Burnham was killed,' Thomas answered.

'Does Mrs Tufton know as yet?' Mrs Lawson asked.

'Yes, and Miss Hayward, you may wish to contact your brother to meet with her?' Thomas suggested.

'Did she... is she a suspect, Thomas, um, Detective Ashdown?' Matilda asked.

'Everyone is, Miss Hayward,' Harry answered.

Matilda nodded her understanding.

'But the reason for our visit, Mrs Lawson, en route to the crime scene, is just to warn you of the dangers first hand and to *suggest* that the interviews, if they are to continue, be chaperoned,' Thomas said, understanding the need for diplomacy and ensuring he was not telling the ladies what to do which might well lead to the opposite action being taken. 'Until we know the motive and find the killer, we don't know who might be a threat.'

Mrs Lawson nodded. 'Of course, I couldn't agree more.'

Harry added, 'Also, if you were intending on going there, the Exhibition is closed to the public today.'

'But we're not the paying public,' Alice said, speaking for the first time. 'Whether Mrs Wilks feels like speaking with us might be a different matter.'

'Agreed,' Mrs Lawson said. 'Thank you both, detectives. We will discuss this now and decide on our next course of action. I assume you don't need to speak with either of the ladies concerning the recent crime given their last interview on the premises was several days ago?'

'Mrs Lawson, I was on site with my brother visiting Mrs Tufton yesterday,' Matilda added.

'A quick word then,' Thomas said, seizing his chance. Matilda nodded. He thanked Mrs Lawson, suggested that Harry meet him outside in five minutes, and indicated the door to Matilda, following her out.

'What do you make of it all, Detective Dart?' he heard Mrs Lawson asked, ever the inquisitive journalist. Thomas didn't need to warn Harry that she was part of the media and he needed to be discreet; Harry had been around a lot longer and knew the ropes.

Thomas followed Matilda to the exit, noticing the glances from the ladies as they walked through. He pushed the door open for her and followed outside.

Once outside, she turned to him. 'Thomas, what has happened?' she asked, alarmed, forgetting all about last night's indiscretion. Thomas hadn't – the image was hard to get from his mind.

He swallowed. 'I won't know until I get to the scene and speak with the coroner, but I believe Tufton was struck in a similar manner to Mr Burnham. Keep that to yourself.'

Matilda nodded. 'Do you think Anna might be involved?'

'I haven't written off the idea. But I don't want to talk about the case for a moment.'

'Oh? You are not going to give me a lecture, are you?' she said, cocking her head on the side as if expecting a war of words.

'No, I wanted to check on you,' Thomas said.

Matilda softened and straightened up. 'Really? Oh well,

that's a relief because I'm sure you want to lecture me though.'

Thomas couldn't help smiling. 'Yes, I'd love to give you a dressing down, speaking of which…' he sobered and did not take his gaze from hers. 'I am sorry last night for trespassing on you in your state of undress and distress.'

She shook her head, blushing slightly. 'I am grateful that you and Daniel were so concerned.' She touched her neck. 'I am sore but fine and still here to talk about it.'

'Thank God. When I think of what more might have happened…'

Matilda swallowed and Thomas noticed it pained her. She admitted, 'It frightened me.'

He softened, wanting to pull her close to him.

She looked down at her hands as she said, 'it was as if everyone I loved flashed before me.' She blushed at what she had just suggested to him.

'Was I amongst the gallery of those you love?' he bravely asked.

She looked up at him. 'Well, of course you were, Thomas. You are my family,' she said.

He reached for her hand. 'Matilda, may I—'

'Righto then, let's get back to the carnival and—' Harry stopped. '–oh, sorry.'

Matilda pulled her hand away.

Thomas cleared his throat and moved away.

'Sunday then, with your nephew, Teddy? A wonderful coincidence.' Matilda smiled.

'Sunday,' Thomas said, offering Matilda a stiff bow, and frustrated, again, he turned to follow Harry.

*Chapter 24*

The two detectives strode towards Burnham's Carnival flanked by half a dozen policemen in uniform that Thomas had secured to undertake a search of the carnival's tents and caravans. As they walked, Detectives Thomas Ashdown and Harry Dart went over what they knew to be true. They stopped as the coroner hurried towards them.

'Can't stay,' he said, 'but the manner of killing was similar. The victim had the same blow inflicted to the throat and had most likely died from choking, but there were no other wounds this time. No beating.'

'So, is it likely that the killers were the same?' Thomas asked.

'Most likely from the blow to the throat. I'll be in my office this afternoon,' he called, giving a wave and taking off at a fast pace to get the omnibus that had just arrived.

Thomas and Harry continued their walk towards the exhibition.

'Perhaps the killer had to use a different technique to strike down their victim – Mr Burnham and Mr Tufton are quite different in size and strength after all,' Thomas thought out loud. 'Or perhaps there was more anger felt towards one than the other, or the killer was interrupted...'

'Someone on the premises or with access to the premises likely committed the crime, but where is the weapon that was used the first time?' Harry said.

'Where indeed. Although I don't think it would be too hard to access the area, the question is why would you? These deaths are very specific and related to the people in the inner circle of the Exhibition,' Thomas said, rubbing a hand over his face which he did often when stumped.

'I agree,' Harry said. 'Who might have dealings with Mr Burnham and Mr Tufton? There are only two clear suspects.'

Thomas nodded. 'Mr Wilks, who wants to run the place according to nearly everyone we've spoken with, and the giantess who wants to leave. Unless there's something we haven't unearthed.'

As they neared the large tent, the two detectives stopped, turned, and waited until the half dozen police officers following them caught up.

Harry gave them a quick briefing of what they were looking for on the grounds of the carnival, the sensitivities, and the need to treat the artists with care and respect.

'There but for the Grace of God go I, or you for that matter,' he told his young charges. 'So remember they've not had an easy life.' Harry's heart was an empathetic one, even after years on the job. 'Detective Ashdown and I will be doing interviews, so track us down if you find anything.'

'And don't go near the current crime scene,' Thomas added.

The detectives headed for the tent, the police officers behind them looking like a small invasion.

Mr Wilks, the manager, stood waiting for them, his arms crossed. Harry greeted him and handed him the notice for entry while Thomas moved to the covered corpse.

Surprisingly, Mr Wilks stood aside and extended his hand in a welcome gesture.

Harry nodded his thanks and waved the officers in. He asked Mr Wilks to wait nearby and joined Thomas at the corpse. The two men studied the area and then pulled back the sheet to study Tufton. He looked angry and bullish in death, as he did in life. After a brief while, the men stood back, and Thomas gave the nod for his body to be removed.

'I'll go have a chat with Mrs Wilks and leave Mr Wilks to you,' Harry said and headed off to the tent entrance.

Thomas re-joined Mr Wilks. 'A quick chat, if you don't mind?'

Wilks agreed, and they remained where they were. No one was around to overhear them – the exhibition was closed, and the only crowds were well back watching the police goings-on.

'Did you see or speak with Mr Tufton last night?' Thomas asked.

Wilks shook his head. 'No. The only reason he would have to be here is to visit his wife. He had no business or appointment with me, so I don't know why he was here,' he said, waving a hand in the direction of where Tufton's body lay.

'Where were you last night?'

'Here, as always, with the wife. We turned in around 10pm. I heard a noise and got up to have a look out. I can't tell you what time that was, but probably a few hours later. I didn't go any further than looking out my caravan door, then when I didn't see anything, I went back to bed.'

'What sort of noise?' Thomas asked.

'Just someone moving around… footsteps on the gravel. Some of the artists take exercise at night when they can do so in private without being seen. Everyone here is an adult, there's no curfew, people can come and go, visit each other, leave and come back.'

Thomas looked surprised.

'Granted, it's only the crew that comes and goes. The artists don't leave the grounds,' Wilks said.

Thomas looked away for a moment as he thought. Mr Wilks stood by in silence.

'Did Mr Tufton know any of your crew or have any dealings with them that you are aware of?' Thomas said, turning his attention back to the carnival manager.

'I've signed off on everyone hired here, and I know them well. I've never seen Tufton talk to them or have any reason to do so,' Wilks said.

Thomas knew that wasn't quite true; he was confident that Wilks did not hire his nephew, rather, the chef did that himself, and Wilks would barely know his nephew from the few days he had worked in the kitchen. Thomas saw Amos arriving and heading to see Mrs Tufton. And that's exactly where he was intending to go next. He thanked Mr Wilks and followed the route that Amos had just taken to the giantess's caravan. He wanted to get there before Amos prepared her responses. He knocked and entered, and they both looked less than pleased to see him. Mrs Tufton at least had the good sense not to act as the bereaved widow.

'Detective Ashdown, I've been expecting you,' Mrs Tufton said.

'It appears everyone has,' he said with a small smile. 'My condolences on the passing of your husband.'

'Thank you,' she said, surprised. 'It wasn't always bad.'

'Of course not,' Amos said, and shook hands with Thomas.

The two men declined her offer of tea and Amos sat. Thomas declined the offer to sit. He could not help being a little repulsed by the enormity of the giantess and her unattractive countenance. It was only her soft voice that reminded him she was a woman.

'I understand you were seeking a divorce?' Thomas asked, cutting to the chase.

'Yes, and I imagine you think Carl's death might be fortuitous for me,' she said.

Amos went to stop Mrs Tufton from speaking, but she shook her head.

'We had a small life insurance policy each that I will benefit from, but it is no more or less than I would have received from the settlement that Mr Hayward had recently negotiated,' she said with a nod towards Amos.

'That's correct,' Amos informed Thomas.

'I will also inherit property – a small farm in the area in which I grew up. It is no longer a working farm so in its current state it will not fetch a substantial sum, but I may choose to live there and revive it. I don't know yet,' she said. 'Regardless, I had my freedom secured before Carl's death.'

Again, Amos concurred.

'Right then. Tell me about your movements last night if you would be so kind,' Thomas requested, and Amos did not interfere.

'It was a usual night for me,' Mrs Tufton said. 'I had dinner with the others in the dining tent, returned here, went for a walk around eight o'clock, then undertook my evening bathing and read for some time before turning in around ten o'clock.'

'Did you see your husband last night on the premises, or hear him for that matter?' Thomas asked.

'Neither. The last time I saw and spoke with Carl was here in this caravan for our separation discussion with Mr Hayward present,' she said with a nod towards Amos who again confirmed he was present on that day.

'So, you do not know why he was here last night?' Thomas asked.

She shook her head. 'When I heard they found here him this morning, I couldn't understand it.'

Thomas shuffled uncomfortably – the giantess's small caravan felt too closed in. He moved towards the window and looked out. His officers were making their way along the row of caravans to inspect them.

'You mentioned to Miss Hayward that there had been some items stolen?'

'Missing, perhaps,' Anna corrected him. 'Two walking

sticks – Mr Burnham's and Mr Jo-Jo's, which is quite special and of sentimental value, I believe.'

'Yes, has anything else gone missing since that you are aware of?'

'Not that has come to my attention,' Mrs Tufton informed him.

Amos moved restlessly, keen to leave but required to endure the interview so he too could talk with his client afterwards about her newfound independence and the required paperwork to achieve it.

Thomas finished, 'Is there anything else relevant that either of you can recall?'

Neither party could offer any insights, and so Thomas bade them both a good day. As he reached the caravan door, Mrs Tufton stopped him.

'Oh, Detective Ashdown, Mr Jo-Jo said the walking stick was not the one he used every day, but an ornate stick. It is likely someone who worked here must have known of it for it to be missing. Perhaps they stole it to sell it?'

'Thank you, that's interesting,' Thomas said, and the thought crossed his mind that perhaps if Mr Jo-Jo did not rely on this stick, he would not miss it if it were used on Mr Burnham's head the night of the murder.

He bade them goodbye again and got as far as two steps down from the van before he turned and went back into the giantess's caravan again.

'Mrs Tufton, did Mr Jo-Jo tell you this information himself?' he asked.

'Yes,' she said and looked confused.

'Do you speak Russian?' Thomas asked.

'No,' she said, surprised. 'Mr Jo-Jo speaks Russian, but very good English too,' she added.

Thomas's eyes narrowed. 'Does he now? Thank you, that has been most helpful.' He turned and left; his pace quickened. Why then did Mrs Wilks need to be with him to translate on the first day they interviewed Mr Jo-Jo? She wasn't just there to comfort or support him or because Mr Jo-Jo was nervous. Thomas distinctly remembered her saying he needed a translator and her acting in that capacity.

He intended to speak with Mr Jo-Jo right this minute. He muttered to himself, 'Is there anyone here able to tell the truth or give me the full picture in one sitting?'

Thomas passed two constables who were on their way to search the giantess's caravan as they made their way through the exhibition and rows of residents' vans.

'Be thorough,' Thomas said to them in a low voice.

*Chapter 25*

Early afternoon, Matilda and Alice alighted from the omnibus near the entrance to the carnival grounds. Passing through the curious crowds watching from afar, they made their way to the large tent. Their editor, Mrs Lawson, had no objection to them continuing their interviews as long as they were constantly in each other's company, including coming and going. Matilda wasn't sure if the carnival's manageress, Mrs Wilks, would see them today given the murder of Mr Tufton on the premises, but she preferred to make a wasted trip than to not try.

The two ladies looked resplendent and accidentally matching – both in shades of blue which were dark enough to withstand the mud and dirt of the exhibition grounds. They were not dissimilar in height but were not similar enough to be confused for sisters.

'There's your detective.' Alice nudged Matilda and nodded towards Detective Ashdown heading away from the caravan area. Tall, handsome and walking with purpose, he was hard not to notice.

Matilda felt a stirring of pride that he was hers, but not officially. He also "belonged" to whomever he chose to see when he went to the clubs with Daniel and his work colleagues.

'Do you think you will make it official?' Alice asked, reading her mind.

'I'm not sure Thomas feels that way, but if I did, then I expect I'll have to play the dutiful housewife and next thing I'll be at home looking after babies. I imagine Thomas won't want me writing for the newspaper in case it reflects on his career.'

'It could help his career, too,' Alice suggested, and then gave a small shrug. 'You are probably right. Most men in his position are conscious of how they are perceived, but I don't know the detective to say whether he is one of those men.'

'He must have been to see Anna,' Matilda said.

They watched him walk away from the row of residents' caravans, turn and make his way to the main tent entrance where they were heading, although he would be there in a matter of moments and the ladies were still halfway across the grounds.

Thomas looked around briefly and then he saw the two ladies. Even from afar Matilda could see the look of surprise, then frustration that crossed his face. He doffed his hat and continued walking, disappearing inside the tent.

They had been so busy watching the detective that at the last minute, Matilda grabbed Alice's arm and steered her away from a large muddy hole and back onto a firmer grass path as they continued across the grounds towards the tent.

Alice lowered her voice. 'Do you think there's any chance she might have... you know, killed her husband?'

Matilda shook her head. 'I confess it crossed my mind, but she just got what she wanted, so I don't know why she would. And, if it is the same killer, then she had to have killed Mr Burnham as well. With Mr Wilks looking to continue the show, I can't see how that would have helped her.'

Alice smiled at her. 'Yes, you've given this some thought.'

Matilda laughed. She looked around just in time to see Amos leaving the area and knew he too must have been visiting Anna this morning. She gave him a wave and he reciprocated, but indicated he had to keep going.

'Now who is that? You know every good-looking man in Brisbane!' Alice exclaimed.

'That's another of my brothers, Amos. He's the eldest and also Anna's solicitor.'

'Oh, yes, I can see the resemblance. You two do look alike, unlike yourself and Daniel. How many of you are there?' Alice asked.

'Four brothers and me.'

'Goodness.' Alice's eyes widened.

'It is not too hard to remember them. Fortunately, my mother had the good sense to name them alphabetically in order of age, with Amos being the eldest, then Daniel, Elijah and Gideon,' Matilda said.

'How eminently sensible,' Alice said, and sighed. 'How lucky you are to have family and brothers. Some days I feel quite alone here.'

'Do you have siblings back home?' Matilda asked.

Alice nodded. 'Two elder sisters back in Kent, both married and with young families. I am here on a grand adventure but some days I worry I am just missing out.'

'Then you must come to lunch on Sunday and immerse yourself in my family,' Matilda insisted. 'We do it every week after mass and after a few hours exposed to my four brothers, plus Thomas if he makes it along, his nephew Teddy, my sister-in-law Minnie, my charming and sensible father, and my outspoken aunt, your homesickness will be cured I have no doubt. Will you come?'

'I would love to, thank you,' Alice said, pleased at the chance to see Daniel again, not that she intended to admit that to Matilda. 'Are you sure there will be room for me?'

'Fortunately, we have a large dining room. We'll make room.'

'How delightful, thank you,' Alice said, excited at the prospect of an engagement to look forward to on Sunday.

They both adopted serious countenances as they approached the entry to the exhibition. Mr Wilks was standing there alone watching as the police officers came and went from different areas.

'Ladies, this is a surprise. I didn't expect to see you today, but I'm sure Mrs Wilks will be happy that you called in. She's inside keeping an eye on the police officers,' he said and waved them through.

The ladies thanked him and found Mrs Wilks only too happy to talk. She was preened and proper, in a dark gown that highlighted a lean figure, and seemed fitting for a matronly woman of managerial discipline. She was an attractive woman but had a hardness about her, as if life had worn her down over the years. She also had an imposing presence and Matilda could understand how the gentle conjoined sisters and the vulnerable Mrs Tufton would be wary around Mrs Wilks.

'No illustrator today?' the manageress asked.

'No, unfortunately. There is so little room for a drawing in our article and as he has another appointment, we will make do with the images of the twins and Mrs Tufton,' Matilda explained. What she did not say was that Daniel had his interview for the court illustrator role and Matilda and Alice were confident that the readers would rather see the illustrations of the sisters and giantess then Mrs Wilks, not that they intended to make that known to her.

As the interview unfolded, Matilda tried to pay attention, but all she could think about was Anna being questioned by Thomas. She pulled herself back into the moment and directed a few questions to Mrs Wilks so that Alice did not carry the whole load.

'What would you say is the most difficult part of your job?' Matilda asked after Alice spoke of Mrs Wilks' Russian heritage.

'The loneliness,' Irina Wilks answered. 'When you are on the road as often as we are, you miss your family, and you don't make friendships except amongst ourselves.'

'Are there many ladies working here other than the artists we've met?' Alice asked.

'No. We had a housekeeper for a while, but Mr Wilks thought that was an unnecessary expense. The ladies of the exhibit are not inclined to go out and socialise, so as you can imagine it can get very isolating at times.'

Matilda smiled, thinking of the conjoined twins. 'They are enjoyable company though, especially Ella and Elvira.'

'Really?' Mrs Wilks asked, surprised. 'They barely say a word when I am around them.'

'Perhaps because you are the manageress, they are a little in fear of you or your position,' Alice added with diplomacy. She glanced at Matilda, encouraging her to move along quickly with the next question.

'I imagine you miss the owner, Mr Burnham,' Matilda said, sympathetically, and hoping not to appear too transparent.

To her surprise, Mrs Wilks became quite emotional.

'Forgive me,' she said and reached for a small white handkerchief that she used to dab her eyes. 'I admired him a great deal.'

'We are so very sorry,' Alice said.

Matilda stored that away to share with Thomas. Did Mrs Wilks miss Mr Burnham just a little too much, perhaps?

*****

Thomas found his partner, Harry, studying a collection of items on a table in the dining tent. They were all shaped with some semblance of a heavily rounded end – a potential death weapon that may have made the indents in the head of Mr Burnham.

'This is as good as it gets,' Harry said, picking up each item one after the other.

Thomas studied them. 'None of them have quite the weight to do the job. And according to the coroner, there was a distinct wave pattern, like an engraving that also left a mark on the flesh.'

Thomas caught Teddy's eye in the kitchen and gave him a barely discernible nod, to not break his undercover persona. He called a constable over to the items.

'Thank you, Constable. None of these items appears to be what we are looking for, so you can return them or let Mr or Mrs Wilks know they can be collected.'

'Yes, sir,' the young man said, and hurried off to find either of the Wilkses.

Harry sighed. 'Chasing our tails.'

'No necessarily, c'mon, we need to speak with Mr Jo-Jo,' Thomas said.

As they strode away from the dining tent back to the main arena to seek Mr Jo-Jo, Thomas briefed Harry on his conversation with the giantess.

'So Mrs Wilks, while translating, could have given us a completely different answer to what Mr Jo-Jo was saying?' Harry shook his head.

'Or since he speaks English and understood the question, she could have been telling him exactly how she intended to answer.'

## Chapter 26

Matilda and Alice returned to the office of the *Women's Journal* to develop their story from the interview with Mrs Wilks. They had interviewed all four ladies now – Mrs Wilks, Mrs Tufton and Ella and Elvira – and the story was almost completed.

'Should we drop into Daniel's work and see if he has finished the two illustrations?' Alice asked, her intent obvious.

'Unfortunately, he has no fixed abode,' Matilda explained. 'He works at the office of whoever assigns him work. Some days he is on site for a merchant, or for a newspaper, and with luck, if his interview goes well today, he will be a regular at the court.'

'Wouldn't that be an exciting career!' Alice exclaimed. 'Imagine all he will hear!'

'I shall give him a hurry along tonight and bring the drawings in with me tomorrow, if he is finished. We can give Mrs Lawson the completed article and illustrations and we will be three days ahead of our deadline,' Matilda said.

'I hope we get to work together on more stories, it's been fun.'

'Well, we will be firm friends, regardless,' Matilda assured her, and Alice smiled with pleasure.

They concentrated on their work and within a few hours, they were both happy with the resulting copy.

'I shall be off then,' Alice said. 'My guardian has a recital he wishes to attend this evening and has invited me along. Well, invite is not quite the right word, insisted is more like it.'

'That sounds lovely, though,' Matilda said. 'Are you reporting on it for the Arts Pages?'

Alice shook her head. 'Mrs Lawson is not a fan of the artist. He's quite obnoxious to quote her.'

Matilda chuckled. 'Heaven forbid.'

Fifteen minutes after Alice departed, Matilda heard the receptionist call her name and turned to find Daniel there with papers in his hands. She waved him through to her desk, introducing him to the nearby ladies whom he charmed with little effort.

'Tell me, how did your interview go?' she asked.

'Very well, I believe, but I won't know until later in the week. They have a few more artists to see and then references and letters of recommendation to consider.'

'I want this so badly for you,' she said.

'Me too!' he said. 'I brought the two illustrations; I wasn't sure how soon you needed them, and I finished them while I was waiting to be called in for the interview. I showed them as part of my portfolio of commissioned work. I hope you don't mind?'

'Not at all and I'm sure Mrs Lawson wouldn't mind either.'
Daniel handed them over, and Matilda inhaled.

'They are perfect, you've captured them as they are to the letter,' she said and looked up at him gratefully. 'And your bill?'

He produced another piece of paper and handed it to her.

'I shall give them all to Mrs Lawson. Thank you, Dan.'

'Thank you, Tillie.' He looked around. 'Where's your partner in this crime?'

'Who might that be?' she teased, and he made a face.

Matilda laughed. 'Alice left about fifteen minutes ago but it will disappoint her to have missed you.'

'Really?' he asked.

'I assure you she has asked after you,' Matilda informed him, to Daniel's obvious pleasure. 'Alice is a little homesick for her family, so I invited her to lunch on Sunday.'

'Excellent. Poor Cook will need to start now, there's so many coming!' Daniel exclaimed.

'Do you think Pa will mind?' Matilda then worried.

'Absolutely not. He loves a crowd. I suspect Cook won't mind, either,' Daniel said. 'So what did Alice ask about me?'

Matilda put her head on the side and looked skyward as she thought. Daniel rolled his eyes, and she laughed.

'She might have said she was looking forward to coming to lunch and meeting all my brothers. And she did ask could we call on you today to check the progress of your illustrations.'

He grinned. 'Good. Righto then, got to run.' With that, he pecked a kiss on her cheek and rushed off with the same energy that he arrived with.

Matilda watched him leave and considered what a suitable match the energetic Miss Alice Doran would make for her brother. Then she turned her attention to his drawings. She sighed as she studied the illustrations of the ladies – so well captured and so memorable. Poor Ella, Elvira and Anna, what hardships they have entered this life with.

*Chapter 27*

For a man who was – according to Mrs Irina Wilks – fearful of the police and strangers, Mr Jo-Jo seemed remarkably composed. Thomas suggested they meet in the far corner of the dining tent, where he could ensure no one was in proximity. Teddy served the gentlemen some refreshments, all the time keeping up the ruse that he did not have an acquaintance with his uncle.

'I just baked that slice, Detectives and Mr Jo-Jo,' Teddy said in good humour, placing it in front of them with a pot of tea, three cups, milk and sugar.

'Looks wonderful,' Mr Jo-Jo said. 'What a treat. I wish you would continue with us when we leave here. You won't reconsider?'

Teddy shook his head. 'Tempting I'm sure, but a man has to put down roots somewhere.'

Mr Jo-Jo nodded. 'One day for sure.'

When they were alone with tea poured and a generous serving of jam and coconut slice in front of them, the "freak" covered completely in soft, long hair studied them with dark eyes.

'I am sorry if I offend. My appearance is not always easy to view,' he said in a well-spoken voice.

'Do not concern yourself,' Harry answered on behalf of the two detectives. 'If Thomas here does not soon find himself a razor, it will be hard to tell you both apart.'

The response got a laugh from both men, and Thomas's hand went to his chin again. He had been remiss on the shaving of late.

'True. But I assure you Mr Jo-Jo, you are not at all offensive.'

Mr Jo-Jo smiled and gave a small nod of thanks. Then Thomas began the interview in earnest.

'We were led to believe that you could not speak English, Mr Jo-Jo.'

'Please, just Jo, the other is a show name. And yes, I was instructed to answer in Russian and to not contradict anything said or to dare speak in English.'

'By Mrs Wilks?' Harry asked.

Jo nodded.

'You were aware that might be obstructing justice?' Thomas continued.

Jo exhaled. 'Of course. But Detective, this is my life and my living. I don't have many options, and to not follow instructions would most likely have seen me cast out. Where would I go? I'm millions of miles from home with very few career paths.'

'Where is home?' Harry asked.

'Moscow. Although I haven't been back there for decades,' Jo said. 'When I was six, my father sold me to a Freak Show.

My grandfather bought me out of the contract, and I lived with him until well into my twenties when he passed away. Sadly, without him and with limited funds, I had to work. Here I am.'

'I'm sorry, that can't have been easy,' Thomas said. 'If we discuss the murders now, are you prepared to speak with us?'

Jo nodded. 'I will if you can assure me of your discretion when speaking with Mr and Mrs Wilks. I need to retain my employment.'

'I give you my word,' Thomas said.

Harry offered his agreement.

'Then yes, what can I tell you, if anything?' Jo asked.

'Where were you the night that Mr Burnham died, what did you see, hear, and I want to talk to you about your missing walking cane.' Thomas laid it all out. It was strange for the detectives trying to focus on the words Jo spoke when he was such an unusual man in his appearance, but soon they fell into the rhythm of the conversation.

'My caravan is the closest to the exhibition tent,' Jo began, 'so I hear and see quite a bit only by fault of its location. On that evening, I saw Mr Tufton and his wife, Anna, walking to the exhibition tent from our row of vans. Her husband was fired up – I could tell because he was walking fast and hurrying Anna along. He looked angry. Mr Burnham was smoking outside the main exhibition tent when they arrived. They shook hands, and it seemed cordial. I sat and read my book. I'm a voracious reader and I did not look up again until almost forty minutes later when I heard raised voices. I looked out of my window and saw that Anna had gone, and it was just Mr Burnham and Mr Tufton.' Jo stopped to sip his tea and then continued. 'Mr Burnham was making platitude noises and also motioning with his hands for calm.' Jo imitated the motion. 'Then Mr Tufton accepted his handshake and strode off.'

'So he did actually leave, but did he come back?' Harry asked.

Jo shook his head. 'I can't say for sure, but Mrs Wilks came out to join Mr Burnham, and they stood and talked and smoked together for some time; I could smell the smoke. That's when I went for my evening stroll. I do several rounds of the oval behind us before bed and late in the evening. I feel safer and it ensures I don't alarm anyone.'

'I understand. Did anyone see you walking and can confirm your movements?'

Jo nodded. 'The security guard saw me twice as I passed him on each lap.'

'Good,' Thomas said. 'What happened after that?'

'I returned to my caravan and prepared for bed. Before I turned out my lamp, I saw Mr Burnham standing there alone, his hands in his pockets looking skyward. He liked his astronomy. I heard nothing more but the next day I noticed my ornate walking cane was gone.'

'What time of the day was it when you noticed?' Thomas asked.

Jo thought about the question. 'Not immediately, because I don't use it as my everyday cane. I need one, but I have a practical one. The cane that is missing is of sentimental value… it was my grandfather's. It has a brass knob and is ornate with engravings and filigree on it – quite beautiful. It is all I have left of his. It was probably after midday when I noticed. Normally, I'd be sitting for an audience, but we were closed because of Mr Burnham's passing.'

Thomas and Harry exchanged looks; it sounded very much like the murder weapon.

'When was the last time you used it?' Harry asked.

'Oh, not for some time. I keep it for ceremonial use such as official portraits. About six months ago Mr Burnham organised for a group photograph for the media – it took some time, but the results were amazing. Perhaps that was the last time I had it out of my caravan.'

'And you had no grievance with Mr Burnham and no reason to harm him or Mr Tufton?' Thomas asked.

Jo shook his head. 'I didn't really know Mr Tufton. As for Mr Burnham, I would not bite the hand that feeds me. Besides, I truly liked him; he was a gentleman and good company. He kept me supplied in books. It's difficult for me to venture into a bookstore without alarming people. That is a loss I feel more than other people's company.'

Thomas felt a wave of sympathy for the poor man which he rarely felt in his occupation, except for the occasional undeserving victim. Jo's eloquent manner surprised him; his English was perfect and rounded for a second language.

Jo continued, 'I am not the biggest man, detectives, and they were both considerably taller and heavier than me. I am not sure I could have felled them if I decided to go down the path of crime.'

'Why do you think Mrs Wilks wanted to control your interview with us?' Harry asked, finishing with relish his last bite of Teddy's slice.

Jo thought for a moment and answered, 'Maybe because she was one of the last people with Mr Burnham before his death. I imagine she did not want that known.'

Thomas's eyes widened and he grunted in surprise. 'Quite right, she has kept that to herself,' he agreed. 'One last question and we thank you for your candour… if your cane was the weapon, do you know of anyone who might want to single you out or try to incriminate you for the crime?'

Jo nodded. 'I've given that some thought should the cane be found to be the weapon… it is extremely solid and could do damage. I have no enemies I know of here, no ambition to be the star or to move in on anyone's territory. But I suspect I'm as good a man as any to frame and truthfully, a vicious crime like that must be done by a degenerate – we freaks are frightening creatures to the public… one can only imagine what we are capable of in their minds.'

Women's Journal
Tuesday, 22 May 1888
Fortnightly edition Vol.1, No.13. Price, 3d.

Special Feature: The ladies of the Carnival

A report by Matilda Hayward and Alice Doran.
Illustrations by Daniel Hayward.

The fate of many a poor woman has been linked with, or left in, the hands of a man to determine her future. We recently had the pleasure of making the acquaintance of three charming and hard-working ladies, who in helpless innocence have been placed on display in a travelling carnival. We also had the pleasure of interviewing the Show's co-manager, a sensible and strong woman who works behind the scenes with her manager husband.

The two young ladies who share one body have all the desires and needs that our readers do – to be safe, loved, happy, and to live their best imaginable life. Misses Ella and Elvira Hove are charming company and perfectly complement each other – Ella being the quieter of the pair and Elvira the livelier.

They share many interests and could find very few vexations despite being in each other's company so permanently. Although Miss Elvira – a capable singer – did claim to listen to her sister sing, left something to be desired which her sister found most amusing and did not contradict. We did not have the chance to appreciate Miss Elvira's lovely alto voice, but we will accept it is a fact.

Miss Ella on the other hand has a passion for drawing and informed us her inspiration comes from, "all things in nature, I especially like to paint birds." One wonders how she attracts a bird to study and paint if her sister should sing loudly next to her, but perhaps they have mastered the art of compromise as well.

Born in Michigan, USA, twenty years ago, their parents abandoned them to an orphanage and later an asylum. Miss Elvira says of the experience that, "for some time we knew the charity of others and received an education in the orphanage." Ella concurred, admitting, "my love of reading has come from the many isolated hours we spent in study out of the view of other children."

It has not been an easy life being conjoined and on display, but as Ella said, they have always had each other.

Elvira explained, "Mr Burnham found us and offered us a role in his show. It allowed us to leave the asylum and afforded us a degree of independence. While we are on display during the day, we have some creature comforts, some adventures, good food and we can enjoy a few of life's pleasures compared to our life at the asylum."

The sisters admitted their greatest fear was dying before the other and being alone. We pray God may take them with the same breath when that day comes.

Mrs Anna Tufton, billed as the carnival's "giantess" brings in an independent income for her family's purse. Her husband, Mr Carl Tufton, manages his wife's appearances and Mrs Tufton has travelled widely from one side of Australia to the other. As part of her performance, she lifts two gentlemen comfortably.

The giantess, as she is known, shared that she is not always at home in the spotlight, preferring her own company and privacy with no stranger to remark about her size. But she delivers upon the obligation to contribute as best she can to their family income.

As a young girl growing up on a farm in country Queensland with three brothers, Mrs Tufton was a strong and valued worker. That strength remains with her but her work these days is up to six appearances a day in front of a paying audience.

Mrs Tufton says the crowd often still surprises her. "I am regularly amazed at the attendees who think I am a fake. I am not sure how I can fake my size and strength but on seeing me they soon change their minds." Mrs Tufton likes to ballroom dance and claims to be light on her feet for one so impressive in size.

Mrs Irina Wilks hails from Moscow, Russia, and works with her husband, Mr Morris Wilks, managing aspects of the show from catering to paying the artists.

When asked to nominate the most difficult part of her position, Mrs Wilks answered, "The loneliness. When you are on the road as often as we are, you miss your family, and you don't make friendships except amongst ourselves."

Sadly, the Misses Hove and Mrs Tufton do not feel comfortable leaving the show and exploring the areas they visit, which increases the need to build friendships amongst themselves.

In a matter of weeks, the ladies will be off again, their lives in a constant state of motion as they survive by the only means they know how.

The pleasure was ours, Mrs Wilks, Mrs Tufton and Misses Ella and Elvira Hove.

## Chapter 28

For the first time at a Sunday lunch, for as long as he could remember, Thomas was seated next to Matilda. Right next to her. He could smell her fresh scent, feel her every movement, and it was excruciating. The fabric of her pale pink gown brushed against his dark trousers. Her hand was in reach, her tresses – adorned with crimson roses and perfectly affixed – he longed to let them down as they were the other evening. To turn and look at her would place her face, her lips, within inches of his own. He cleared his throat and sat back, distancing himself a little more from her.

There were three faces at the Haywards' Sunday lunch table that weren't Haywards – himself, his nephew Teddy, and the young English lady, Alice. She was quite a beauty with her light brown hair, intelligent blue eyes and English pale skin. She was also not short of an admirer around the Hayward table.

Alice bowed her head and accepted the honour of saying grace as the nominated guest; Thomas gave a silent prayer of thanks that he hadn't been asked to do it, or Teddy for that matter who might have resorted to something less than reverent. Teddy's last "prayer" several nights prior came to mind – *Good bread, good meat, good God, let's eat!*

Alice began:

*'Be present at our table, Lord,*
*Be present in our souls,*
*For those without family, friends and food,*
*Let faith and heart console.'*

'Amen and pass the potatoes,' Gideon said as Alice finished.

Mr Hayward, sitting beside Gideon, shook his head but joined in the laughter as he passed him the dish as requested.

'Really, Gideon, our guests will think you are a heathen,' Aunt Audrey said, giving him one of her best stern looks, and then hiding a smile as he gave his aunt a wink.

Teddy, who was placed beside Aunt Audrey, spoke up. 'Yes, we will, Gideon, and I can only speak for Uncle Thomas and myself, but I hope you don't corrupt us,' he joked, and flashed Gideon a grin. Gideon immediately liked Thomas's nephew, who was only a few years older than him.

'Too late,' Thomas added.

'I nominate Gideon to say grace next time as penitence for his less than gracious outburst at the end of my prayer,' Alice said in her English accent, and all heads turned to her and then to Gideon. Then Alice laughed, and everyone relaxed.

'I think the young lady may have actually shamed you,' Mr Hayward said, 'and we don't see that often with the rascal of the family.'

Gideon grinned. 'Daniel said you were a handful.'

Daniel spluttered. 'I did no such thing, I merely said that Alice – Miss Doran – was very independent.'

'There are worse things to be called,' Matilda said, smiling at Alice and enjoying her brothers' attentiveness to her guest.

'Although I would have preferred, charming, beautiful, clever, witty even,' Alice suggested, her quick wit a match for the men. She had directed her comment to Daniel, and all heads turned to him for a response; he looked unsure of whether to flatter her now or what the appropriate course of action might be.

Mr Hayward laughed again. 'I think Miss Doran has claimed another scalp.'

Alice smiled, and Aunt Audrey nodded her head with approval.

'Well done, young lady,' she said. 'These boys need a bit of pulling into line and the firm hand of a woman. It can be quite exhausting trying to keep them in line.'

'Goodness, we're all in our twenties, not ten,' Elijah said. 'Although Gideon might act that way,' he said, and ribbed his twin.

'But while you are sensible and a credit to your family, Elijah,' Aunt Audrey added, 'the same cannot be said for the rest of your brothers, with the exception of Amos.' She managed to work both of her favourite Hayward boys into her compliment.

'There's no hope for us,' Daniel sighed with a glance to Gideon.

'None at all,' he agreed.

Thomas was happy to be out of the limelight and to focus on eating quietly beside Matilda and observing her smiles and laughter.

'So where are Amos and Minnie today? I'm sure someone told me, but I've forgotten,' Mr Hayward said from his seat at the head of the table directly opposite Aunt Audrey in the matriarch's seat. He passed the gravy-boat along the side of the table where his sons sat and up to Daniel as requested.

Matilda answered, 'Minnie's niece is being christened and there's a family gathering after the ceremony.'

'Lovely,' Aunt Audrey said, pleased at the recruitment of another soul. She thanked Teddy, who held a platter of mixed roast meats for her to select from and gave him a warm smile afterwards, once served.

'So, Thomas,' she said as she turned to the detective sitting a few seats down whom she had known since he was a boy. Thomas bristled to find himself called into conversation action. 'You are playing host to this charming young nephew of yours?'

Thomas studied his nephew and smiled.

'I am indeed, and I am proud of him, Aunt Audrey.' He addressed her by the familiar name she had invited him to use as a boy.

'How is it you can have a nephew so near your age?' she enquired, with no thought of there being any potential delicacy to the situation.

Thomas was not embarrassed and responded, 'My mother married at eighteen and promptly had my brother, Sewell,' he explained, 'and then they were not blessed with a second child for another thirteen years.'

'Good grief!' Matilda said. 'So your mother was two-and-thirty when she conceived you?' She blushed after saying the words that blurted from her mouth.

Thomas gave her a nod and smile. 'Indeed, and not excited by the prospect of a new arrival – but there I was. Hence, my brother is now nearing forty with his own adult son whom he has entrusted my way,' he said with a nod to his nephew. 'With luck, Teddy will find work soon and settle here for the long-term.'

Aunt Audrey turned to Teddy. 'Oh, what do you do, young man?'

'I am an apprentice cook looking to finish my apprenticeship, Mrs Bloomfield,' he said.

Her eyes widened with interest. 'Is that so? Well, I shall ask around.'

He gave her a nod of appreciation. 'Thank you, Mrs Bloomfield.'

'Teddy's a wonderful cook and a hard worker,' Thomas added.

'Like his uncle, except for the cooking part,' Daniel jostled his closest friend. 'Oh, and Teddy got the looks too.'

'Except for those things, he's a lot like me,' Thomas agreed good naturedly. He could see Aunt Audrey's eyes studying his nephew. She had a plan, and she desperately wanted a good cook, so he suspected she'd be calling Teddy for a trial soon.

'I happen to think handsome runs in your family,' Matilda said to Thomas and, caught by surprise, he thanked her, further adding to his agonies of sitting beside her. As laughter broke out between Alice and Daniel, she whispered to Thomas, 'I have something to tell you, about Mrs Wilks.' There was no work talk at the table, but Thomas couldn't finish lunch soon enough to hear her news, and have her focus entirely on him while she shared the news.

Matilda returned her attention to the group. 'But we must show you around while you are here, Teddy, and help you make new friends.' She turned to her brothers to put that plan in motion. 'Daniel, Gideon, Elijah...' she enlisted them. Thomas bristled beside her; did Matilda want to see more of his nephew since his heroic rescue of her?

'Consider it done, sister,' Gideon said, needing no excuse for a social outing.

'Much obliged,' Teddy answered, and Thomas sighed.

'Just don't be ending up in my station at the end of your night and if you do, don't say your name is Edward Ashdown.'

'And when did you become so sensible?' Daniel asked him.

Thomas nodded at Teddy. 'Since my brother gave me responsibility.'

'I won't embarrass you, Uncle. And what of Miss Doran then, Alice? Are you not in need of new friends too?' Teddy asked.

'Indeed, I am,' she said, 'and I am so fortunate to have met Matilda.'

'I'll take that in hand.' Daniel jumped in gallantly and selfishly before the rest of his brothers could answer. 'Matilda and I will ensure you see the better part of our town, not where this lot is likely to go,' he said with a nod to Elijah and Gideon.

Alice smiled a charming smile, and Daniel was smitten. Meanwhile, Aunt Audrey studied the young people and gave her brother, Mr Hayward, a satisfied look. Yes, soon they would all be paired, and her job would be done. But first, a job for young Edward.

*****

The Hayward family was not overly traditional and the men at the table did not want to retire to a room, smoke and drink port while the ladies were in another room. Daniel for one had his sights set on Alice; Thomas and his nephew, Teddy, were watching Matilda astutely; and Aunt Audrey was the source of all town gossip. Nevertheless, Thomas did get a quiet moment with Matilda.

'What do you know?' he asked her, exhausted by his proximity clashing with his desire. He wanted to grab her and kiss her, but such impropriety would be outrageous and never see him invited to a Hayward Sunday lunch again.

With a subtle glance around, Matilda told him, 'It is only one small little matter and nothing more, but when Alice and I were talking to Irina Wilks for our interview, I mentioned Mr Burnham to her and she became emotional, quickly. She began to cry. She apologised but I think it is fair to say she had strong feelings for him.'

Thomas nodded. 'Yes, I just received some more information that would confirm their companionship. Thank you, Matilda.'

'You are welcome, Thomas. I hope you get an outcome

soon; it is frightening for all involved to think who might be next. Plus, you look exhausted.'

He softened. He felt jaded and depleted of energy from thinking about the case. It was nice to have someone worry about him.

'I don't sleep well during a case.'

'Goodness, then you mustn't sleep much at all,' she said, her large blue eyes studying his face.

'It is for want of other distractions,' he said and realised that sounded as if he was seeking something fun and casual, a night at his club, a casual liaison. Before he could correct himself, Alice and Daniel joined them.

'I'm trying to persuade Alice that she must come along for the opening night of Marlon Dominey's Art Exhibition this Saturday at Gideon's gallery. Gideon has tickets for us – it's a by-invitation-only,' Daniel said.

'Oh, you must,' Matilda said.

'We could all go if Gideon could throw a few more tickets our way,' Thomas suggested to his best friend, and held his breath.

'Yes, let's do that,' Matilda said enthusiastically. 'Some time away from work, Thomas, will do you good, I'm sure. Unless someone gets murdered or assaulted at the exhibition while we are there,' she added drily.

'I'll try my best not to attract crime for the night,' Thomas said and returned her smile. And just like that, he realised he wouldn't be sleeping tonight either.

## Chapter 29

Mrs Wilks asked not to be interviewed in her husband's presence and in consequence, she hurried the detectives outside towards the dining tent. At the back of the tent, Thomas could see his nephew at work in the kitchen. Teddy was on by himself today and looked busy.

'I hear you've got a new assistant cook,' Harry said, making conversation as they moved to sit down. Thomas glanced at him – a mixture of curiosity and confusion.

Mrs Wilks waved her hand as if it were of no interest to her. 'Yes, Chas – the chef – tells me he is very good. He'd have to be a miracle worker to make a reasonable meal on the budget that he's been given.' She shook her head.

'The budget Mr Burnham set?' Thomas asked, sitting once she had taken her place.

'Oh, no,' she said, smoothing back her hair and retaining a calm countenance. 'Mr Burnham was generous to a fault; my husband is quite the opposite.'

Thomas sat forward, webbing his fingers and watching Mrs Wilks for her emotions and listening to her responses.

'It has come to our attention that you and Mr Burnham were... close,' he said.

Mrs Wilks' face hardened as if she was holding a winning card and did not want to reveal it.

'He was a friend, a truly lovely man. I had great respect for him. I also thought the conversation I was having with the ladies of the *Women's Journal* was private.'

'Really? But they are writing for a published newspaper,' Thomas said, surprised.

Mrs Wilks raised her chin with defiance, realising her comment was ignorant but she had not expected her reaction to the death of a dear friend to be reported to the police.

Thomas lowered his voice in deference to indicate he understood her dilemma. 'The ladies are in my acquaintance. They were not reporting on you, rather sympathising that Mr Burnham was indeed a loved and respected man in his community and ensuring that we were aware of his standing.'

She nodded but said nothing. Thomas continued.

'He was the one that kept you going?'

She could be strong if he talked with her severely, even accused her of an affair, but his sympathy was unexpected. Tears ran down her face. She whispered so low that the men barely heard the words, 'I loved him.'

Thomas nodded. 'Were you lovers?'

Her voiced hitched. To admit it, the shame, and what might become of her if her husband demanded a divorce for infidelity? She couldn't get the words out, but gave a curt nod, without making eye contact with either of the detectives.

Harry cleared his throat and asked, 'Did Mr Wilks know?'

'No! Absolutely not. We were discreet. No.' She looked around and regained her composure. 'He can't know, not even now.'

'I understand. We assure you of our discretion,' Harry said.

'If Mr Wilks found out, would he go to the extreme of removing his competition, of killing Mr Burnham?' Thomas asked.

'No,' she said and straightened. 'He is many things, but he is not capable of that.'

'We are all capable of it in the right circumstances, Mrs Wilks, even women, especially women,' Harry said.

'Well, I didn't kill him, I loved him!'

Neither of the detectives spoke for a moment, hoping Mrs Wilks might say more, but she was savvy and held her silence.

Thomas ran a hand over his face. 'If not your husband, if not you, who do you think might have committed this act, Mrs Wilks? You were close to Mr Burnham, was he in fear of his life? Did he owe money? Did he have enemies?'

'No. If it were my husband murdered, I could give you a list of offenders,' she scoffed, 'but not Alfred – Mr Burnham – not him. Everyone liked him, he was kind and fair, he tried to make this a family even though neither my husband nor I agreed with that.'

'Why not?' Harry asked.

'Because it is a business and if you don't keep it as such, people will take advantage of you. Like the giantess's husband… always trying for extra money and believing his wife made for the success of this carnival.' She scoffed at the thought.

'Do you know why Mr Tufton was here on the premises the night he died?'

Mrs Wilks shook her head. 'No, I was in the caravan with my husband from 10 o'clock onwards. It is true what my husband told you, that he heard a sound and got up to look but saw nothing and came back to bed.' She was giving signs of impatience now, and adjusted herself in her seat. 'I have a business to run, will that be all today?'

'One more question please, Mrs Wilks,' Thomas said. 'Why did you translate for Mr Jo-Jo when he was perfectly capable of speaking English?'

Thomas watched as the question caught her by surprise and she struggled to formulate an answer.

'I thought he might be more comfortable speaking in his native tongue, so there was no confusion, and he didn't give the wrong answer,' she said.

'I recently discovered that he speaks excellent English,' Harry said.

She shrugged. 'That was my reason.'

Thomas sighed. 'Thank you, Mrs Wilks. As we've said to your husband, the Exhibition is to stay in town until we give you clearance to leave.'

She nodded, rose, and the men stood as she turned back to the main exhibition tent.

Thomas and Harry watched her depart before sitting back down.

'What do you make of that then?' Harry asked.

'Can't fault her story, even so, there's something not right about it,' Thomas said, watching her in the distance. 'She is savvy, not intimidated by authority.'

'Yeah, that's how my gut feels, too,' Harry said.

'The husband is still the most likely suspect with a motive – if he knew his wife was having an affair, then he's taken his revenge by killing Mr Burnham, and if Tufton came demanding a rise for his wife as he did to Mr Burnham, Wilks might have lost his temper and killed him then and there.'

'It's unlikely that anyone here is going to risk talking about Wilks. It appears he rules with an iron fist,' Harry said.

'I agree. I think it might be time to speak with everyone individually, and away from other eyes and ears.'

'You're not going to try and take them to the station, are you?'

Thomas shook his head. 'No, but we could set up an interview area here somewhere and see them, one at a time. That way Mr Wilks does not think we have singled anyone out and he'll never know who said what.'

They rose to leave, and Thomas looked over to Teddy, who gave a barely discernible sign to come over. Thomas nudged Harry and they went towards the kitchen.

'You're the new cook, I hear?' Harry said, trying not to grin.

'Assistant cook,' Teddy corrected them. 'We met briefly the other day when you were talking with Mr Jo-Jo. I'm Teddy Clements,' he offered his name. 'Sorry I can't shake, but

I've got my hands full.' He continued chopping vegetables, giving the knife and cutting board his full attention.

Thomas kept up the charade, should anyone be watching or listening in. 'Detectives Ashdown and Dart. A few questions?'

'Sure, if you don't mind if I keep working while you ask?' he said, and placing down the knife, he swept the vegetables into a large pot.

Harry wandered outside the area, had a glance area and came back.

'All clear,' he said.

'You wanted to know of any strange comings or goings?' Teddy said and continued without waiting for an answer. 'There was a man here this morning who was looking for Mrs Wilks. He looked down on his luck and I saw her slip him something. I'd be guessing it was money. He stuffed it in his pocket and walked off.'

'Can you describe him?' Harry asked.

'A few inches short of six-foot, wiry and thin, but strong, if you know what I mean? His nose looked as though it had been rearranged a few times. I wouldn't put it past him to box a bit. He had that look, and his hands were sporting cuts,' Teddy said.

'Did you hear anything they said?' Harry asked.

'No, but he muttered something as he went past and I'm pretty sure he was speaking a foreign language, don't know which one, I didn't recognise any words. She responded in the same language, so if she speaks Russian, I'm guessing that's it.' Teddy wiped his hands on the apron he wore and glanced around again to ensure they were alone.

'Good job,' Thomas said. 'Anything else?'

'Yeah, the butcher delivers here twice a week, every Monday and Thursday; the milkman's here daily, and vegetables and groceries as needed but usually they come from Compton's store twice a week. So, there's a few comings and goings but the man who was talking with Mrs Wilks had no delivery to make.'

'Met many of the crew yet?' Harry asked.

'I've seen them eat, but that's as close as I've got. There's only a handful and they keep to themselves, avoid the management. They don't even eat at the same time.'

'You've done well, lad,' Harry said.

Thomas agreed. 'Mrs Wilks' visitor is worth checking out. If he's not one of the servicemen, who is he and what is he being paid for?'

They bade Teddy goodbye and headed to the main road – across the grass and patches of mud that had been well trodden by the curious – to their ride.

'That's Miss Hayward alighting from that omnibus,' Harry said as they neared the edge of the grounds.

'And she's alone,' Thomas said, annoyed. As he said the words, her gaze found him and she smiled, pleased to see him. It was hard to continue being frustrated with her when she looked at him with delight.

They made their way to her.

Matilda looked radiant in lilac. Her gown was cut and fitted to highlight her slight and nicely proportioned figure, her hair was delicately plaited and tied into a becoming style under a straw hat with a black band. She carried a small box with a home-baked slice within from Cook.

'Detective Dart, Thomas, have you made an arrest?' she asked.

'I wish, miss,' Harry answered with a dip of his hat.

'Are you alone?' Thomas asked.

Matilda looked behind her and then to the other side.

'Apparently so, Thomas.'

Harry chuckled, and Matilda smiled for half a second.

'I'm here to see Mrs Tufton,' she continued.

'The giantess?' Thomas asked, surprised.

'The one and the same. I promised I would call in to see how she was. She can't leave the Exhibition until you release her husband's body, and she gets the death certificate and burial finalised. Only then will the insurer pay.'

'They can be ruthless,' Harry agreed. 'I shall walk you over and perhaps you can ask Teddy to walk you back to here afterwards.'

'I don't want to pull you away from your work,' she said, knowing she was annoying Thomas.

'No, actually I have a book for Jo – Mr Jo-Jo – he's a keen reader.' Harry patted his coat pocket. 'I almost forgot.'

'That's a good idea, Harry, thanks,' Thomas said, as if taking responsibility for Matilda. 'Lucky you are not working, or I would be having a chat with Mrs Lawson about allowing you to come unaccompanied. Regardless, Matilda…'

'I know, Thomas, and I appreciate your concern. But the man who attacked me is dead, and I'm hoping that the man who killed him isn't after me too,' she said and sighed.

Thomas made a sound that translated to 'Hmph.' He

turned to Harry. 'I'm going to visit a few local boxing rings,' he told his partner. 'I'll see you back at the office.' He doffed his hat and said her name, 'Matilda.'

'Thomas,' she said, and then added, remembering, 'Oh, the gallery exhibition is confirmed for this Saturday evening at 7pm if you are not working. Detective Dart, you and Mrs Dart are most welcomed to join our small party. I'm sure I could secure a few more tickets.'

'Most kind, Miss Hayward, but we'll leave you young ones to it. Thom and I see enough of each other during the week, despite how good the company might be,' he said, and Matilda laughed at his joke.

'I'll ensure I am free,' Thomas said and watched as Matilda accepted Detective Dart's arm and they walked across the unlevel grass.

With another huff of frustration and a churn of pleasure, he decided he would start on foot to visit a few of the local boxing gymnasiums. The walk would do him good and give him thinking time.

*Chapter 30*

Mrs Tufton's caravan came into sight, and Mr Jo-Jo's van was at the start of the next row. Matilda turned to Harry as he led her down the row.

'How kind of you to bring Mr Jo-Jo a book, Detective Dart,' Matilda said, as Harry finished telling her of Mr Jo-Jo's love of reading, but his inability to go to a bookstore.

'I'd love to take him to a bookstore and let him browse to his heart's content,' Harry said with a sigh.

Matilda had an idea; she was rarely without one.

'Detective Dart, if you were prepared to collaborate, I might be able to make that happen for Mr Jo-Jo!'

'Indeed, let's collaborate and give the poor man a happy memory.'

'Done! I'll talk to my Aunt Audrey in confidence and let you know the outcome. Is he social if we were to have a private supper to follow?' Matilda asked.

'Indeed, and very articulate, good company. We might have to hasten; I understand from Teddy that the exhibition will leave as soon as they are cleared to do so.'

'Aunt Audrey will love the challenge. She has a heart of gold under that tough exterior.'

Harry smiled, delighted. 'Bless her. Wouldn't that be lovely to do that for him?'

'You have a kind heart, Detective Dart. You need to impart some of that to your protégé,' she joked.

'Ah Thomas, an intense young man, but he has a soft spot for you. He's waiting for you Miss Hayward, but I am speaking out of turn to say that.'

Matilda flushed. 'It's odd for us both after a lifetime of friendship to think like that. And Thomas does like the ladies,' she said.

'Necessity not choice, my dear. He would ask for your hand in a heartbeat if you gave any sign you were ready. But of course, I never said that.' He tapped his nose and Matilda laughed. Then he knocked on Mrs Tufton's van, gave Matilda a small bow, and departed after greeting Mrs Tufton.

\*\*\*\*

Matilda stepped into the caravan and the two ladies greeted each other with a hug; a sign of their growing closeness. Unbeknown to Matilda, before the afternoon was done, she would make an important discovery on the case, but for now, she accepted the offer of tea.

'I am so glad you came,' Anna said. 'It is so hard being in waiting. Waiting to leave, waiting to bury Carl, waiting to find a killer, waiting to do my last show…'

'I can only imagine,' Matilda sympathised. 'I've never been good at sitting still either and you've had much more worldly experience than me.'

She accepted the offer of tea and produced the slices baked by Cook.

'How thoughtful. Please thank her on my behalf,' Anna said.

'Of course. So tell me, have you plans in place yet? Where shall you go? We must correspond,' Matilda said.

The ladies enjoyed tea and banter for some forty minutes until Matilda rose to return her cup and saucer to the tiny kitchenette.

She paused, seeing Mrs Wilks through the curtains. She was wandering to the small copse of trees behind the exhibition tents, looking back several times as if she thought someone was watching or following her.

'That's odd,' Matilda said, and Anna rose and joined her at the window, catching a glimpse of Mrs Wilks walking into the forest area.

'It is,' Anna agreed, 'she looks nervous.'

'What is in there?' Matilda asked.

'Just dense greenery. Carl and I took a turn of the grounds several times.'

Matilda noted she said her deceased husband's name with absolutely no emotion.

'It is a pleasant walk through there,' Anna continued. 'Quite dense in places and there are a few boggy areas. You certainly wouldn't want to be in there at night,' she told Matilda.

'I'm going to follow her,' Matilda said.

Anna gasped. 'That could be dangerous. Let me come.'

'No, you are kind to offer, but she will see us both, and I will move quickly. I promise to be careful.'

'I'll keep watch and listen. If you have not returned in a brief time, I will get help. Yell or scream and I will hear you and come.'

'I will,' Matilda assured her and opening the caravan door, headed down the few stairs of the van and darted around the back towards the small forest. She glanced back to find that Anna had followed her to the back of the caravan where she could see the area and hear if she were needed.

Matilda headed towards the forest, staying close to the trees as she entered. She could see Mrs Wilks' blue gown in the distance as she weaved her way through the trees. Little did Matilda know that behind her, Teddy had seen her and also followed; he had given a brief wave to the giantess and pointed that he intended to follow.

Anna had no option but to trust he was honourable.

Matilda heard her name and looked around. She didn't see him at first and then Teddy emerged from behind a tree, his finger across his lips warning her to hush. She nodded, and they fell in together.

'I was worried I might frighten you and we'd alert Mrs Wilks to our presence,' he whispered.

'Thank you for following me,' she said. 'Do you think it is odd?'

'Definitely,' he answered. 'She looked around quite a bit before entering as if she was out to do something.'

They trod quietly, following and keeping Mrs Wilks in sight, and then she stopped. Matilda and Teddy moved closer without showing themselves and watched.

Mrs Wilks looked around again, ensuring she was alone and squatting down, she moved a couple of large stones and ran her hand along the earth feeling for something. She visibly relaxed and then moved the two stones back in place, stood, brushed off her hands and turned to walk out the way she came in, but this time much more briskly, as if her work were done.

Teddy and Matilda scurried quietly behind cover and waited until she passed.

When they were safe, Matilda asked, 'Should we go see what is under there before notifying your uncle? It might not be relevant.'

'True, but we might also unearth or ruin something that's a clue and then find ourselves in trouble with the law,' Teddy said, less interested in a scoop than Matilda, and mindful of the wrath of his uncle.

'Then we'd best get Thomas.'

'I agree,' Teddy said, 'but I'm worried that if we don't watch the area, it might be different on our return.'

Matilda nodded. 'If you are happy to stay here, I will rush back – Anna is watching for me. I'll have Thomas sent for now.'

'Perfect,' Teddy agreed.

'Be careful. I'll be as fast as I can,' she assured him, and standing, hurried back the way she had come to help solve a case of murder.

*Chapter 31*

As Matilda broke free from the trees and rushed back across the grounds, she saw Anna still waiting for her. Then she stopped suddenly. Standing with her arms folded watching Matilda was Mrs Wilks. She was some distance away, but there was no doubt that she saw where Matilda emerged from. Matilda froze.

Scenarios rang through her mind: if Mrs Wilks were hiding something related to the murders and Matilda went to Anna, Mrs Wilks would see, and it might put Anna in danger. It would also leave Teddy vulnerable and alone. If Mrs Wilks returned to the rock area, she may well attack him, and he was unprepared and had no weapon. Matilda thought if she were to confront Mrs Wilks, she might draw harm upon herself. Of course it could be completely innocent, and Mrs Wilks may have other reasons for visiting the area, but Matilda couldn't risk that.

As she stood frozen, Mrs Wilks turned and walked away. What to do now? Matilda looked to Anna, who had stayed out of sight and appeared to understand the risk.

Was Detective Dart still here? Unlikely, it had been close to an hour. Matilda saw an opportunity; one of the crew was coming towards her carting a rope and some tools.

'Miss,' he said, with a nod.

'Can you help me please?' she asked.

'I'll do my best, miss. What do ya need?' he said, keen to help the attractive young lady.

'Could you please give Mrs Tufton an urgent message for me?'

He looked confused.

'Anna, she is just over near her van and expecting me.'

He looked over and then back at Matilda. 'Oh, the giantess, no problem.'

Matilda continued, hurriedly, 'Could you ask her to call the detectives and let them know I am still on site? They were expecting me to do a story on them.'

'Ah, you'd be one of those lady writers. Right then. So, tell her to call the detectives and tell them you're not coming?'

'That will do perfectly, thank you kindly.'

'Pleasure, ma'am,' he said and strode towards Anna. Matilda didn't wait to see if he delivered the message or Anna's reaction. She would understand what it meant and would know who to trust to deliver it. She hurried back towards Teddy and the forest, as fast as her dress would allow her, and not taking her eyes off her surroundings in case she should see Mrs Wilks coming.

'What's happened?' Teddy asked, rising and appearing before her from behind a tree.

Matilda told him what had transpired.

'Perhaps we should move the rocks and see. It might be nothing and we can explain that to Uncle when he gets here... but if she returns with support and outnumbers us...'

Matilda nodded. 'That's what I was worried about, too. Let's do it.'

She allowed Teddy to lead the way, constantly watching and listening to the surrounding forest. He knelt in the area where Mrs Wilks had been and moved the two large stones. The earth underneath was fresh and not compacted like the soil around the surrounding rocks. With his bare hands, Teddy dug away the top layer, and then glanced at Matilda.

'What is it?' she asked, leaning over, keen to get a glimpse.

'I think we've found the two missing walking canes.'

Teddy dug a little deeper and sure enough, two long sticks appeared, one with a distinct metal globe on the end, encrusted in the dirt.

'Should we get them and go?' Matilda asked.

'Uncle Thomas will have my head if we touch them. I know that much from his stories, but we may have to,' he said and looked around.

'If only Anna, the giantess, were a man, we could secure the scene and have our own personal guard,' Matilda said with a sigh.

'I can lift two men,' a voice said and made them both jump and swing around.

The giantess stood there.

## Chapter 32

The forest area was quiet. The giantess had moved with stealth – an impossible feat one would have thought for a person so large but yet neither Matilda nor Teddy had heard her approach.

'Anna! We didn't hear you!' Matilda said, shocked, her hand racing to her heart. Had she sent a message to the detectives, or had Matilda misjudged Anna? Were Anna and Mrs Wilks involved in the murders of Mrs Wilks' lover and Anna's husband?

Anna smiled. 'There's a small path behind you that I discovered on one of my afternoon walks,' she said. 'It's been used regularly, and the path is clear of branches.'

'Right,' Teddy said, 'and here I was thinking you were a stealth expert.'

Anna laughed.

Matilda realised Teddy had not made the connection; he didn't think they could be in trouble.

'I am surprisingly light on my feet,' Anna said and smiled. She returned her attention to Matilda. 'I had a message sent to your friend,' she said subtly, with a glance at Teddy and then back to Matilda, not sure about Teddy's involvement.

'Thank you,' Matilda said, breathing a sigh of relief. 'I knew you would understand. You have met Teddy, have you not?'

'I'm the new assistant cook,' he said, 'and we've seen each other in passing, Mrs Tufton.'

'Yes, indeed. Please call me Anna.' She looked at the small unearthed trough. 'You've found something?'

Teddy explained about following Mrs Wilks and unearthing the walking canes as they watched and waited. Matilda thought it might still be possible that Anna warned Mrs Wilks and she would come with reinforcement, instead of the expected detectives. But it wasn't long until Matilda saw Thomas and Harry entering the caravan lane and she relaxed.

'I'll go to them,' she said. 'Thank you, Anna.' Matilda raced out of the treed area and waved her arms until they noticed her. Both men picked up speed and ran towards her, Thomas well in the lead.

'I'm fine, it's all fine,' she assured him, holding up her hands. Thomas's look of panic subsided. He slowed down and drew large breaths, and Detective Dart caught up.

'For the love of God, Matilda, I thought you were attacked again,' he snapped, scanning her and taking a measure of his anger when he saw her eyes widen at his display of temper.

'No, I'm fine. I'm sorry, Thomas,' she said and explained, 'I had to be a little cloak and dagger. I wasn't confident of whose side everyone was on.'

'Very smart indeed,' Detective Dart said to her between pants.

'We've found something,' she said. 'Mrs Wilks went into the bush, and we followed.'

'We?' Thomas asked sharply, his eyes narrowing.

'Teddy and I, and Anna called for help and came back to watch over us.'

'Thank Christ,' Thomas swore under his breath. They followed Matilda into the copse of trees and coming upon Teddy and Anna, Thomas and Harry acknowledged them before looking into the area that had been dug out.

Thomas nodded. 'I think you've unearthed a murder weapon.'

*****

Mrs Wilks sat in the gaol cell, tight-lipped and waiting for legal counsel. She had said little in her police interview, but Thomas guessed a night in the cells would make her feel a little more talkative the next day. Mr Jo-Jo had identified one cane was his and the other was the deceased Mr Burnham's cane.

Thomas paced around his office, stopping only long enough to look at the canes displayed on the table before beginning his pacing again. He had only just retrieved them from the coroner, who had confirmed that Mr Jo-Jo's cane was indeed a positive match for the skull wounds received by the first victim. Why beat one and not the other? Was it the same killer, or was he interrupted before he could deliver his modus operandi?

Thomas wanted to see Matilda. He pondered why she seemed to find herself in the middle of trouble. Did it seek her, or did she draw it to her? As if he didn't have enough to worry about, he sighed. He couldn't even call in on her this evening on the pretence of seeing Daniel – she was at some bookshop outing with Harry and Harry's new charity recipient, Jo from the carnival. Going home was no consolation when Teddy had been commissioned at a handsome rate by Aunt Audrey to produce her menu for Harry's evening. He paced around his office for a while longer before deciding to have one more crack at Mrs Wilks. He found the night desk clerk and ordered her returned to the interview room. He made his way there at his leisure.

He had to give Mrs Wilks credit, she had more front than Finney Isles Big Block Emporium in Adelaide Street and that had front. Most ladies, except for the street girls, were fearful of the law and revealed their hands without any pressure needing to be added, but Mrs Wilks had Russian stoicism, a healthy distrust of men and the law, and self-preservation working for her. Sitting opposite her, Thomas took a different tack.

'I do not believe you killed Mr Burnham yourself,' he said.

Irina Wilks placed her hands on the table and exhaled, gratified.

'I do, however, believe you know who did and you may be protecting them. What other reason would you have to hide the two canes?'

She looked down at the table and did not speak.

'You know this does not bode well for you,' Thomas continued. 'If you are protecting yourself or your husband, or even someone in your employment, you did lead us to the weapons, which a jury will see as guilt. You were in a relationship with the deceased, and Mr Tufton was a bully trying to coerce more money from a business that you manage and now run. Are you protecting your husband?'

Mrs Wilks laughed at the suggestion, but did not answer.

'Did you witness Mr Jo-Jo and Mr Burnham in a fight, and are you protecting Mr Jo-Jo?'

She sighed and, breaking her silence, said, 'I assure you, Detective Ashdown, neither of those *gentlemen* would fight to the death.' She emphasised the word *gentlemen* and Thomas gave that some thought before phrasing his next question.

'So if it was not you, and as I said, I don't believe you to be the killer, the light has to fall on your husband or Mrs Tufton as the likely suspects.'

'Anna, the giantess!' Mrs Wilks exclaimed with surprise. 'Good lord, there's an original idea. Would she need to beat them though, or could she just crush them to death?' She gave a wry laugh.

Detective Ashdown pushed himself out of his chair and moved to the exit door, turning and leaning against it.

'I get the impression you would be happy to see your husband charged and locked away, Mrs Wilks. If Mr Burnham felt the same way about your husband and wanted you to himself, was he intending to bump him off, but was overpowered and Mr Wilks won the fight?'

She appeared to think about this for a while and then answered, 'I guess that's as good a scenario as any.'

Thomas sighed. 'Mrs Wilks, I'm not looking for your help to come up with a reason to arrest your husband. I'm looking for the truth.'

She gave him a wry look; her lack of fear again surprised him, particularly in a foreign police station.

'How many languages do you speak, Mrs Wilks?' Thomas asked out of the blue, remembering Teddy overhearing her respond to the boxer.

'English and Russian,' she retorted.

And then he cut to the chase, bluffing just a little. 'I have in the cells a man that was brought in earlier today. The man you were seen paying money to at the Exhibition.'

She sat upright, and her head snapped to look at him. It was the reaction he was hoping for and he was not disappointed. This man was involved and now Thomas just had to find him.

'I need to speak with him,' she said.

'I'm afraid that is not possible. Is there anything you would like to tell me now?'

He waited as she wrung her hands, all the while staring at the table, and then in a faint voice she answered, 'No.'

Thomas nodded and left the interview room, instructing the guard she could be returned to the cell.

He had no luck earlier wandering through the Valley district and enquiring about boxing tournaments, but a night visit might produce a different result. He had to find that man.

## Chapter 33

The hansom cab pulled up outside the shopfront; a slip of lamplight peeked through the closed curtains of the Corner Bookstore. Inside the hansom, Mr Jo-Jo waited for the signal, as Detective Harry Dart exited first, paid the cabman and opened the door of the bookstore. Getting the nod, in the dark, Mr Jo-Jo slipped from the hansom into the shop unnoticed.

When he entered, he gasped in surprise. He knew to expect Miss Hayward and Mrs Therese Dart, but the setting was breathtaking. By the window, Teddy had set a table for four with candlelight and a small table nearby featured dishes, each covered with silver domes. Teddy stood by the dishes, dressed in a suit, and gave a small bow.

'Mr Jo-Jo, welcome,' Matilda said as if greeting an old friend. She offered her hand, and he took it, bowing over it but not presuming to kiss her hand.

'This is my wife, Mr Jo-Jo,' Harry said, 'Mrs Therese Dart.'

Mrs Dart, a woman of round proportions, kindly face and donned in a comfortable floral print, stepped forward and offered her hand. If she was at all alarmed by the countenance of the abundantly small and hairy man in front of her, she hid her surprise well.

'Madam.' Mr Jo-Jo took her hand and offered a small bow. He was a man well-versed in gentlemanly behaviour, courtesy of his grandfather's upbringing.

'Mr Jo-Jo,' she said, 'I am so pleased to meet you.'

Teddy and Mr Jo-Jo exchanged greetings.

Matilda spoke up. 'Let's not stand on formality tonight. Shall we go by Harry, Matilda, Jo and Therese? And Teddy of course?'

Therese Dart laughed. 'Indeed, like old friends.'

'You have gone to so much trouble,' Jo said, emotion is his voice. 'Thank you.' He encompassed all the guests in his thanks, and then let his eyes travel around the setting so handsomely complemented by the lamps lit in each corner of the bookshop.

'Now don't you be fretting about that,' Therese said, warmly. 'I'm as much a guest as you are. I've arrived at the same enchanting sight and not lifted a finger.'

'Nor have I,' Harry admitted.

'And be assured, Jo, I have done very little,' Matilda said. 'I'll explain while we enjoy dinner.'

'With Harry's irregular work hours, it is a treat to have a night out and enjoy new company,' Therese said, as excited as Jo for the evening ahead.

'Shall we be seated and dine while the dishes are fresh and warm and then we shall leave you and Harry to browse the books?'

'Yes please,' Teddy said, not keen to have his cooking ruined.

'I'm starving,' Harry said, pulling out a chair for his wife, and Jo did the same for Matilda.

Jo looked at Teddy. 'You must be exhausted, Teddy, you've worked today as well.'

Teddy shook his head. 'It's not a demanding job, Jo, not by any measure. I do only five hours, so it is a pleasure to cook something a little more refined.'

'Then join us,' Matilda said, and the party agreed. Teddy tried to talk them out of it, but they insisted. A fifth chair and a place setting were found and soon Teddy introduced each dish and the banter, wine and conversation flowed.

'This is a beautiful spread. I hate to think of you out of pocket,' Jo said.

Matilda explained. 'No one is, I assure you, Jo. My Aunt Audrey is a benevolent lady, and she likes to organise and give. It's one of her most enduring traits but there's often a trade involved.'

'Do tell,' Harry encouraged her.

'Well,' Matilda continued, 'The bookstore's owner wants his daughter introduced to a certain society person and Aunt Audrey has the connections. In return, he has offered his store tonight and a book budget for your pleasure.'

Jo gasped but Matilda assured him, 'It is a small price for an intimate introduction that could be fortuitous to the family.'

Harry continued, 'When we have finished dinner, Therese and Matilda will head home in a hansom, and you and I, Jo, will browse to our hearts' content. You have to select five books to take home with you and we can't leave until you do.'

'No, that is too generous, and you should accompany Therese home—'

'—Truly Jo, you do not want to argue with Aunt Audrey, you won't win,' Matilda said.

Harry laughed. 'It's the truth. I've had the pleasure on a few occasions of meeting Mrs Bloomfield, and she is not to be trifled with. Besides, she must get her end of the bargain.'

Jo dabbed his eyes. Such kindnesses were few and far between in his world.

'And don't you worry about Harry wanting to get home,' Therese said, patting her husband's hand. 'There's been many a time I've had to pull him from this bookstore with threats of a cold supper. You'll be like peas in a pod.'

The meal, conversation and company continued, and it was for all present a most memorable and enjoyable evening.

For Mr Jo-Jo, it was one of the happiest nights of his life.

*Chapter 34*

The City's Fortitude Valley area had its share of respectable places, less at night. But it wasn't a respectable venue that Detective Thomas Ashdown was seeking. He was too wired to go home, and he knew the best chance of finding this man – the potential boxer – was in the underground clubs and fighting halls at night. He had little to go on but that the man was shorter than he, wiry, might have been a boxer, mature, and had a nose that had met a fist a few times. It was enough.

'So where are you taking me since we're obviously not going to our club?' Daniel asked his best friend. They stepped down from a hansom in the heart of the Valley area.

'Well observed, Dan,' Thomas said, teasing his friend. 'I'm working, but I thought you might like to keep me company. I'm looking for a man, probably Russian, who boxes, and might be a link in one of my current cases.'

'Well that's exciting – the murder at the Freak Show?'

'That's it,' Thomas said, lowering his voice as they walked along.

Daniel moved out of the way of two men brawling and kept stride with Thomas.

'I know of a place where the boxers wear gloves. Is that what you're seeking?' Daniel asked.

'No. I'm thinking he's more likely to fight at one of the less than legal venues where bare-knuckle boxing is popular.'

'You know of these?' Daniel asked.

'I've made a few arrests.'

They walked a little farther, turned down an offer from several ladies of the night, and then Thomas nudged Daniel into a discreet laneway. Ahead of them was a rowdy party of three men, and Thomas and Daniel followed them towards a small set of iron stairs.

The two men slipped down the stairs behind the group of men as if they were part of their company, and entered a surprisingly large room lit by lamps, with dark curtains covering all the windows. On the far side of the room was a boxing ring, and a bar with numerous tables and chairs filled the remaining space. The two men equipped themselves with a glass of whiskey each not long after. They stood at the back of the room, blended in and watched a few rounds of the fight in the ring as bets were being made and the alcohol flowed.

'No great talent there,' Daniel muttered to his friend.

'True, but some men will bet on anything,' Thomas said. He scanned the crowd several times, plus the trainers, bookmakers and fighters, and found no one to match his description satisfactorily.

'We're out of here,' Thomas said, and gulped the last mouthful of his whiskey.

'What? I was just warming up. Thought I might get a round in myself.'

Thomas gave him a wry look, and Daniel chuckled. Leaving the smoke-filled den, Thomas engaged the doorman in some banter, while Daniel lit a cigarette, offering one to the doorman, who accepted, recognising its quality.

'I saw a good fighter the other night, a wiry Russian he was,' Thomas said casually. 'But I don't remember where I saw him fight, I'm blaming the whiskey.'

'I know the man,' the doorman said with a curt nod. 'Angry bastard.'

'Is that so?' Daniel said. 'Still, we're not looking to befriend him, just keen to throw a few more dollars on his fights. Is he a regular here?'

The doorman shook his head in the negative. 'You'll find him at Ray's Club. But I'll give you a tip for nothing,' he added. 'Best to bet on him fresh, because after a few fights he gets a bit punch drunk and starts on a losing streak. He's all front no stamina.'

'Appreciate that,' Thomas said with a nod, and adjusted his hat.

The two men moved away as another group arrived, and before Thomas could be recognised by anyone he might have arrested. They made their way to Ray's seedy joint whose reputation preceded it especially as far as Thomas was concerned. He would have felt better having Harry with him. His partner might have a few decades on him, but he'd boxed a bit in his younger years and could still swing a good punch. Daniel was great company, but his fighting ambitions and bravado didn't match his talent; he was an artist, after all. The last fight he had was probably in the school grounds. Even another officer by his side would have been helpful – it wasn't the most savoury of joints, but Thomas conceded it was easier to blend in as two men friends out on a gambling night.

'It's been a few years since we've taken each other on, but we could have a go in the ring,' Daniel suggested. He was itching for a fight, needing to release some steam.

'If I remember, that was your idea then, too. I flattened you and got in serious trouble from your family.'

Daniel laughed. 'Yes, you are a bad influence, apparently. Anyway, you are probably right, I need to protect my hands as I expect to be hearing about the court appointment in the next few days.'

'You're just worried I'll thrash you again,' Thomas cut to the chase, 'but if we're going to fight anyone tonight, save your energy, because I suspect the Russian will not agree to come in for questioning without a fight.'

They moved around some ambitious traders and the well imbibed until, after a good ten minutes' brisk walk, they arrived at Ray's boxing establishment – not that there was a name or sign over the door promoting it.

'Just in time. I need a drink,' Daniel said.

Thomas spotted a few of the younger police officers patrolling nearby. He didn't want to risk drawing attention to himself, but he noted their location should he need back-up. He grabbed Daniel's arm and pulled him back.

'A moment,' Thomas said, 'just to observe.' They stood

back on the pretence of having a cigarette outside and studied the entrance to the club. The guests that entered appeared not to be scrutinised by the door staff, and on spotting a well-inebriated party of four, Thomas nudged Daniel, moved behind them and found their way into the smoky and noisy den in a matter of moments. The club was much bigger, and inside were the extremes – gambling men dressed to kill and splashing money around like it was going out of fashion, to the down-and-outers keen for cheap entertainment or to feel and inflict a bit of pain themselves for a quid. Daniel ordered another round of whiskey; fortunately, they had the constitution for it and were well-practised at drinking, as it would be another few rounds until the man in question would present himself.

Thomas settled in to study the crowd, watch, and wait.

'Oh, get him off!' Daniel yelled, joining in the chorus of calls, as some poor man was pummelled too many times for comfort. He was dragged out, and a new contender slipped under the ropes to take on the reigning champion.

'A quid on the newcomer,' Daniel said.

'You're on,' Thomas took the bet and despite the valiant effort of the current champion, lost the bet and slipped Daniel his winnings. It was forty minutes later when he spotted a likely contender for his Russian boxer.

'That could be him.' Thomas nodded toward a newcomer. He watched the man's every move as the boxer studied the competition, not taking part, yet. Nearing ten o'clock, the man rose and went to the side of the ring. Thomas watched as the Russian man spoke with another, appearing to negotiate for a few moments and then he moved to the back of the ring, stripped off jacket and trousers and in a singlet and shorts approached the ring. He was rough and angry, a man who would inflict damage just because he could, but there were contenders happy to take him on.

Thomas finished his drink and was tempted to place a bet on him. And then with a cheer, the current match ended with a man flat on his back and the angry Russian stepped into the ring with another contender. He had little flair, but his raw energy attracted the crowd, and he had his own following. They knew him and started chanting a word. Thomas leaned forward to pick it up – killer. They were chanting, "Killer".

# Chapter 35

Matilda lanced out the window of the hansom cab to the passing street. 'Good grief!' she exclaimed. Only ten minutes earlier, she had dropped Mrs Dart home and was now riding the hansom alone to her residence when she caught sight of her brother and Thomas looking the worse for wear and dishevelled. She could have sworn Thomas was bleeding. She rapped on the ceiling of the hansom.

'Stop please, stop.'

The hansom pulled over and Matilda opened the door.

'Daniel!' she called and confirmed her sighting. He turned at the sound of her familiar voice and raised a hand. Thomas did not look as pleased to see her.

'What on earth...' she enquired as the two men approached her hansom.

'I could ask the same about you,' Thomas said. 'What on earth are you doing here at night in this area?' He almost shouted the last few words, and Daniel put a hand on his chest to calm him.

'I'm returning home from my dinner with your colleague. I've just dropped Mrs Dart home.'

'And your cabman chose to come past this way,' he said, glaring up at the driver who seemed not to realise that he might have put his lady passenger in any danger.

'What happened? You're bleeding, Thomas, and Daniel, you're completely dishevelled. You have been fighting in public!'

'It's fine,' Daniel said, straightening himself and brushing down his suit as if he regularly fought in the streets on his nights out. 'We were looking for a man, a boxer, and we found him.'

'Well, yes, I can see that. Did he win?' Matilda asked, the ghost of a smile on her face.

'He did not, thank you, Matilda,' Thomas said with a smirk.

'But it was rather exciting following him and then putting him on the spot!' Daniel said, grinning like a child on Christmas morning.

Matilda sighed. 'Well, best you stem that blood then,' she said, not at all squeamish. Growing up with four brothers had cured her of that many years ago.

Thomas withdrew a handkerchief from his pocket and dabbed at his nose. Behind them, a young constable arrived.

'We've detained him, sir, and will take him to the lock-up.'

Thomas turned. 'Thank you, Constable. He is not to be released until I question him in the morning.'

'Understood, sir,' the young man said and departed.

Matilda watched Thomas in authority and felt a stirring of pride and something else that made her blush slightly in his presence.

He returned his attention to her brother.

'Perhaps you could accompany Matilda home now, Dan, our work is done here, and I should head home too and clean up. Thanks for coming out.'

'I'd do it again anytime. But the night is young, Thom,' Daniel said, fired up. 'I think I will find Gideon. Do you wish to come?'

Thom shook his head. 'I've had enough. Besides, nowhere would admit me now. I'll see your sister home then.' He tried not to sound too enthusiastic about the suggestion.

'I am right here,' Matilda reminded them. 'The mute sister,' she said.

Thomas ignored her comments and asked. 'Did Teddy leave the bookstore when you did?'

'A little earlier, so he should be at your home now unless he's taken up street fighting as well,' Matilda said.

'Here's another hansom. I'll take this one if you are happy to share Tillie's?' Daniel asked but not waiting for an answer, hailed the driver and gave them a wave of goodbye.

Matilda moved over to allow room for another passenger and stared at Thomas as he watched her through the open hansom door.

'Well, come on then, or are you going back for another round?' she asked.

He looked at his bloodied hands and dirt-ridden suit and, sighing, climbed in beside her. She tucked her gown close around herself and sniffed. Whiskey.

'If I offend, I can get another cab,' he said, sitting as close to the hansom door as possible.

'You offend no more than usual, Thomas,' she teased him, and he chuckled.

He closed the door, and the hansom moved off.

'Let me see your hands,' she said.

'No, I'll get blood on your gown. They're fine,' Thomas assured her.

'My gown is dark, blood won't be noticed,' she said of her dark navy gown with white trim. Matilda tugged out a white lace handkerchief that was tucked between her breasts and reached for his hand.

'You'll ruin it,' Thomas said.

'It's to be used,' she said, and he reluctantly gave her his hand. She dabbed at his bloodied knuckles, and studied his hand, before releasing it and requesting his other hand. Thomas watched her with great attention. He wasn't used to being cared for; his mother did not welcome his late arrival and held little interest in running after an infant or putting up with the adventures of a young boy. His father, when not at work, was at his club, and his brother was so much older that he had left home when Thomas was a young boy. The most affection he received was when visiting and staying with Daniel and the Hayward family.

She dabbed the white lace onto his skinned knuckles and secured the lace handkerchief around his thumb where a cut continued to bleed.

'Thank you,' he said.

Matilda studied his face and blackening eye. 'Why did you take the brunt of it? Where was Daniel?'

'I was trying to arrest the man, so I met his fists first. Besides, it is best if Daniel preserves his hands for his occupation.'

'Is the man you arrested the murderer?' she asked.

'I am not giving you a headline for your newspaper, Matilda,' Thomas answered.

'Well, I'll remember that next time I find out some information and give it to you first and foremost,' she said.

'And I thought you shared that with me to help my career along as a close friend and a good citizen,' Thomas said, watching her, a hint of amusement in his eyes.

'No,' she answered bluntly.

Thomas laughed, shook his head and looked out of the hansom cab window. She always managed to disarm him.

Matilda continued. 'I told you the information I knew hoping to get a murderer off the street,' she said and catching his eye, smiled. 'And to help you advance I suppose.'

Thomas grinned.

'Besides, I don't write for a daily newspaper, Thomas, in case you have forgotten, so your headline will be of no advantage to myself and Mrs Lawson.'

'Ah, right then,' he continued to tease her in the fashion that he had done for well over two decades. 'So, you don't want some insider information?' he asked, as she sat back, having released both his hands and had begun rummaging through her handbag.

'Well, I wouldn't say no,' Matilda said. 'Who was he?'

'We don't know yet,' Thomas answered and saw the disbelief cross her face. 'No, that's the truth. He was seen with Mrs Wilks, so I want to know why.'

'Odd.'

'Indeed,' Thomas agreed.

'Here it is,' Matilda exclaimed, and pulled out another white lace handkerchief and a small wrapper of ointment. She studied his face again. 'How is the eye?' It was black and red and looked terrible.

'It's fine,' he said stoically.

Matilda reached for her throat, running her hand down to her neck muscles, and gently touched the bruises that had now almost faded underneath her dress collar. Thomas's gaze followed her hand.

'I know for a fact, Thomas, how much a good hit can hurt.'

'Well then, it is painful,' he conceded.

She gave him a sympathetic look and opened a small paper wrapper. 'Allow me.'

'What on earth is that?' he said, objecting to the dark cure-all stick and its smell.

'You should know,' Matilda said, turning the paper wrapper towards him so he could read it – *Bates' Salve*. 'Harriet put it on every bump and scrape that you and Daniel had growing up. It has many good properties which I could recite to you, but better still, close your eye.'

He grimaced.

'I won't get any in your eye, it's supposed to go on the broken flesh around it. It numbs the area and stops the infection.'

'Why on earth are you carrying it around with you, and what else have you got in there?' Thomas nodded at her handbag, which resembled a small doctor's bag in shape and design.

Matilda clamped her bag shut and removed one of her gloves. Thomas's eyes widened in surprise.

'Harriet made me carry it around in case my neck and throat became painful, so I could dab a little on.' She placed her gloves in her lap and looked up at him to administer the ointment.

Thomas looked unconvinced. Matilda sighed and put her hands in her lap, giving him an impatient look.

'Fine,' he said, and closed his eyes, waiting for her touch. 'Just be careful you don't poke me in the eye every time we hit a bump.'

'Then keep still,' she said. 'Lean right up against the edge.'

He did so and waited; momentarily he felt her gentle touch as she dabbed the ointment around his eye. Thomas swallowed, she was too close, it was too intimate. He didn't dare open his eyes, but he could feel the skin of her fingers on his flesh, feel her warm breath upon his face. He was inches from kissing her.

'There,' she said, and just in time as the hansom jerked to a halt, pushing them closer together. Thomas opened his eyes and helped straighten Matilda back in her seat.

'Thank you.'

'You're very welcome,' she said with a satisfied smile.

The cabman had leapt down from his higher seat and appeared at their door. Matilda wiped her fingers on her handkerchief and put on her glove.

'Right, your stop, Matilda,' Thomas said and alighted to assist her.

She stepped down capably and thanked Thomas and the cabman.

'I'll walk you inside,' Thomas said, glancing up the pathway to the house as the front door opened.

'No need, there's Harriet,' Matilda said with a wave and a smile to her housekeeper at the ajar front door. 'Perhaps you should come in and let us both clean you up and ply you with tea.'

'As tempting as that is, I'll be fine,' he said, with a nod to Harriet, he re-entered the hansom. He was in pain, exhausted and dirty, and did not want to make it harder for himself to leave in an hour or so.

'Goodnight Thomas.'

'Matilda,' he said and watched her until she reached the front door. He tapped the roof for the cabman to depart. He glanced back to see Matilda watching after him. Thomas sat back and sighed, sore, tired and frustrated as he often was after an encounter with Miss Hayward.

On the way home he imagined coming home to her every night, her face the last he saw of an evening and the first in the morning, her small, warm body next to his. Agony.

*Chapter 36*

As they shared tea and cake at Bowen's Tearoom, Matilda finished telling Alice all about her adventures last night at the bookstore and then running into Daniel and Thomas on her journey home.

'Goodness, the Gallery Exhibition Saturday evening will be quite dull for the three of you after last night,' Alice said. 'Perhaps we should go back to Fortitude Valley with Daniel and Thomas.'

Matilda laughed. 'I am sure they will be quite happy with an uneventful night, but I am not sure Thomas will be welcome at the gallery with a black eye. I must ask Gideon will it be a concern for his patrons. Thomas was angry when he saw the route the cabman had taken me.'

'Of course he was,' Alice said. 'He's very protective of you.' She lifted the dainty teacup, sipped and returned it to the saucer before stabbing her fork with anticipation into a beautiful jam sponge dessert.

'I have to say,' Matilda began, lowering her voice, 'it felt strangely comfortable caring for Thomas last night, as a wife might should he return from duties needing attention. I couldn't sleep for thinking of him.'

Alice gushed, 'That's wonderful, Matilda.' She squeezed Matilda's hand.

'It's odd is what it is.'

'Why?'

Matilda finished a mouthful of her sponge cake and said, 'Because it is Thomas. I have grown up with him. He has pushed me into creeks, thrown bugs at me, beaten me at races – and been most angry when I've beaten him – we've fought like brother and sister and now...'

'Now?'

'Well, it is fair to say there is an attraction. But yet he did not want to come in for a cup of tea last night or to allow Harriet and me to fuss over him. I think sometimes he is pleased to have me off his hands and he finds me a duty.'

Alice scoffed. 'He is in love with you, Matilda, and I am sure you feel the same, if you let yourself admit it. I envy you; I want to be loved and love.'

Matilda looked surprised. 'But I thought you wanted a career first.'

'I want both,' Alice said, finishing her slice of cake and declaring it, 'light and delicious.'

'Indeed,' Matilda agreed.

Alice continued. 'My father wants me to marry his oldest friend's son, Joseph. He said we had been promised to each other at birth. Well, not me and I'm sure Joseph feels the same, we have nothing in common and no attraction to each other.'

'Is that why you are here?' Matilda asked. They stopped to admire a lady going past in a fashionable hat.

'Yes. I told my father that I had a calling and was going to join a nunnery.'

Matilda's jaw fell open.

'He was furious, but my mother was thrilled. So I negotiated with him that I would have a year in Australia with my guardian to see if perhaps I could fall in love instead of becoming a nun.' She laughed.

'Alice, you are positively wicked and brilliant,' Matilda said.

'A girl must do what a girl must do. We have so few options available to us, but there are ways to get around them.'

Matilda looked at her new friend with great admiration. They accepted a fresh pot of tea and Matilda poured.

'Do you think you might like my brother? I won't be offended if you feel you are unsuited.' Matilda held her breath, hoping for a positive response.

'I like them all,' Alice assured her and laughed at seeing Matilda's expression. She clarified. 'What is not to like about Daniel? He's handsome and lively, talented and charming, very much like you.'

Matilda blushed, unused to taking compliments.

'Thank you, Alice. Oh, imagine if we were sisters-in-law, wouldn't that be exciting,' she said.

'You, me and Minnie, and whoever else comes along. You will have four of them.' Alice lowered her voice and leaned forward slightly. 'Tell me, what prevents you from loving the detective?'

Matilda sighed and placed her cup back on her saucer. 'I guess I have loved him like a brother, like my fifth brother for so long, that should I change our relationship to more and we fall out, I will lose him forever.'

'But you might have him forever. How would you feel about someone else being his wife?'

Matilda's breath hitched. 'Well, when you put it like that…'

*****

Thomas expected and endured the remarks from his colleagues as he walked along the second floor of the Roma Street Police Barracks en route to the stairwell, and the cells below on the first floor. He looked as if he had done ten rounds in a boxing ring but assured his colleagues that he was fine and won the battle, despite the throbbing eye and bruised face.

'You did well, Thom, bringing him in.' Detective Harry Dart slapped his partner's shoulder as they walked towards the interview rooms to talk with the Russian boxer. 'I feel terrible that I was dining on your nephew's cooking and enjoying the bookstore while you were fighting for justice.'

Thomas smiled at his partner. 'I think you've paid your dues many a time.'

They entered the interview room to find the boxer – sullen, sitting with his arms crossed and glaring at them.

'You have no right to hold me overnight for fighting when you started it,' he said, his accent thick.

'Requesting that you accompany me to the police station for some questions is not starting a fight nor an invitation to one,' Thomas said and sat opposite the man.

The Russian laughed when he saw Thomas's face. 'Who are you both, what do you want?'

Harry answered. 'Detective Dart and Detective Ashdown, and you are?'

'You should know that if you arrested me.'

'You haven't been arrested yet,' Thomas answered.

'So I can leave?'

'No. Your name?' Thomas asked, exasperated.

The Russian drew a long breath, cracked the knuckles on his hands and then spat the words out, 'Georgievich Melnikoff.'

'Write that down, plus your address,' Harry said, pushing a notepad and pencil to the boxer.

'And what was your business with Mrs Irina Wilks at the carnival?' Thomas asked.

The question caught the Russian by surprise. He sat back; his eyebrows raised as he stared at the detectives.

'Wilks? The woman at the Freak Show? That's why I'm here? Not illegal boxing?'

'That's why you are here,' Detective Dart said.

The Russian's countenance changed; he ran a hand over his mouth, he glanced towards the exit and then he ran his tongue over his lower lip.

'We're not waiting for you to invent an answer. Why did you meet with her?' Thomas continued.

He shrugged. 'She had some work for me, around the show.'

'Go on,' Thomas prompted him, relieved the Russian had admitted the acquaintance, and he didn't have to get Teddy in to identify him.

'Manual work.'

'Is that so? Odd when she has a crew on hand. How much did she pay you for this work? And before you say you did it out of the goodness of your heart, we have witnesses who saw you accepting money from her.' Thomas embellished the truth as Teddy saw him accept something from Mrs Wilks but couldn't be sure it was money.

'A small amount for odd jobs.'

'How did you meet her?' Harry asked.

'The Russian community always welcomes people when they come to town. I met her at the Russian Centre. It is a small community, but we extend a welcome to all with our heritage,' he said proudly.

Detective Dart stood. 'We have Mrs Wilks in another room so we will need you to wait here until we ask her the same questions.'

The Russian sat back, bluffing that he was fine with them doing so, and crossed his arms across his chest again. Thomas rose and the two men departed. They stopped outside to glance back at him through the small window that the room afforded. He was worried – the bravado had departed from his countenance.

'How do you want to play this?' Harry asked as he and Thomas walked towards the room where Mrs Wilks was being held.

'She's shrewd,' Thomas said, 'and she will know that the

boxer will not go to gaol for her unless they have a history or are family. According to the boxer, they have neither.'

'Now that we have his name, give me five minutes while you get Mrs Wilks upstairs to the interview room and I'll see if he has a record for anything,' Harry said, and turned off, taking the stairs back up to the records department.

Thomas went and got himself a cup of tea while he waited. He'd felt better – his eye ached and his head throbbed – but the thought of his time in the hansom with Matilda last night and the promise of the gallery event this weekend was cheering him up no end. Luckily, Teddy appeared to have withdrawn any interest in Matilda... he's a quick learner, Thomas thought.

Harry was back before he had finished and with a shake of his head confirmed, 'there's no file for him here at this station, but that doesn't mean he hasn't been involved in something elsewhere – in other colonies or overseas,' he said.

'Right, let's get this over with,' Thomas said and, after tipping out the remains of his tea, followed Harry to the interview room to press Mrs Wilks for answers.

*Chapter 37*

Despite the fact that Matilda had ventured to the carnival on her own recently, today she was working under the guise of the *Women's Journal*, thus she travelled with Alice as they promised Mrs Lawson. Matilda and Alice were visiting the giantess, Anna, to drop in the latest issue of the magazine featuring the profile piece and Amos's bill for his services. It was also a good opportunity to stop, rest and take tea; Matilda was not expecting her visit to be dangerous. As Matilda sat opposite the two very different ladies, she could not help being amazed at her two new, independent and fascinating friends.

'We've received a wonderful response to our interviews and story about yourself and the ladies of the Exhibition,' Alice said.

'Most sympathetic and supportive,' Matilda agreed.

Anna smiled with pleasure. Matilda could tell she was a little uncomfortable in the company of two smaller and dainty ladies, and she did her best to relax her, but Alice soon put Anna at ease.

'You are far more patient than me, Anna,' she said, addressing Mrs Tufton informally, as she had been invited to do so. 'I'm sure I would have crushed several of those men just because they could leave and be independent and we struggle for the same right.'

Anna chuckled. 'I confess there were a few gentlemen that I would have liked to have done that to, but I didn't have the fortune of lifting them during my show.'

Matilda smiled at her friend.

'You're too kind-hearted for that, Anna, you don't fool me.'

Anna blushed, uncomfortable with kindness. She returned to tending the kettle as Alice placed an apple tea cake that she had baked on the small table.

'That looks delicious!' Matilda exclaimed.

Alice smiled. 'I do have some womanly skills, Mother insisted.'

'Goodness, look,' the giantess said, pausing in the tea making for her guests.

The young ladies rushed to join her at the window.

Detectives Thomas Ashdown and Harry Dart, flanked by half a dozen policemen in uniform, were approaching the Exhibition.

'There's Mr Wilks,' Anna exclaimed as the business manager and heir of the carnival emerged from the tent to meet them.

'He seems nervous,' Alice said, and they watched Mr Wilks glance around before he moved back inside the big tent. Moments later he appeared again with his wife,

Irina – only released from police questioning earlier that morning. It was nearing ten o'clock, thirty minutes before the Exhibition was due to open in its last week – if they were allowed to pack and leave, which was still very much at the mercy of the police. Fortunately, at that hour there were few members of the public present, many scared away by the recent murders.

'Oh, let's see what is going on,' Matilda said, and found no resistance – Alice was at the door before her. The three ladies made their way over to the gathering, staying far enough back not to attract the ire of the detectives and police force.

*****

Thomas took charge, looking completely calm and in control, Harry by his side. Mr Wilks greeted the detectives. The ladies moved a little closer to hear what was being said.

'Detectives, may I assist you?' Mr Wilks asked, his eyes travelling to the police party fanning out behind the detectives.

'Mr Wilks,' Thomas began. 'We are here to make an arrest and to search your wife's possessions again.'

A small gasp rose from the viewing gallery – the artists and crew of the Exhibition had wandered out to see what the commotion was about. Present were Mr Jo-Jo, Elvira and Ella – the conjoined sisters who gave a discreet wave to the ladies on seeing them, Unzie the albino man, several crew members, and the chef, Chas, along with Teddy. The amassed group remained hushed, keen to know who the murderer was in their midst and riveted by the drama playing out before them.

'You want to arrest Irina?' Mr Wilks asked and turned towards his wife as though the concept of her being a criminal was outrageous.

'Your wife,' Thomas said, again with a nod towards her.

Harry stepped forward along with a police officer and cuffed Mrs Wilks' wrists in front of her body.

'There must be some mistake. I'm sure there's a reasonable explanation,' Mr Wilks said and then he laughed. 'Trust me, she would not have killed Alfred Burnham, she loved him.'

Mrs Wilks looked at him, her countenance shocked.

'Oh yes, my dear, I knew. I'm sure everyone did. You must think I'm an idiot if you didn't think I could see what was happening under my nose, but I'm prepared to save your skin because I know you wouldn't kill him,' Mr Wilks said knowing he would truly own her after this admission and he had always wanted to own her.

Thomas looked from Mrs Wilks to her husband.

'You are correct, Mr Wilks; your wife loved Mr Burnham and did not kill him. However, she hired a Russian boxer – a wharf worker – to kill you.'

Mr Wilks stepped back, shocked, and an audible gasp went up from the gallery. He glared at his wife, expecting her to be appalled. She was not.

Thomas continued, 'Mrs Wilks told her hired assassin your routine – what time you came out to check the grounds were locked – but unfortunately Mr Burnham appeared on that evening. The wrong man was slain.'

'You were going to remove me and be with Burnham. Run this place together?' he asked, spitting the words out angrily, his face reddening.

Mrs Wilks was not at all upset by his anger. She stared at him coldly.

'But what about Mr Tufton?' Wilks asked and Thomas noted every eye turned to Anna, and then hastily away. He saw Matilda amongst the group, along with Alice, and momentarily frowned. Here, again, she's managed to be in the thick of it when she should be at home away from this scene and the dreadful findings he was about to deliver. He shook his head slightly, clearing his mind and returned his attention to Mr Wilks.

'Apparently, Mr Tufton was too smart for his own good,' Thomas said, and with a nod to Anna added, 'my apologies Mrs Tufton, I am now going to speak of your husband if you wish to return to your caravan.'

Matilda took Anna's arm.

'Thank you, but I wish to stay, Detective,' the giantess responded.

Thomas turned and continued addressing Mr Wilks. 'He knew of the affair and told Mrs Wilks that he would inform the police that she was the killer if Mrs Tufton's increased fee and top billing was not actioned.'

'He didn't know the truth, he was bluffing,' Mrs Wilks spoke for the first time. 'But I couldn't risk that. We were all better off without him.' She glanced to Anna momentarily and then was warned to quieten down by the officer who had cuffed her.

'So where is this hired killer?' Mr Wilks asked.

Thomas ignored him while he sent several of the uniform officers to Mrs Wilks' caravan to ensure they had missed nothing that might serve as evidence.

Harry responded, 'We have him in the lock-up.'

'Detective.' A small voice spoke up from the crowd. Mr Jo-Jo said, 'Why were my walking stick and Mr Burnham's used? I heard you found them and that you believe them to be the murder weapons. How did that man get them?'

Thomas then pulled off the second surprise for the morning and motioned to the constable, who moved behind Mr Wilks and cuffed him.

'What? Unhand me! What are you doing?' he protested.

Again, the group gasped and tittered, but not one protest arose from the small gathering of onlookers.

'Your act of genuine surprise was impressive, Mr Wilks,' Thomas said, 'but the cause of death for both men was a single blow to the throat, which collapsed the larynx and caused both victims to choke. A blow that an experienced boxer would know how to deliver.'

'Then you have your man, the boxer,' Mr Wilks said incredulously.

'We do,' Thomas agreed. 'But when you found Mr Burnham, he was choking, but still alive. You delivered the final blows with Mr Burnham's cane in revenge for the affair with your wife. Then, fearful that we might trace his death back to you, you stole Mr Jo-Jo's cane and delivered another blow to the skull, hoping to incriminate Mr Jo-Jo. I can only hope that Mr Burnham was deceased by that stage.'

There were gasps of shock and cries as the watching group became animated with anger; Matilda felt distressed for Mr Jo-Jo and Mr Burnham's friends.

Mr Wilks sneered at the group. 'It's not as if any of you have a future. What would it matter if Jo is behind bars in gaol or behind bars in a travelling show?'

'I imagine it would matter a great deal to Jo, who is a free man, and a man of integrity,' Harry snapped at Mr Wilks.

Thomas continued. 'You told your wife what you did and why, and she had no choice but to keep your secret. But she wanted to reveal where you had buried the canes. The day we saw her near them, she was checking to see they were still there. Your wife intended to deliver them to us.'

'And she'd have lied and said she had nothing to do with it, and I'd killed the men because of her affair. Oh, you are good,' he said, sneering at her.

'Nothing would make me happier than to see you locked away or dead. One more day was all I needed, and that stupid woman writer ruined everything.'

The group glanced to Matilda, with Alice standing beside her. Thomas also looked her way, and she gave him a small smile and a barely discernible shrug of her shoulders.

He sighed. No doubt he would hear about how much of a help she was in time to come. Thomas motioned to the remaining officers. 'Take them both away.'

Harry sensed the rising panic amongst the remaining group. This was their livelihood, all they had, and now the owner and managers were gone. He held up his hands.

'Ladies, gentlemen, please your attention.'

The group quietened down.

'Detective Ashdown and I know this leaves you without management. Can we suggest that this evening you gather and discuss what you wish to do? If you wish to continue in the Exhibition, I am sure Miss Hayward and Miss Doran could help you with running an advertisement seeking management or to sell the business as an ongoing concern.'

'Of course,' Matilda responded, and Alice nodded her agreement.

'Or if you wish to depart, we will assist you with securing passage home,' Harry added.

The two detectives turned to depart – Harry with a quick word to Mr Jo-Jo to assure him that his cane would be returned – and Thomas with a doff of his hat to the ladies.

Another case solved, and one of his most interesting ones, he mused. Not to mention that he and Detective Dart had both been rewarded with a large bonus of five pounds for their recent results. He intended to invest that in his house, to make it habitable for a lady. By choice, he had spent long enough as a bachelor, but it no longer held the same appeal, and he knew just the lady he wanted to inhabit with for the rest of his days.

*Chapter 38*

Harry shook his head. 'Unless your face changes dramatically in the next two days, you can't possibly go to the gallery exhibition looking like that,' he kidded his younger colleague as he studied Thomas's black and yellowing face wounds.

Daniel agreed. 'It looks worse now than it did on the night. I'm sorry, my friend, but they'll throw you out for sure for street fighting.' Daniel chuckled, and Teddy did his best to offer a sympathetic look to his uncle.

'You are probably right,' Thomas said, and sighed.

He sat on the veranda of his house, which had not hosted guests for years or seen a paintbrush for about the same time. But now, with Teddy's minor improvements, the timber Queenslander home with its corrugated zinc roof was starting to look respectable, and the neighbours were indeed pleased. The four men – Thomas, Daniel, Harry and Teddy – sat enjoying a lager at the end of a warm Brisbane day.

They all had their own reasons for celebrating. Thomas and Harry had successfully closed another case; Daniel got the coveted court sketch artist job, and Teddy had secured himself a cook apprenticeship to finish his last qualifying year, thanks to Mrs Bloomfield – Aunt Audrey. The dinner he had cooked for Mr Jo-Jo had sealed the deal, as Aunt Audrey had sampled the wares that evening unbeknown to the other guests.

Thomas put his feet up on the veranda rails and turned to Daniel. 'You might have to take the ladies on your own.'

'I have four tickets!' Daniel complained. 'I'll have to find someone to fill in if you can't go. Gideon will be angry if I waste them given, they are the hottest tickets in town.' Daniel remembered his two friends and suggested, 'I could ask William or George if they wish to attend. I know both gentlemen were keen to call on Matilda.' He knew it would stir Thomas into action. He felt his friend stiffen next to him.

'I would hate for you to miss out,' Thomas said. He knew what his friends were up to, trying to get him to reveal his feelings for Miss Matilda Hayward.

'If you were desperate, I could accompany you, Daniel, and escort Miss Hayward,' Teddy offered.

Thomas felt strangely relieved at this suggestion. At least Teddy knew how he felt about Matilda and with luck Matilda might think Teddy too young to form an attachment with.

'That's a good idea,' Harry contributed. 'After all, Teddy, you have come to Miss Hayward's rescue once before.'

'So gallant,' Thomas added drily.

The men chuckled.

'I know what you are doing, so don't think you are so very smart,' Thomas said, emptying his glass and glancing at his guests who were grinning, enjoying their humour. 'I'm sure by Saturday I will be presentable enough to attend.'

'If not, Uncle, we could spread the story of your heroism catching a murderer, so everyone will admire your face on the night instead of running a mile,' Teddy offered.

'Let's focus on that,' Thomas agreed and accepted a refill from an amused Daniel.

'Your house improves every time I see it.' Daniel diverted the conversation.

'Teddy's work. It is returning to its former glory,' Thomas agreed with a glance around.

'Got to earn my lodgings,' Teddy said with a grin, 'and besides, I enjoy seeing it come to life.'

'You are a creator – food, renovations, well done Teddy,' Harry praised him. 'This house might be fit for a lady soon if you keep this up.'

All eyes turned to Thomas again, and he groaned as they laughed with fondness at his expense.

*****

Matilda read the advertisement a final time and with Alice's agreement that it would do the job, she booked it to run in the daily paper and the *Women's Journal*.

# Advertisement: For Sale – Travelling Carnival

ATTENTION THEATRICAL MANAGERS AND CIRCUS PROPRIETORS. SHOWMEN, SPECULATORS, AND OTHERS – FOR SALE, A CARNIVAL COMPLETE.

In good working order and condition, running requiring no money spent on it for some time, and with dedicated performers and crew. With little capital, a business owner and proprietor could make a fortune in a short time. The new owner undertakes to engage the artists under their existing employment arrangements at the same wages and favourable conditions.

The artists number eight in total with other persons employed include three travelling crew, one cook and one maintenance man. An inventory of goods is available and includes four complete tents, sidewalls, wagons, caravans and tools.

The Carnival cost the former proprietor over 1,000 pounds but will be sold below valuation.

Bona fide purchasers only need apply and seller seeks haste.

Apply with particulars to Mr Amos Hayward, Hayward & Bruce Solicitors, AMP Chambers, Edward Street.

## Chapter 39

As required over the years, Harriet had assisted Matilda to dress, but tonight was different. Tonight, Harriet helped Matilda and Alice as they prepared to be seen with the men of their future. It was Alice's idea to dress together – Matilda had not known the joy of dressing with a sister and sharing each other's clothing and jewellery, and Alice's two sisters were across the ocean.

'You look so beautiful, the pair of you, you will be the belles of the art gallery opening,' Harriet said, admiring them both, and putting a final touch to Alice's hair.

The two ladies wore evening dresses to complement their colourings – Matilda in blue accessorised by pearls and Alice in red with diamonds. Both wore a hint of fragrance and a touch of rouge, as the occasion required. It wasn't every day they got to wear gowns for an exclusive art exhibition opening – it helped that Gideon was co-owner of the gallery and had generously allocated four of his opening night tickets. The ladies were well aware of his motive – he hoped Matilda and Alice might write a story for the *Women's Journal*.

'Are you nervous?' Harriet asked Matilda.

Her breathing gave her away.

'I can't wait to see him,' Matilda said.

'I can't wait to see both gentlemen in their evening wear,' Alice said, 'especially Daniel.'

The ladies smiled as Harriet went to the window, hearing the hansom cabs coming to a stop outside. She pulled aside the curtain and announced, 'Daniel and Thomas are here.'

Alice did one last turn in front of the mirror and sighed, satisfied. 'Thank you for all your help tonight, Harriet, you're wonderful. I was homesick for my sisters, we always dressed together.'

Harriet flushed with pleasure.

'You are wonderful,' Matilda concurred. 'Look at us, we're stepping out after our fairy godmother has made us sparkle.'

Harriet became sentimental as she looked at the tomboy who had now become a beautiful young woman. Mr Hayward's voice carried up the stairwell.

'Ladies, your escorts have arrived,' he called.

'Coming Pa,' Matilda called back. 'Shall we?' she asked Alice, who smiled and nodded.

Harriet opened the bedroom door and stepped back as the two ladies exited and descended the stairs. She stood at the top of the railing, watching as proud as punch.

Daniel, Thomas and Mr Hayward waited in the foyer, the men laughing over a shared joke until the ladies came in to view. Thomas looked to the stairs, and Harriet watched him as his eyes settled on Matilda. He watched her walk towards him.

Alice paused midway and said in her English accent, 'Oh my, don't you two look handsome?' Her eyes lingered on Daniel.

'Yes we do,' Daniel said, and grinned at her, making the party laugh.

Thomas cleared his throat but did not speak. Mr Hayward opened the door for the group.

'Have a lovely night, be careful and please have the ladies home at a respectable hour,' he said to Daniel with paternal solemnity, but gave a wink to Matilda. She kissed him on the cheek as she passed.

'Goodnight, Pa, don't wait up.'

'I may not since you are in such excellent hands,' he agreed. He closed the door behind them and invited Harriet to join him at the window to watch the young couples' departure. She hastily descended the stairs to do so.

\*\*\*\*\*

Thomas studied the ease at which Daniel addressed Miss Doran, and his natural charm that made them both comfortable. Thomas acknowledged he did not possess the same skills. Whether it was his nature or the job that had made him more reclusive, he could not be sure, but he would do his best tonight to be the gentleman Matilda deserved tonight.

When they arrived at the awaiting hansom cabs, Daniel moved to the first one and offered Alice his hand to assist her in. He instructed the cabman to wait so they could depart together.

'You look absolutely beautiful tonight, Miss Doran,' he said, and she laughed, delighted.

'Thank you, Mr Hayward, that was the effect I was trying for indeed.'

He saw her seated inside and followed, leaving Thomas to assist Matilda, into the hansom behind him.

Thomas felt the need to compliment Matilda now, as they both overheard the conversation. He swallowed, offered his hand and said, 'As do you Matilda, look beautiful, that is.'

She gave him a nod and smile at his awkward compliment.

'I can probably manage,' she said, used to pulling herself in and out of cabs.

'But you will take my hand because you are a lady,' he said, continuing to offer it.

'And because you are a gentleman?' she asked.

'Precisely.'

'Even though you look as if you've been brawling in the alley,' she teased him.

'I am hoping my dapper evening wear distracts from my face,' he said, falling back into their familiar banter.

She placed her small hand in his, and before he assisted her in, Thomas stopped her. He could hear Alice and Daniel having an animated conversation in the hansom in front of them, so he took the opportunity to have a moment with Matilda.

'Matilda, I need to say something to you.'

'Oh?' she said. 'Should I expect to be on the receiving end of a lecture about interfering in your case?'

The seriousness of Thomas's countenance said otherwise.

'Whatever is the matter, Thomas?' she asked, and bit her bottom lip anxiously.

'I want you to reconsider our friendship,' he began. Thomas had given this considerable thought. 'I would like to court you.'

Matilda's eyes widened in surprise.

Daniel called out. 'Are you two intending to come with us?'

'A moment,' Thomas answered, and on hearing them resume their lively discussion, he continued. 'Matilda,' he said, and raised her hand to his lips, kissing it. 'May I love you?'

For a moment she was silent, and Thomas lowered her hand and looked into her eyes. This was it. It would be difficult to continue now if she laughed and turned him down outright. He realised he should have had this discussion later in the evening so as not to endure a night in her company after being rejected. But he found her eyes full of tenderness, and a small smile traced her lips. She nodded.

'Yes, Thomas, yes. I would like that very much.'

Relief spread across his countenance, and they smiled at each other.

'Thomas!' Daniel called.

He rolled his eyes and assisted Matilda into the hansom. She slipped slightly and his firm hands caught her around her slim waist. She sighed with frustration.

'If I didn't have this gown on, I would be much more capable. I most likely would beat you in,' she said.

'I doubt it. I'm still stronger and faster,' he responded.

'Stronger maybe, but faster, I doubt it. Do you want to test that theory?'

'No Matilda, we are all grown up now and you are a lady. Remember?'

He followed her in and sat beside her. He shook his head.

'You are the most beautiful woman I have ever seen and the most frustrating.'

'Really?' she asked, and brightened. 'Thank you, Thomas.'

He sighed. 'You're welcome, Matilda.'

And the hansom moved taking the four young people on their first official outing together.

## THE END

I hope you enjoyed Matilda's adventures. If you would like to read Matilda and Thomas's next story featuring her brother Gideon and the missing artist's muse, read on for the first two chapters of *The Artist's Missing Muse*.

*The Artist's Missing Muse*

## *Chapter 1*

Matilda Hayward inclined her head to the side and studied the painting in front of her. She was no artist or art critic nor did she take a great interest in art – writing was her passion and since securing a position with the Women's Journal and working with the respected editor, Mrs Dora Lawson, she felt rather pleased with herself. She was a woman with a career path despite the less than enthusiastic acceptance of her new role by her family matriarch, Aunt Audrey, and Matilda's new beau, Detective Thomas Ashdown. In all fairness, he didn't discourage it but didn't encourage it either.

Looking at the painting Matilda tried to keep a neutral countenance but, truth be told, the painting was awful and it shouldn't be – it was a Marlon Dominey original.

'Well then,' her friend and fellow writer, Alice, said as she joined her.

Matilda looked to Alice for her thoughts.

Alice lowered her voice. 'It's rather awful, don't you think?'

Matilda stifled a laugh. 'Thank goodness. Yes, awful is kind. I thought it might have been brilliant and I was too ill-advised of the art world to know the difference.'

Alice studied it some more. 'I too am no art expert, but my father has a fine collection. This is not nearly as good as Marlon Dominey's past collections – I saw one of his exhibitions in Sydney before I arrived here.'

'I wonder if he has lost his inspiration?' Matilda whispered.

'Hmm, he's lost something,' Alice agreed, and the ladies moved on to the next of his paintings hanging in the exhibition. Matilda glanced around for their dates. Her eyes easily found Thomas Ashdown, Detective, in the room. Tall, dark, lightly bearded and handsome. His eyes met hers for just a moment and softened. Her brother Daniel broke their gaze, distracting Thomas with a nudge as he passed him two filled flute glasses of champagne – one for Thomas and the other to give to Matilda. Daniel picked up another two for himself and his date, Alice, on this, their first outing together. Matilda watched two of her favourite men walking towards them bearing the flutes.

'Champagne for you, Miss Doran,' Daniel said, offering the glass to the young English beauty who had escaped a less than desirable partnering in England to spend some time in the colonies – Australia. Having taken a job at the Women's Journal as well, she had become firm friends with Matilda. As a consequence, she was warmly welcomed into the breast of the Hayward family, to Daniel's great delight.

'Cheers,' Thomas said, raising his glass. 'This might help us discern if the art is any good or not,' he said in a low voice.

'It's not something I would want hanging in the drawing-room,' Daniel responded in an equally low voice. 'Have we seen enough? Shall we depart and find somewhere to dine?'

'Best idea you have had tonight,' Thomas agreed.

'Daniel and Thomas, before the speeches?' Matilda scolded them, and Alice laughed.

'No, you are right of course, Matilda,' Thomas said with a wry look to Daniel, his childhood friend whose sister he had just officially asked to court after years of friendship. 'Let's make our way around and enjoy the exhibition… we might find one we like,' he muttered.

'Thank the Lord they're serving alcohol,' Daniel said, swallowing half his glass in two easy gulps. His comment earned him another stern look from his sister Matilda. He gave her a wink.

'It was so good of your brother, Gideon, to get us tickets for tonight,' Alice said in her British accent. 'Everyone is talking about the exhibition.'

'God knows why,' Daniel continued, and earned a glare from a fellow guest. 'Poor Gideon has a disaster on his hands.'

'I feared as much,' Matilda agreed, 'and the showing does not seem to be overrun with patrons. Gideon has sold very few of the paintings.'

Matilda dropped her programme and Daniel and Thomas both reached to claim it for her. Her brother rose, leaving

Thomas to be chivalrous. Thomas dusted off the program and returned it to Matilda. Her small, slim hand touched his for a moment, the warmth of his skin, the strength of his hand. Her eyes rose from the programme to look at him.

'Thank you, Thomas,' she said, holding his gaze as if no one else was in the surrounding room. Daniel noticed, cleared his throat, and Matilda dropped her gaze. Thomas stepped back slightly, giving his best friend a smirk – Daniel was hardly one to lecture on impropriety.

With a little colour rising on her cheeks, Matilda turned to Alice. 'Mrs Lawson is quite happy for us to co-author a small article on the exhibition for the *Women's Journal*.'

'Let's do so!' Alice exclaimed. 'It can be our second co-authored piece.' She lowered her voice. 'However, it might be difficult to write the piece, when I can't, in all honesty, say I like any of the works.'

'Hear, hear,' Daniel agreed and raised his glass.

'There's your brother, Gideon, now,' Alice said, looking across the room to a young man who looked like her date, Daniel.

'Yes, he doesn't look happy,' Matilda said. 'He's only managed the gallery for a short while,' she explained to Alice, 'but he's attracted some big names for showings.'

'He does look a lot like you, Daniel,' Alice said, looking from one brother to the other.

'He is devilishly handsome,' Daniel agreed, and Thomas smiled and shook his head.

'If you ask me, he looks somewhat agitated,' Thomas added, studying Gideon's expression and movements.

Matilda nodded. 'I think you are right, Thomas. I imagine the response to this showing hasn't been all he hoped.' She bit her lower lip as she watched her brother from afar.

'But Marlon Dominey is still a big name in the art world regardless of what we think,' Alice said, looking at the nearest painting hanging on the wall.

'They are saying he's the most talented artist of his generation,' Thomas agreed, and Matilda gave him a surprised look.

'I do my homework,' Thomas told her.

'I can't see it,' Daniel said.

Thomas gave a small shrug. 'Me either. The art world is in trouble if this is our best offering.'

'Oh, and what was the last thing you painted?' Matilda teased Thomas as she turned and looked up at him.

'My house,' he retorted and made the group laugh.

'A fine job you did of that too,' Daniel said. 'You're good with a brush.'

'Thank you, it's been said before,' Thomas agreed.

Matilda laughed again and shook her head at their antics. 'But what did the critics say of your house painting?'

'A masterpiece in white,' Daniel quipped. He turned his attention to his date. 'Speaking of masterpieces, did I mention you looked beautiful tonight, Miss Doran?' He admired her red evening gown, which set off her blue eyes.

'Why, I think you might have, Mr Hayward, but thank you again,' Alice said coyly.

The matchmaker in Matilda couldn't help but smile; they looked most handsome together and Daniel was smitten.

Thomas cleared his throat. Daniel's ease at complimenting put him in the awkward position of now having to compliment Matilda again. But Matilda stepped in before he formulated a sincere response.

'I think we all look rather splendid, even if I say so myself,' she said and then nodded towards the front of the room. 'Gideon's coming our way.'

They turned to see the youngest male of the Hayward family coming towards them. It intrigued Matilda – it wasn't every day she got to see the rascal of the family, one year her senior, looking so mature and sensible. He shook hands with a few gentlemen and bowed to the ladies as he made his way to her group.

'Miss Doran, Matilda, Thomas, brother, glad you could make it,' he said.

'Thank you, Mr Hayward, for the tickets, it's very exciting,' Alice said, all manners. 'But where is the artist?'

'Where indeed,' Gideon said under his breath. 'He was due here some time ago and we are late for speeches.'

Just as the words left his lips, there were noises from across the room, and spontaneous applause broke out. The group looked to the entrance where a confident man had walked in with a beautiful woman on his arm.

'That's him, is it not?' Matilda asked, 'Marlon Dominey?'

'It is, excuse me,' Gideon said and left the party to go greet and organise the guest of honour.

Matilda's eyes widened. Marlon Dominey was the most handsome man she had ever laid eyes on. His dark hair brushed back from his face highlighted a square jaw, deep brown eyes, and a smile that could best be described as seductive. She felt herself blush. The woman on his arm was a match for his beauty – dark-haired, full red lips and tawny eyes. She sashayed in, her hand looped through his arm. Her figure was a perfect hourglass, and her red gown showed it to perfection. She did not leave his side as they made their way to the front of the gallery, accepting greetings and applause on their way. They made a handsome couple with an air of mystery. Matilda was mesmerised; they appeared so glamorous and worldly, so European, perhaps. She felt like a young girl in their presence.

'Oh my, isn't she glamorous,' Alice said, eyeing the woman on Marlon's arm.

Thomas did the gentlemanly thing and feigned disinterest, and Daniel took the question figuratively.

'She's a little too showy for my liking,' he said.

'If only the paintings had as much presence as the artist,' Thomas said for Daniel's ears, but Matilda overhead.

She agreed, her thoughts interrupted by Gideon introducing the guest of honour for the evening. A robust round of applause welcomed him, and Marlon gave a small bow before speaking.

'Ladies and gentlemen, I apologise for our tardiness,' Marlon began and the guests all appeared to have forgiven him immediately as they watched him, enamoured. He continued, 'the dusk light on the beautiful river of your city inspired me, and Sapphire and I had to admire it.'

A small murmur of appreciation rose from the audience, and spontaneous applause broke out. Matilda glanced to Thomas, who gave her a raised eyebrow and restrained himself from rolling his eyes. She gave a small smile and returned her attention to studying Marlon's muse. Sapphire, so exotic and womanly – full-figured and glamorous. Matilda could not imagine what it must be like to be someone's muse, to inspire their work and creativity. It did not occur to her that beside her, Detective Thomas Ashdown, who had known her since they were children, stared at his own muse: Matilda, his first thought every morning and last thought at night. The woman he wanted to keep safe from harm, provide for, and make happy. She looked at him again to find him staring at her. Thomas righted himself and returned his attention to the speeches.

'I am glad to be here, to extend my stay in your beautiful country for another season and my thanks to the owner of this fine establishment, Mr Steinman and the Fine Art Gallery Manager, Mr Hayward for the opportunity to display my art for you,' he began. 'I cannot with a clear conscious say that I have sacrificed everything on the sacred altar of art, for I have not.'

'That would appear obvious,' Daniel muttered.

Marlon continued. 'My muse, Sapphire, and I have enjoyed ourselves too much to call our visit and my creations suffering. To gaze upon the beauty of your city—'

Matilda tuned out as she looked around the room. The audience was in the palm of Marlon's hand as he charmed with his words and beautiful face. But a glance at Thomas, Daniel, and some other young men showed the men dragged along to the event under sufferance were not quite as enamoured.

Thomas leaned towards her and she whispered, 'His inspiration and creativity from our city does not seem to have met the canvas. I wonder if all is well between Marlon and his muse.'

'Will you be writing that in your article?' he whispered.

'Heavens no!' She returned her attention to the speaker.

Marlon was finishing his speech: 'My enduring creative partner reminds me that the best part of any speech is brevity and so be it. Thank you again.'

There was much applause as the artist and his muse gave small bows and then began to meet the guests.

'Can we get out of here now?' Daniel asked.

'Yes,' Matilda said, 'your duty is done.' She took one more look at Mr Dominey's beautiful muse, never imagining for a moment what might befall Miss Reubens in the very near future.

## Chapter 2

Detective Harry Dart arrived at the office not long after his younger partner, Thomas. The pair had a comfortable routine – Harry, a few years short of hanging up his badge and enjoying his retirement – had been teamed up with the young gun. Thomas's ambitions sat well with Harry who could mentor and not feel the need to be in the limelight or line of fire. He also recognised the young gun's talent and wasn't averse to rising on the success of their crime-solving rate to see out his career.

'The Mrs made you a sandwich,' Harry said, entering and passing over a wax-wrapped bundle. 'I told her your nephew, Teddy, was a chef and living with you now, but she appears to have this soft spot for you.'

'She's a saint is Mrs Dart.' Thomas said, gratefully reaching for the sandwich. 'Thanks, I'm starving,' he muttered and took no time unwrapping it and taking a large bite.

'So, did you buy a painting?'

Thomas snorted and tapped the small headline on the bottom of the newspaper front page. Swallowing his bite, he exclaimed, 'God no, I could have done better myself after a few stiff drinks.'

'I'd like to see that then. Let me know when you'll be taking up the brush,' Harry joked. He leaned over the edge of Thomas's desk and read the headline aloud: 'Artist's work unredeemable.'

'That's being kind,' Thomas said.

'Oh dear,' Harry said and proceeded to read the review: 'The last time I saw work as deluded as Mr Marlon Dominey's recent collection, I was in a children's playground and could excuse it. Scrambled and wasteful, it may be time to rinse out the brush. Harsh!' Harry said.

'But close to the truth,' Thomas said. 'There was little to admire amongst the lot except for the ladies in our company, of course.'

'Ah, the delightful Miss Hayward and her writing friend. And to think you got to spend the entire evening together uninterrupted with not one dead body or a good mugging to interrupt you,' Harry joked.

'Good of the city,' Thomas agreed and started on the second half of the sandwich.

A knock at the door made both men turn sharply to the intruder.

'Ah, don't bother taking off your coat, Harry, you've got a body, a dead one,' the crusty desk sergeant clarified and handed him a slip of paper. 'That's the address. The coroner said he'd meet you there.'

'Thanks, John,' Harry said, taking the paper as Thomas rose and wrapped his sandwich.

'I'll finish this on the way.' He grabbed his hat and coat and followed his partner down the hallway.

'Well, that was a short-lived reprieve from crime,' Harry sighed.

'Where's the body?' Thomas asked as he caught up and they descended the office stairs into Roma Street to fetch a hansom cab.

Harry looked at the note with the victim's name, address, and a few scribblings of explanation on it. 'Just across the river. Oh, there's a coincidence,' Harry said. 'The deceased is an artist. Maybe your artist?'

'His works weren't good but not bad enough to bump him off, surely,' Thomas said and Harry chuckled.

A hansom cab pulled to a stop in front of them and Harry gave the driver the address.

'What was your artist's name again?' Harry asked.

'Marlon Dominey.'

'Hmm.' Harry shook his head as they stepped into the carriage and seated themselves. 'He couldn't have a normal name like Fred, could he?'

'That would be most unartistic,' Thomas agreed. 'So, is it him then?'

'No, we're off to the studio of Benjamin Bannon,' Harry said, pocketing the slip of paper. 'I wonder what the poor bloke did to deserve a visit from the grim reaper.'

'A disgruntled customer, an unhappy lover, a muse misrepresented,' Thomas guessed, and finished the last bite of his sandwich, pronouncing it excellent as he balled the waxed paper.

'A jealous rival with a critical review in today's paper,' Harry added, and got a look of interest from his partner.

The hansom took the Victoria Bridge across the river to South Brisbane and, exiting at their destination, Harry settled the fee with the driver. 'Not short of a dollar then,' Harry said, taking in the area. 'This is the studio and residence, I believe.'

Two young police officers stood at the entrance to the small terrace house and already neighbours and interested parties were hovering around outside.

'No reporters yet,' Thomas said, relieved.

'That'll be short-lived,' Harry agreed. 'What do we have, lads?' he asked the constables.

The senior of the two policemen spoke up.

'Sirs, the dead man is an artist who lives on the right of the terrace house. His studio is on the left. The housekeeper who comes early every morning to prepare his breakfast could not find him when she went to announce his breakfast was ready. She did not enter his room when she saw his bathroom door closed but called us immediately after not being able to get a response.'

'How did she even know he was home?' Thomas asked.

'They had a system, Sir,' the younger constable answered. 'He left his keys and hat at the entrance when he was in, but she was not to disturb him until breakfast was ready. If she arrived and they were not there, she cleaned and left.'

'Righto.' Harry nodded. 'Where is she?'

'She's next door with a neighbour, Sir, having a cup of tea.'

'Where's the body?' Thomas asked, cutting to the chase. His partner always looked after the matters of the heart where others were concerned.

'We found it in the bathroom, Sir, in a most unusual pose, but we have touched nothing,' he assured the detectives.

'Good work, men, thank you,' Thomas said and, with a nod to the two constables, he entered the building with Harry on his heels. They took the stairs to the top floor, as advised. The building was beautifully outfitted, rooms to the right of the staircase, and a large room that appeared to be the studio to the left.

'Strange,' Harry muttered at first sight from the doorway. The room was pristine, not their usual death scene. The white and cream embossed wallpaper was amplified by the light streaming in through the windows.

'Good light for an artist, I imagine,' Harry said.

The body was not in sight from the living area, and Harry entered tentatively while Thomas remained in the doorway, studying the room. Nothing was out of place – the desk was neat, the paintings were straight, the curtains tied back, the ornaments and lamps upright and intact, and not a mark on the flooring.

'Ready?' Harry asked after a few minutes, and Thomas nodded. They made their way to the bathroom and Harry pushed the door open wider. The room was large, adorned with glossy white bricks and gold fittings.

Both men's eyes widened with surprise. Sitting in a large green enamel claw-footed bathtub was the victim, the artist Benjamin Bannon. He sat as if alive, perfectly still and looking forward, his hands placed on either side of the bathtub. The detectives moved closer to find there was no water in the bathtub and the artist was naked or appeared to be from the waist up. His lower body was buried under leaves – autumn leaves of every colour that filled the bathtub to a quarter full.

'Well, that's one of our better death scenes. Perhaps you'd expect that from an artist or his murderer,' Harry said, thinking aloud. 'No obvious sign of death unless we burrow through those leaves,' he added reluctantly.

Thomas studied the tub, sniffed, and moved a few handfuls of leaves.

'There's no obvious wound or blood evident. He has got a strange tint to his skin, don't you think? He might have been poisoned,' Thomas suggested, studying the stiff, pale body of the victim.

'Detectives?' A voice called from the other room and Thomas stuck his head out of the bathroom to find the coroner had arrived. Dr Patrick Nevins entered, his cane tapping lightly on the parquetry flooring.

The men greeted each other.

'The stairs give you hell, Patrick?' Harry asked the coroner, ten years younger than Harry, but looked the same vintage with his grey mop of hair, glasses and a limp courtesy of a childhood accident.

'Always,' he sighed, 'I just wish they'd all die on the ground floor.'

The men chuckled.

'Well,' Dr Nevins said, pausing in the bathroom doorway. 'A most considerate death scene, so clean.'

'Indeed, even artistic, one might say,' Thomas agreed.

Dr Nevins tapped his way over to the bathtub and looked in. He nodded and smiled.

'What? What does that expression mean?' Harry asked him.

'I understand this is the artist, Benjamin Bannon?'

'Correct,' Thomas said.

'I think you will find this is a self-portrait, emulated.'

Thomas snapped to look at the doctor, his breath hitching. 'Where is it now, the portrait?'

'I don't know,' Dr Nevins said with a shrug, 'but Bannon's manager or agent may know.'

Harry spoke up. 'The Hayward brother who manages the gallery…'

'Yes, Gideon Hayward,' Thomas said. 'He could find it for us. One moment, Doctor, please.'

Dr Nevins nodded and stepped back. Thomas explained: 'I just need to take in the scene now that it has a different interpretation.'

Harry and the doctor exchanged looks, well used to Thomas's quirky traits. After a few moments, Thomas stood straighter, exhaled, and looked at the two men.

'Thank you, I'm done if you are Harry?'

'I'm finished,' Harry agreed.

Dr Nevins began his observation of the body. 'The portrait, it's called something like An Artist Bathing in the Season or similar. Quite lovely, I saw it and some of his other work when he was on tour last year.'

Thomas paced. 'An artist killed in a style emulating his own successful work.'

'I'll have a time and cause of death to you later this afternoon,' Dr Nevins said as he moved the leaves from the body. A small, red puncture wound in the lower leg was barely visible, and he made a knowing sound. 'Looks like he might have been injected with a substance.'

The two men glanced over the edge of the tub at the mark and then left the coroner to his work and went to question the housekeeper and neighbours.

'I wish all our death scenes were as gentle,' Harry said.

'It's odd,' Thomas said. 'No clothes lying around, perfectly positioned, no evidence of a struggle, and someone knew his work. Why that painting?' He continued to mutter as he went down the stairs.

'The timing on the back of Marlon Dominey's exhibition and bad reviews is interesting,' Harry added.

'Indeed,' Thomas agreed. 'I just hope Matilda and the ladies of the Women's Journal don't feel the need to report this crime.'

His eyes scanned the small group waiting outside and, on this occasion, it relieved him not to see the woman who filled his thoughts every waking moment.

*****

Continue reading *Miss Matilda Hayward and the Artist's Muse* now. Available from Amazon or free in Kindle Unlimited.

# Author's note:

While this is a work of fiction, I try to be as accurate to the era as possible, in this case – 1889. It has been fascinating to research and write in this era, especially in my own city of Brisbane, and the National Library of Australia (Trove) is a wonderful source of information and newspapers of the day. Sadly, the touring carnivals were accepted entertainment and advertised as 'Freak Shows'. My giantess was loosely based on the real giantess, Mrs Auguste Rewald of Boonah, Queensland. The following advertisement appeared in a 1907 Australian newspaper:

*"NOW ON EXHIBITION in Premises opposite Kenmure's, Liverpool-st., for a Few Days only, the Most Marvellous Woman of the Age, AUGUSTE REWALD, the Queensland Giantess, whose weight is 42st. 10lb., and measures 90 inches around the body. ADMISSION - 6d. Open from 10 a.m. to 11 p.m."*

These 'Freak Shows' such as those toured by Barnum and Bailey, travelled the world in times when disabilities were flaunted and abnormalities earned a living for the subject and their handler with sometimes complex relationships. They provided a home for 'oddities', and it was considered perfectly accepted entertainment for the culture of the time.

For some of the performers and entertainers, it was a lifetime of fame; for others, it was a means of survival in a time with no welfare and where abandonment meant destitution.

The crowds were fascinated by the performers and a lack of understanding of illnesses such as microcephaly (a small head and brain), hypertrichosis (excessive hair growth), dwarfism, missing limbs, conjoined twins, or anything not deemed 'normal', meant that people born with disabilities became curiosities, and as such were ripe pickings for the carnivals.

Augusta, the giantess, was capable of great strength, and her enterprising husband found a way to earn a source of income from his wife and her unfortunate size. She wasn't unloved, abandoned or without family. So, was she a willing participant in being exhibited, or was she forced by her husband to participate? Did she enjoy the opportunity to travel widely, even overseas to pose as a giantess? We will never know.

Matilda's editor, Mrs Dora Lawson at the *Women's Journal,* was based on the trailblazing Mrs Louisa Lawson, owner and editor of *Dawn: A Journal for Australian Women* (1888-1905). Mrs Lawson was one of a number of Australian women in the 1880s who worked as journalists but were often confined to the social pages. Thus, founding her own magazines for a female readership, Mrs Lawson employed female writers and production staff – it was a commercial success.

The stories discussed by the ladies of the *Women's Journal* in this book were based on real stories taken from the pages of newspapers in Queensland, Australia, in 1889 and the articles featured in Dawn. I hope you enjoyed Matilda and Thomas's first book.

**Books in a similar genre by Helen Goltz:**

**Miss Hayward and the Detective series:**
Murder at the Carnival
The Artist's Missing Muse
Mystery at the Asylum
The Mortician's Clue
Murder in Bridal Lane

**The Lady Mortician's Visions' series:**
The Missing Brides
The Fake Child
The Dastardly Debutante

**The Jesse Clarke cosy mystery series:**
Death by Sugar
Death by Disguise
Death by Reunion

**The Mitchell Parker thriller series:**
Mastermind
Graveyard of the Atlantic
The Fourth Reich

**Writing as Jack Adams** (mystery suspense):
Poster Girl
And the Delaney and Murphy childhood friends' series:
Asylum
Stalker
Cult
Hitched (coming soon)

*About the Author:*

Helen is a hybrid-published, Amazon best-selling author. After studying English Literature, Media, and Communications at universities in Queensland, Australia, and obtaining a Counselling Diploma, Helen Goltz has worked as a journalist, producer and marketer in print, TV, radio and public relations. Born in Toowoomba she has made her home in Logan Village, Australia with her journalist husband, Chris, and Boxer dog, Baxter.

Connect with Helen:

Website: www.helengoltz.com
Facebook: www.facebook.com/HelenGoltz.Author
BookBub: www.bookbub.com/authors/helen-goltz